Praise for Robert Thorogood

'Very funny and dark with great pace. I love Robert
Thorogood's writing'
Peter James

'Deftly entertaining…satisfyingly pushes all the
requisite Agatha Christie-style buttons'
Barry Forshaw, *The Independent*

'A treat'
Radio Times

'Fans of the Agatha Christie-style BBC drama *Death In
Paradise* will enjoy this book from the show's creator'
Mail on Sunday

'This brilliantly crafted, hugely enjoyable and
suitably goosebump-inducing novel is an utter delight
from start to finish'
Heat

'A brilliant whodunnit'
Woman

Robert Thorogood is the creator of the hit BBC One TV series *Death In Paradise*.

He was born in Colchester, Essex, in 1972. When he was 10 years old, he read his first proper novel – Agatha Christie's *Peril at End House* – and he's been in love with the genre ever since.

He now lives in Marlow in Buckinghamshire with his wife and children.

Death Knocks Twice

Robert Thorogood

ONE PLACE. MANY STORIES

HQ
An imprint of HarperCollins*Publishers* Ltd
1 London Bridge Street
London SE1 9GF

www.harpercollins.co.uk

HarperCollins*Publishers*
Macken House, 39/40 Mayor Street Upper
Dublin 1 D01 C9W8 Ireland

This paperback edition 2022

2

First published in Great Britain by
HQ, an imprint of HarperCollins*Publishers* Ltd. 2017

Copyright © Robert Thorogood and Red Planet Pictures Limited 2017

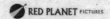

RED PLANET PICTURES

Robert Thorogood asserts the moral right to be
identified as the author of this work.
A catalogue record for this book is
available from the British Library.

ISBN: 978-1-84845-927-4

For Penny and Jack

CHAPTER ONE

Detective Inspector Richard Poole was in a bad mood.

This wasn't in fact all that unusual. Not to say that he was *always* in a bad mood, far from it. Sometimes, he simmered without quite boiling over. And at other times he felt too worn down by the whole shooting match of life to get a proper grump on. But today wasn't one of those days. Today he was in a fury so complete that he was in grave danger of going 'the full Rumpelstiltskin'.

As was so often the case, the object of Richard's ire was Police Officer Dwayne Myers.

'Then how about you try this one, Chief?' Dwayne said as he stood by his desk holding up a brightly-coloured Hawaiian shirt.

There was a stifled laugh from the direction of Camille's desk.

'What's that, Camille?' Richard asked.

'Nothing, sir,' Camille said in her most grown-up

voice. 'But I think Dwayne's right. That shirt would really suit you.'

'It wouldn't,' Richard said.

'I think it would, sir.'

'It wouldn't, Camille. I just said.'

'But why not? It's fun.'

'*Fun*?' Richard squeaked in a high falsetto that, frankly, surprised all of them. He coughed to put the gravel back into his voice. 'You call that aberration of a shirt "fun"?'

'I reckon so,' Dwayne said. 'And Camille's right. You'd look great in it.'

'Right, that's it,' Richard announced, standing up from behind his desk. Having commanded his team's full attention, he shot the cuffs of his white shirt, did up the middle button on the jacket of his woollen suit and stepped out into the centre of the Police Station.

A trickle of sweat slipped down from Richard's hairline, and he glanced at Police Officer Fidel Best's desk, to check that he had gone back to his work. As the youngest member of the team, Fidel generally stayed out of the skirmishes and outright civil war that could sometimes engulf the office. Richard was pleased to see that Fidel was looking at his monitor in a way that suggested that he was indeed keeping himself to himself.

Richard pulled a hankie from his jacket pocket, wiped the sweat from his face and turned to face Dwayne.

'I'm your commanding officer, and I'm telling you to put that…garment down. Right. Now.'

'But seriously, Chief,' Dwayne said. 'I'm only trying to help. You have got to get into some lighter clothes. That woollen suit in this climate will be the death of you.'

Richard jutted out his jaw. He found his subordinates' desire to get him into more casual clothes deeply irritating. Didn't they appreciate just how very elegantly he was already dressed? And hadn't they any idea just how hard it was keeping his black brogues polished to a parade ground sheen when most of the island was covered in fine grade aggregate – or, as the tourist brochures were so intent on calling it, 'sand'?

'I've worn a suit every day of my working life, and I'm not going to stop now just because I've had the misfortune of being posted to the bloody Caribbean.'

Dwayne exhaled.

'Okay, Chief.'

'Thank you.'

Dwayne's face brightened as he grabbed up another shirt from the pile of clothes on his desk.

'Then how about you try this one?' he asked, before realising that the shirt he was now holding was a billowing confection of gold satin with silver tassels.

Even Dwayne was surprised.

'Okay, maybe not this one. But how about this?' he said, putting the disco shirt down and picking up a far more acceptable shirt in a sky blue colour.

'Dwayne,' Richard said with the rattle of death in his voice. 'That shirt doesn't even have sleeves.'

It was true. It wasn't so much a shirt as a vest with ideas above its station.

Richard strode over to Dwayne, grabbed the shirt from his hands and dashed it back onto the pile of clothes on the desk.

'Dwayne. Let me be clear. Hell would have to freeze over before I'd wear any of these clothes.'

'Although, sir,' Fidel said, finally joining the conversation. 'If hell *did* freeze over, you wouldn't want to be wearing shorts and Hawaiian shirts anyway.'

Richard turned and looked at Fidel to see if he was winding him up. It was clear from his helpful smile that he wasn't.

'Tell you what,' Dwayne said. 'The guy on the market said there was no rush getting these back to him. He was having problems selling them anyway. So how about I just put them in the back office? You can look at them another time, when you've got a moment. What do you reckon to that?'

As though Richard had just agreed with his plan, Dwayne picked up the pile of shirts and shorts from his desk and went through the bead curtain that led to the cells.

Richard finally let out a breath that he hadn't even known he'd been holding. At least that was that problem dealt with.

'Good morning, team,' a mellifluous voice announced, and the island's Commissioner of Police, Selwyn Patterson, saundered into the room, his hands thrust deep into the trouser pockets of his rumpled khaki uniform.

'Good morning, sir,' Richard said, knowing that the Commissioner's arrival was never good news.

Selwyn removed his peaked cap, held it delicately between forefinger and thumb, and gave the office a once over.

'So,' he said. 'Busy?'

'Of course, sir,' Richard said, knowing that he and his team were nothing of the sort. In truth, things had been frustratingly quiet for the last few weeks. The only incident that had required any proper policing was a dispute between two neighbours, one of whom owned a cockerel that had taken to crowing every night from midnight to dawn. The dispute had threatened to escalate into violence until Dwayne had taken the offending rooster into custody, killed it, cooked it, ate it, and then pronounced the case closed. Such was island life sometimes.

'Then I'm sorry,' Selwyn said, looking nothing of the sort, 'but I'll be adding to your burdens.'

'What have you got, sir?'

'A very important case.'

'Of course,' Richard said, reaching into his inside jacket pocket and pulling out his notebook and silver propelling pencil. He flicked the notebook open to a fresh page and waited in anticipation.

'You see,' Selwyn said, 'I was at a charity rum tasting yesterday afternoon, and I got into conversation with the man who owns the Fort Royal Hotel.' Richard knew the hotel well, having once solved the murder of a bride there. 'And he says his hotel guests are being scammed by a ruthless criminal with no concern for the consequences of his actions.'

'They are, sir?' Richard said, his interest piqued. Finally, was this going to be a case worthy of his and his team's talents?

'Apparently so.'

'And what's this criminal doing?'

'Well, he's set up a roadside stall and he's selling bottles of bootleg rum.'

Richard's pencil remained hovering above his notebook.

'He is, sir?'

'It's affecting sales in the bar at the Fort Royal.'

'And... that's it, is it?'

Selwyn pursed his lips.

'We rely on tourists on this island, Inspector.'

'Of course, sir.'

'And the tax revenue from duty being paid on legal alcoholic beverages.'

'Yes, sir.'

'And above all else, we still make rum on Saint-Marie. I won't have the island's reputation as the best rum producer in the world tarnished by this man and his dangerous, third-rate product.'

'Well, sir, we'll look into it,' Richard said, somewhat

disappointed. When was he going to get a decent criminal case?

There was a 'ting' from the front desk of the office, and Richard and his team turned and saw a woman with her hand hovering over the little brass bell on the counter top.

'You've got to help me!' she said in desperation.

Knowing that his team would have to attend to the young woman, Selwyn put his peaked cap back onto his head and smiled for Richard's benefit.

'I'll expect a report on the bootleg rum seller,' he said, before sauntering out of the office.

'Yes, of course, sir,' Richard said, already heading over to the woman. She was about thirty years old, had pale skin, straight black hair and was wearing an old black cotton dress that was now faded to grey. But what Richard noticed most was how jittery she was. She looked like a startled deer who could bolt at any second.

'Can I help you, madam?'

'You've got to,' the woman said, her voice breaking as she spoke. 'There's someone stalking me. Up at my house. And I've just seen him and chased him. But he got away. You've got to come with me!'

'Someone's been stalking you?' Richard said, unable to keep a note of excitement out of his voice. *This* was more like it. A proper case.

'And he could still be there,' the woman said in desperation. 'We've got to get back at once. See if we can catch him.'

'Of course. Do you live nearby?'

'I'm sorry?'

'Do you live nearby?' Richard repeated. 'Have you come to the station on foot?'

The woman looked at Richard in surprise.

'Don't you know who I am?' she asked.

'Should I?'

'You're Lucy Beaumont, aren't you?' Camille said as she joined Richard at the desk.

Richard realised he'd heard of the Beaumont family when he'd first arrived on Saint-Marie, but he'd never really listened to what he'd been told. All he could remember was that they were some kind of ancient British family who'd been on the island for generations, and they ran a coffee plantation half way up the south-western slopes of Mount Esmée, the island's active volcano. Oh yes, Richard realised, that's why he'd never been interested in finding out any more about the Beaumonts. They lived on an active volcano.

But if this young woman was being stalked, then it was their duty to investigate, volcano or no volcano. Richard turned to Dwayne.

'Dwayne. Take Fidel to the Fort Royal hotel. See what you can find out about the Commissioner's bootleg rum seller, would you?'

'Yes, sir,' Dwayne said.

'Which leaves you and me, Camille,' Richard said. 'And I suggest we accompany Ms Beaumont back to her house and find out exactly what's going on.'

★★★

After Richard had first arrived on Saint-Marie, it had taken him quite a few months to get his head around the fact that there was a live volcano on the southern half of the island. Admittedly, Mount Esmée was such a huge geological feature that it could be seen from everywhere on the island, but it seemed so improbable to Richard that people would share an island with an active volcano that he'd presumed that, at some level, it wasn't real. Even when he heard about the Great Eruption of 1979, which had apparently shot lava hundreds of feet into the air and sent a terrifying pyroclastic flow down the side of the mountain at a hundred miles an hour – wiping out dozens of homes and killing 34 people – he remained in denial.

Now, as Camille drove the Police jeep up the tight hairpin bends towards the Beaumont Plantation, Richard found himself suffering an existential crisis. He was sitting in the sweltering heat of a vehicle that he knew hadn't been serviced for over a decade while a Frenchwoman was driving it ever-higher up a real life volcano. What had gone wrong with his life?

'Watch out!' Richard shouted as an oncoming motor-bike took a wide line around a tight bend in the road.

'Will you please calm down,' Camille said.

Richard could sort of see Camille's point. After all, she was an excellent driver and he knew it probably didn't help that he kept shouting 'Brake! Brake! Brake!' as they approached every corner, so he instead decided to grab hold of the dashboard and not let go.

He was still holding onto the dashboard when, ten minutes of stomach-sloshing fear later, Camille brought the Police jeep to a juddering halt by a row of wooden farm buildings half way up the mountain. Richard took a moment to calm himself. It seemed even hotter – if that were possible – this high up the mountain. There wasn't a hint of a breeze, and all he could hear was the ticking of the jeep's diesel engine as it started to cool down. Richard looked through the windscreen and saw that there wasn't a cloud in the sky. Typical, he thought to himself. He was about to get roasted by the scorching heat again. With a weary sigh, he opened the passenger-side door and stepped out of the jeep.

It started raining. And not just any rain, either. Richard found himself standing in a full-on torrential downpour. He looked up at the sky, but couldn't see anything close to a cloud either directly above his head or even nearby. He was always prepared though, so he went to the boot of the jeep, grabbed his emergency umbrella and put it up with a satisfying *whomp*. There, he thought to himself, that was better.

It stopped raining.

Only now did Camille step out of the jeep, and Richard had a brief out of body experience where he could see that his partner, Detective Sergeant Camille Bordey – who was wearing dark green cotton trousers and a short-sleeved checked shirt – was now standing next to a pasty-faced middle-aged Englishman who was wearing a black suit, black brogues and was holding a funeral umbrella in the bright sunshine.

'It's not raining, sir,' Camille said.

'I know that, Camille,' Richard said, trying to keep his dignity intact as he lowered his umbrella and returned it to the boot of the jeep. There still wasn't a cloud in the sky, but Richard knew that he hadn't imagined the brief tropical downpour. His woollen suit was damp with water, and he could see that the dry mud he was standing on was now covered in little craters where the raindrops had drilled hard into the ground. When would the tropics ever make any sense to him?

'Okay, sir, so what do you know about the Beaumont family?' Camille asked her boss as they watched Lucy park her car a little way away.

'Not much,' Richard replied, trying to ignore the fact that his suit was now steaming. 'Other than the fact that they're very rich.'

'Very rich and extremely secretive. Sir, could I say something?'

'Of course. What is it?'

'You seem to be on fire.'

'It's not fire, Camille. It's steam.'

'Oh, I see. You're steaming, sir.'

'It's the rain in my suit. The sun's making it evaporate, okay? It's just basic physics.'

'Of course it is, sir.'

Ignoring the smirk on his partner's face, Richard turned and looked at the plantation buildings as Lucy headed over. There were old barns, workshops, and other structures all made from the same grey stone, and they were all arranged around an ancient cobblestoned yard. In fact, if it wasn't for the palm trees and jungle pressing in on all sides, Richard could imagine the farm buildings fitting just as well into a village scene back in Dorset. Oh, and the active volcano looming above the plantation, Richard noted to himself – that was the other clue that he wasn't on a farm in Dorset.

As Lucy reached the Police, Richard took charge.

'We'd better not waste any time,' he said. 'So can you tell us what you saw and when?'

'I'll try,' she said, nervously. 'But I don't really know where to start.'

'That's okay,' Camille said, knowing that if her boss was all clanking metal cogs, she had to be the oil. 'Just tell us what happened in your own words.'

'Well, I suppose it started a couple of weeks ago,' Lucy said. 'And I didn't know it was happening at first. If you see what I mean. It was just a feeling I got. That someone was watching me. You know, that feeling where your skin prickles?'

'How do you mean?' Camille asked.

'You know, when your skin creeps because you think someone's looking at you? Well, I had that feeling a couple of weeks ago. When I was down here. But I couldn't work out if anyone was actually looking at me. It was just this sensation I had that I was being watched. So I told myself I must be imagining it – even though it's happened quite a few times since then. Mostly when I'm down by these buildings. Or out in the coffee fields.' Here, Lucy indicated the land as it sloped down the mountain from the courtyard, and Richard could see that the whole hillside was covered in neat rows of densely-packed bushes, each about ten feet high.

'Oh, are those coffee bushes?' Richard asked.

'They are.'

'Where the coffee berries grow?'

'We call them cherries, but yes, that's where they grow.'

'I see,' Richard said, none the wiser. 'Sorry, why do you call them cherries?'

'Because the fruit of the coffee plant is red like a cherry. Don't you know how coffee is made?' Lucy asked, surprised.

'Well, I know it comes in jars,' Richard said before realising that this was probably the wrong thing to say.

'It's a bit more complicated than that.'

'I'm sure it is,' Camille said, trying to get the interview back on track. 'But you were telling us that you felt you were being watched when you were down by these farm buildings?'

'That's right. And a couple of days ago I thought I'd got proof. I was just getting into my car when I had the feeling again – that someone was spying on me – and when I spun round, I caught this quick flash as whoever it was ducked behind that wall over there.' Here, Lucy pointed at a stone wall that separated two buildings. 'I was shocked, I can tell you. But I made myself go over and look behind the wall. If I'm honest, I was really scared. But what I saw was kind of the worst thing possible.'

'Why?' Camille asked. 'What did you see?'

'Whoever it was had gone. They'd just vanished into thin air. It was really spooky. Because I was sure I'd seen someone, but they were no longer there. And after that moment, I started to doubt my own shadow. It even occurred to me that maybe I'd been seeing things. But then this morning, I finally saw him. The guy who's been stalking me. Plain as day. Let me show you.' Lucy led them off to a clump of vegetation that pressed up against the side of one of the old buildings. 'I was just coming back from the fields when I looked over and saw a man standing to the side of this bush here.'

'And it was definitely a man?' Richard asked, eagerly pulling his notebook and pencil from his inside pocket.

'Oh yes. This old guy with a beard and straggly grey hair down to his shoulders. He looked like a tramp if I'm honest.'

'What time was this?'

'I don't know. Something like 10am. Or just after.'

'What colour was his skin?'

'I think white.'

'Did you recognise him?'

'No. But I only saw him for a split second. Because the moment he realised that I'd seen him, he ran back into the jungle just beyond the bush here. And then I did a pretty stupid thing. I chased after him. Look.' Lucy went over and indicated a couple of thin branches on the edge of the jungle. They were snapped back, and Richard could see the white sap seeping from the exposed wood inside.

'You followed him into the jungle?'

'I did.'

Richard could see how anxious Lucy was.

'And did you catch him?'

'No. He had a head start on me, and the jungle's pretty thick around here, so about ten steps in, I lost him altogether. That's when I came back out here, got straight into my car and came down to the Police station to report the incident. Because, whoever he is, it's got to stop.'

'So,' he said, 'this man could be anywhere by now?'

'I suppose so.'

'Well, let's see about that,' Camille said, and before Richard could stop her, his partner had pushed through the broken branches and started to wade into the thick jungle.

'Camille, what are you doing?' Richard asked, unable to keep the panic out of his voice.

'Police work,' she called back, at which point Richard saw her stop dead in her tracks. Oh God, he thought to himself, what if a giant spider had just jumped at Camille's face? Fortunately for Richard, before he had to pretend that he was about to come to his partner's aid, Camille headed off at a new bearing, and he realised that she'd only paused to check that she was on the right track before continuing on her way.

As the dense vegetation finally swallowed Camille, Lucy turned to Richard.

'We'd better follow her,' she said, before pushing into the jungle and soon disappearing herself.

Richard looked about himself in a panic. While he felt just about okay-ish letting one woman go into the jungle on her own – especially seeing as she was a trained Police Officer – he felt he couldn't very well let *two* women vanish into the unknown while he stayed back here on the fringes, even though that was precisely where he wanted to stay. So, taking a deep breath to steady his internal shriek of terror, Richard stepped into the jungle.

Within seconds, he was lost. The vines and vegetation pressed into his face, the fetid smell of the jungle was revolting – it seemed to be a pungent mix of rotting fruit and decaying animals – which, when Richard thought about it, was very possibly because the jungle was full of rotting fruit and decaying animals. He felt whole rivers of sweat run down his back. Where had the women got to? Richard heard some branches snapping up ahead of him, and he made himself push through the sticky vegetation another ten or so paces until he saw the figures of Camille and Lucy through a thick screen of vines. Before he lost his nerve entirely, Richard covered the remaining distance like a mad marionette – his legs and arms lifting as high and wide as possible – until he burst through the wall of vines into a little clearing.

As Richard dashed the burrs, berries and sticky god-knows-whats from his jacket and trouser legs, he could see Camille looking directly at him and smiling broadly. He gritted his teeth. As far as Richard was concerned, it wasn't his fault he didn't function well in a tropical jungle, was it? His last posting had been in Croydon, for heaven's sake.

'You okay, sir?' Camille asked, pretending to be concerned.

'Yes. I'm fine,' he said.

'Then I think you need to see this. I've found something.'

Richard went over and saw that Camille and Lucy had found an area of ground that was littered with empty water bottles, paper bags that had once contained fresh food, crushed cigarette packets and an empty bottle of cheap vodka.

'Someone's been here,' Camille said, indicating the food.

Richard saw a column of bright red fire ants – each seemingly the size of his thumb – marching up to and engulfing a bag that had once contained a pastry of some sort, and he took a couple of steps back.

'Although I don't see any evidence of anyone sleeping

out here,' Camille said, looking about herself. 'No tent's been pitched. Or bivouac. Or rain cover of any sort.'

'I see,' Richard said, lifting his feet up one by one to check that an army of fire ants weren't already marching up his legs. 'So tell me, Ms Beaumont, is there anything else you noticed about the man you saw earlier today?'

'I'm sorry,' Lucy said. 'I've told you everything I can remember. He was definitely a man. And he was definitely old. I didn't really notice his clothes, but he had this beard – sort of whitish, sort of grey – and long-flowing grey hair. That's all I saw. And I had no idea that he had any kind of camp in the jungle here.'

Richard looked about himself. It wasn't much to go on, was it? An old tramp had been spying on Lucy from the jungle. And when Lucy had tried to confront him, he'd run away.

There was a sudden bang from nearby – followed by a flock of parrots squawking into the air above the jungle.

'What was that?' Lucy asked.

'That sounded like a gunshot,' Camille said to her boss.

'What?' Lucy said, panicking.

'Quiet!' Richard ordered, trying to work out where the sound had come from. Like Camille, he'd already guessed that the sharp retort had been from a gun of some kind. But where had it come from?

There was a second bang, and, without thinking, both Camille and Richard started running towards the noise – Richard this time pushing through the vines and vegetation without any thought for his personal safety – or that of his suit – and they soon burst out of the jungle and back into the blinding sunlight of the cobbled yard. There was no-one nearby. So where had the gunshot come from?

Lucy joined them only moments later.

'What do you mean, that was a gunshot?' she asked.

'Stay here,' Richard said, before turning to Camille. 'There might still be a shooter on the premises. We need to check the farm buildings.'

Camille marvelled at how a man so personally timid could be so apparently brave when there was clear procedure to follow, but Richard was already heading off to investigate the nearest farm building.

'Saint-Marie Police!' he called out before entering the open door.

Over the next few minutes, Richard and Camille announced themselves before entering the nearby farm buildings one by one, but there was no sign of anyone who might have fired the two gunshots, let alone any sign of what the gunshots might have been aimed at.

Richard reconvened with Camille in the centre of the cobbled yard.

'It was definitely a gunshot, sir.'

'Two gunshots, Camille. I agree'.

Lucy came over to join the Police, and Richard turned to her.

'Do you have any idea why we just heard gunshots?'

'No,' Lucy said, but even as she said this, Richard and Camille could see the young woman's gaze slide towards one of the few buildings they hadn't yet searched. It was a long stone barn – a bit like a stables – with five evenly-spaced openings along the side, although Richard could see that the middle opening had a thick wooden door built into it. And while there was a gabled roof of red tiles running the length of the building, the area of roof directly above the central wooden door rose high into the air in a cone-shape that was shorn off at the top in a way that reminded Richard of the main body of a windmill. Or perhaps – more accurately – a Kentish oast house. But it was as Richard was looking up at the cone structure in the middle of the building that he realised he could see puffs of smoke or steam gently rising out of the top of it.

'What's that building over there?' he asked Lucy.

'It's the old drying shed,' she said.

'Let's check it out,' Camille said, and started jogging towards the building.

Richard and Lucy followed, and by the time they arrived at the building, Camille was already trying the handle to the heavy wooden door, but it wasn't budging.

'It's locked,' she said.

'Is there a key to this room?' Richard asked Lucy.

'I don't think so. There's just an iron bolt you slide across on the inside.'

Richard looked at the door and could see that it was

ancient – maybe over a hundred years old – and it had wide black iron hinges holding it in place. It was the sort of door you'd expect to find on a safe-room in an old castle. Entirely solid, entirely impregnable, and with a locking mechanism that could only be accessed from the inside.

'Saint-Marie Police!' Richard called out. 'Open up this door!'

There was no answer. As Richard saw Camille go to investigate through one of the open doorways nearby, he turned to face Lucy.

'Is there another way in?'

Lucy shook her head. 'No, it's just an old room we've converted into a shower room. This is the only way in.'

Richard stepped back from the door and looked up at the raised area of roof. Steam was now very definitely billowing out of the cone. So he took a deep breath, steadied himself a moment, and then ran for the door and shoulder-barged it.

His left shoulder exploded in pain, and he recoiled in a whimper.

'Bloody hell, that hurt.'

Then, as he rubbed his shoulder to get some feeling back into it, he saw Camille re-appear from the nearby doorway, but now she was holding a massive sledgehammer. Where the hell had she got that from?

'Is there any other way in?' he asked her.

'Not that I can see, but I found this,' she said.

'A sledgehammer?'

'We need the strongest person here to smash that door in.'

'And you think that's me?'

'As it happens, no, but you'd be offended if I didn't ask you first. So please be as quick as you can, sir, we need to get in there.'

Camille shifted the weight of the sledgehammer over to a now speechless Richard and went to stand with Lucy.

Richard now realised that he was wearing a beautiful woollen suit while also holding a super-heavy weapon of destruction. The sort of super-heavy weapon he'd always seen manly men use. The tiniest hint of a smile appeared at the corner of his mouth.

He turned to face the door and took a moment to steady himself. And then, knowing that he was now holding hundreds of pounds of power in his hands, Richard opened his mind to all of the resentments he felt at being posted to the tropics. How he couldn't get a decent pint of bitter, a slice of bread, or even a proper cup of tea. How he'd found a black scorpion lurking in one of his slippers that morning. Then Richard thought about how bloody hot it was at all times, and how desperately he craved just one morning of crisp winter, with mist hanging in the air, and frosted grass crunching underfoot. And, as he gave in to his normally-suppressed feelings of frustration at the almost infinite vicissitudes of his life, Richard felt a powerful wave of emotion rise up inside him and, before he even knew he was doing it, he was swinging the sledgehammer through the air and thumping it dead-eyed into the door just beneath the handle with a thunderous crack.

Richard exhaled. Oh, that had felt good. But had it worked?

Richard saw the door swing back an inch on its hinges, and he could see that the frame had splintered where the bolt had torn free of its housing.

Richard caught a look of wonder on Camille's face, but she was quick to hide it when she realised that her boss was looking at her, and she pushed past him to enter the shower room. Richard dropped the sledgehammer to the ground as Lucy entered the room after Camille, and then he followed .

As he stepped into the room, Richard was almost instantly swallowed by a fog of hot steam. Remembering that Lucy had called this building 'the shower room', Richard guessed – and could also hear – that a powerful shower was turned on somewhere nearby.

Richard wafted the door open and shut a few times to help clear the steam, and he was soon able to see that the room was empty – although, now he was looking, he could see that there was an object slumped on the floor to the left hand side of the room.

The object looked like a human body.

A human body that wasn't moving.

As Camille went to inspect the body, Richard was pleased to see that Lucy had kept her distance and was standing on the other side of the room.

'Please don't move or touch anything,' he told Lucy,

indicating that she was to stay exactly where she was, and he went over to the shower that was built into the side of the wall, and which was thumping hot water down onto the mosaic-tiled floor to the side of the body. As Richard twisted the dial on the wall to turn the shower off, he saw that the body belonged to a man.

'He's dead, sir,' Camille said.

Richard saw that the dead man looked to be in his sixties. He was wearing old jeans, a cheap grey shirt that was frayed at the collar and seams, and a tatty old pair of trainers that had once been white but were now grey and falling apart. Richard also saw that the man had matted grey hair that went down to his shoulders, and a nicotine-stained beard that was similarly straggly.

But what was perhaps most noticeable was the handgun that Richard could see was loosely held in the dead man's right hand where it lay on the floor. And seeing as there was no-one else in the room when they'd smashed the door in, Richard realised that it was pretty obvious what had happened here. The man – whoever he was – had come into the shower room, bolted the door from the inside, and then committed suicide by shooting himself with the handgun.

Before Richard rolled the body over to reveal the dead man's face, he briefly noticed that the man lay on the floor directly between the shower and the drain that was set into the centre of the mosaic-tiled room. And although the water from the shower had run down to the old man on its way to the metal-grilled hole in the floor, his body had formed something of a barrier, and the water had gone around him on either side on its way to the drain. In other words, Richard realised, the shower hadn't been running long enough to really drench the man's clothes and start seeping underneath the body as it ran away. The area of floor that lay directly between the body and the drain was still bone dry.

This briefly puzzled Richard. After all, it made sense that the man would have turned on the shower *before* committing suicide. It was a well-known – if somewhat macabre – fact that most suicides were carried out with some consideration for those who were about to discover the body. This was why so many gun suicides happened in bathrooms. The person about to commit suicide knows that bathrooms are altogether easier to clean of blood than any of the other rooms in a house. And the fact that this man had turned on the shower and positioned himself by the drain before he shot himself suggested that this suicide was no different. The man had wanted to make sure that whatever blood he created with his death would be sluiced away afterwards.

But if the shower had been turned on before the man had taken his own life, the tiles should have been wet all the way between the shower and the drain. After all, while it was plausible that the body became a barrier to the water after it had collapsed to the floor, it didn't seem possible that no water at all had made it to the drain before the man had killed himself. And yet, the tiles between the dead body and the drain were entirely dry. Maybe there was some kind of timer on the shower that had turned on after the man had killed himself, Richard wondered to himself. Either way, Richard filed away the puzzle of whether the shower had been turned on *ante* or *post mortem* for later consideration.

It was time to turn the body over and discover the man's identity.

Richard took hold of the body's shoulders, and Camille looked over at Lucy.

'I think you should leave.'

'I want to see his face.'

'But we don't know how damaged the body is.'

'I don't care,' Lucy said desperately. 'I have to see.'

Camille looked at Richard. He nodded. It was okay by him.

With a grunt of effort – cadavers were always surprisingly heavy – Richard turned the body over, but he and Camille needn't have worried about gore. There was only the smallest of blooms of blood seeping onto the man's grey shirt above the heart area. But, once again, Richard noticed that although the back of the body was wet with water, the clothes to the front of the corpse – where the body had been touching the floor – were still bone dry. It was looking increasingly as though the man was dead and on the tiles before the shower had been turned on.

As for the body itself, Richard could see that the man's face was hollow-cheeked and craggy-lined from age. And although his skin was greyish-white, his cheeks and nose were a purple starburst of burst veins. He had clearly been a drinker. Adding to the impression of an old man who didn't look after himself was an unruly pair of grey eyebrows and a long beard that seemed almost yellow rather than white, and which was very distinctly nicotine-stained around the mouth – from the cigarettes, Richard could smell from the man's clothes, that he smoked.

'It's him,' Lucy said simply.

'This is the man you saw stalking you this morning?'

'It is.'

'And who you then chased into the jungle?'

'That's right,' Lucy said, but Richard could see that something was making her frown.

'Are you sure?'

'Yes. It's definitely him. It's the man I chased into the jungle.'

Lucy was still troubled by something.

'What's wrong?' Richard asked.

Lucy kept on looking at the man on the ground.

'Ms Beaumont, what is it?'

'It's just, I don't know who he is.'

'How do you mean?'

'Well, I only got the briefest of glimpses of him before now. But I always reckoned I'd maybe recognise him if I ever got up close.'

'And you don't?'

'I don't,' Lucy said. 'In fact, I've no idea who that man is at all.'

Richard looked at Camille.

And then he looked from Camille back to Lucy.

'Then who the hell is he?'

CHAPTER TWO

'You're sure you don't recognise him?' Richard asked.

Lucy was troubled as she looked at the old man.

'I don't. But he's definitely the man I saw this morning.'

'Then, is there anyone else at the plantation who might recognise him?'

'I don't think there are any workers on the plantation at the moment.'

'There aren't?' Richard asked, surprised.

'It's the wrong time in the growing season. But the rest of my family should be up at the house.'

Richard looked at Camille, who got the message.

'I'll accompany you back to the house,' she said. 'We'll need to bring whoever we can down here to see if they can identify the body.'

'Of course,' Lucy said.

'And call Dwayne and Fidel, Camille,' Richard said as Camille led Lucy out of the room. 'Pull them off the bootleg rum case. We're going to need them and the Crime Scene Kit up here pronto.'

Once Camille and Lucy had left, Richard started to work the scene. First he took stock of the room. It was about forty feet across, entirely circular, and the walls and floor were constructed of stone. And from the way that the stone on the walls and floor was worn away, Richard could tell that the building was very old. Halfway around the room, there was an old metal-framed window to let light in, and on the far side of the room there was a slatted bench with a neatly-stacked pile of white towels waiting to be used.

The shower area itself consisted of two tall sheets of glass, one either side of a mosaic-tiled area where the shower and control unit were.

Richard went to the centre of the room and looked up at the cone-shaped roof as it rose high above his head. He could see that the wide opening at the very top of the cone had been blocked off and there was now just an old metal vent of some sort. There was no way a human could have come in or out of the building through the 'chimney'.

Richard had only seen the one bullet wound in the man's chest and yet he'd definitely heard two shots being fired when he'd been in the jungle, so he decided to see if he could discover what had happened to the other bullet.

Richard 'walked the grid' of the floor and soon found two bullet casings where they'd skittered to a stop on the tiles about five feet from the body. So if two bullets had been fired – as the two bullet casings suggested – where was the second bullet? Richard returned to the body, and it was only as he crouched down and really started checking it over that he found the second wound.

When he unclasped the dead man's right hand from the handle of the pistol, he saw a bullet hole in the base of the man's right palm. Richard hadn't noticed it when he'd first seen the body because the man's hand had been holding the gun. And the hand had been in the wash of water that was flowing around the body, so most of the blood that had come out of the wound had been washed away. But now, as Richard looked more carefully, he could see a red sheen to the tiles that lay in between the man's hand and the plughole.

Now he thought about it, Richard realised he'd failed to notice this wound the first time around because, although there was an entry wound as the bullet had punched through the man's palm and into his wrist, there was no exit wound. Richard guessed that the bullet had maybe hit the bones inside the wrist, and then stopped dead in its tracks.

This was puzzling. If two shots were fired by this man, then he must have shot himself in the wrist first before shooting himself in the heart – seeing as the shot to the heart would have been the killing shot. Therefore, it was only logical to presume that the shot to the heart had come second. The shot to the wrist must have come first.

But seeing as the man had died holding the gun in his

right hand – suggesting that he was right-handed – how on earth did that first bullet get into his right wrist? The man would have to have been holding the gun in his left hand to fire it. And why would a right-handed man fire a gun with his left hand? And, having smashed the bones in his right wrist with that first bullet, the man would then have had to transfer the gun over to his right hand, somehow grip the gun with his broken hand, and then pull the trigger, firing the fatal shot into his heart.

It didn't seem in any way possible, did it?

And now that Richard was thinking about it, what sort of suicide attempt was so botched that the first bullet missed the heart and hit the wrist instead?

As Richard looked down at the body, he remembered how the area of tiles between the body and the drain had been dry when he'd broken into the room, suggesting that the shower had perhaps been turned on *after* the body had hit the ground.

When understanding came to Richard, it was almost as a physical shock.

This wasn't suicide.

This was murder.

But what exactly had happened here? Richard took a step back and imagined a shooter aiming his gun at the old man. It seemed only natural that he would try to plead for his life, or – yes, maybe this was it! – he'd even try to grab the gun out of the killer's hand. But when the old man raised his hand to grab the gun, the killer fired the shot that drilled through the man's palm and shattered the bones in his right wrist. Then, before the old man could run away or shout for help, the killer fired the second shot, and this time the bullet went straight into the old man's heart.

Jesus, Richard thought to himself. This wasn't a murder. This was an execution. But it was an execution that hadn't quite gone to plan. The killer had been forced to use two bullets rather than the one. And then what had happened next? Well, Richard considered, seeing as he'd just found the victim in an empty room with the gun in his right hand, it was pretty obvious that the killer's plan had always been to make this murder look like a suicide. And even though there were now two bullets in the victim, the killer would have known that the gunshots had been very loud. Loud enough for anyone nearby to come and investigate. He or she would also no doubt have been panicking at the fact that the murder had been botched. There wouldn't have been time to finesse the situation. So the killer had decided to go through with the plan of making the scene look like a suicide – and hope that the Police didn't work out the truth.

So far, so understandable. But there was still an aspect of the scene that didn't quite make sense. Having committed murder – when time was surely at a premium – why did the murderer then linger at the scene long enough to turn on the shower? Was it to wash away the blood? It seemed a possibility, but Richard couldn't see how washing away the blood might be of any benefit to the killer. After all, it didn't wash away the body or the two bullets, did it?

So what *was* the killer trying to wash away?

Richard went over to the shower controls and inspected them. There were two dials. One that turned the water on and off, and one that controlled the temperature. There was no timer. So it hadn't come on automatically, Richard realised. It could only be turned on manually. As Richard peered at the second dial, he saw that it was twisted all the way around to its highest setting. Richard was surprised. Why was the shower set to its hottest temperature?

There was a discreet cough from the doorway. Richard looked over and saw Camille.

'Sir. I've brought the occupants of the house to identify the body.'

Richard could see a clutch of people waiting behind Camille. 'How many people are there?'

'Three, sir. But a fourth is on the way. He was out in the coffee fields.'

Richard tried to work out the best way of proceeding.

'Okay, then would you send them in one by one please.'

The first person to enter was tall, thin, had a glossy mane of blonde hair, and was wearing a faded pair of blue jeans, a long-sleeved shirt in blue denim, and very old Converse trainers. Richard guessed that the man was about fifty years old, and from the way that he was carrying himself – and the patrician way he swept his eyes over the scene and the dead body – Richard guessed that this was maybe the plantation owner.

'Hugh Beaumont,' the man said with a smile as he went over to Richard and shook his hand firmly. 'I'm Lucy's father. I'm in charge here.'

'Detective Inspector Richard Poole,' Richard said, quietly impressed by Hugh's bearing. After all, it took a certain type of person to make sure that introductions were completed satisfactorily while a dead body lay only a few feet away.

'So, this is Lucy's Peeping Tom, is it?' Hugh said, turning to look at the victim.

'Apparently so,' Richard said.

'Amazing. We all thought she was making it up.'

'You did?'

'Well, only in the sense that none of the rest of us saw anyone lurking down here. Anyway, I'm sure you'll have plenty of questions in due course, but let me see if I recognise him.'

Hugh took out a pair of gold-rimmed glasses from his shirt pocket and put them on. He then walked a couple of paces to the side so he could better see the dead man's face. He bent over to get a closer look, shook his head sadly to himself, and then stood up again.

'I'm sorry. I've no idea who he is.'

'You don't?'

'I've never seen that man before in my life.'

'I see. And you're sure?'

'Quite sure.'

'Might he perhaps be a plantation worker who used to work here?'

'I don't think so. I don't recognise him. And I'm pretty sure I would. I've got a good memory for faces. Sorry not to be more help. Shall I send the next person in?'

'Yes please. Thank you, Mr Beaumont.'

'Please,' Hugh said with an easy smile. 'It's Hugh.' He then left, saying, 'I'll send Sylvie in next. She's my wife.'

A few moments after Hugh left, a woman – also in her fifties – entered. And whereas Hugh was tall and thin, Sylvie was far shorter, far rounder, and she was wearing a dark blue trouser suit that wouldn't have been out of place at a cocktail party at Government House. Richard had the suspicion that Sylvie had put it on specially to meet the Police.

'So this is the man who's shot himself?' she said in plummy tones that were ninety-five per cent regal, Richard realised, and five per cent... what? He wasn't sure. But there was maybe something forced about just how posh Sylvie was being.

'How macabre,' she said, pronouncing 'macabre' with a suitably French roll to her tongue. 'I mean, it's ghastly, isn't it? Finding a dead man in one's shower room. Although, I suppose you're used to this sort of thing.'

Richard recognised a put-down when he heard one, and decided that he didn't much like Sylvie.

For her part, Sylvie turned from the body and looked at Richard.

'You're that British policeman, aren't you?'

'If you mean, am I Detective Inspector Richard Poole, then yes I am. Could you tell me if you recognise the body?'

'I'm so sorry, but I don't,' she said without a hint of regret.

'Are you sure?'

'I'm not the sort of person who consorts with tramps.'

'So that's who you think this person is? A tramp?'

'Or vagabond. I never know the difference. I suppose you do?'

Richard decided that he'd had enough of Sylvie.

'So you definitely don't recognise him?'

'I don't.'

'Then thank you very much for your time. If you could send the next person through?'

'Of course,' Sylvie said with a superior smile, and left the room.

Richard briefly considered the differences between the welcoming charm of Hugh and the dismissive manner of his wife, but he was interrupted by the arrival of the third witness.

He was a young man – a boy, really, Richard thought to himself – aged about eighteen years old.

'Oh,' he said in a light voice as he saw the dead body on the tiles, and Richard took a moment to notice that the man seemed to be a perfect copy of Hugh, but thirty years younger. In fact, as Richard looked at the man's smart haircut, slender build, and easy manner, he wondered

– not for the first time – how a certain class of Brit managed to breed effortlessness into their children. But, more troubling than that, Richard saw that this boy-man was wearing the sort of casual clothes that Richard wished he had the confidence to wear: an old pair of brown suede shoes, khaki chinos smartly held up with an old leather belt the same shade of brown as his shoes, and a somewhat billowing white shirt that was tucked in at the waist, rolled up at the sleeves, and open at the neck. Before he could stop himself, Richard had a little epiphany. He realised that this elegant young person – who had only uttered one syllable so far – embodied pretty much all of the conflicts he felt about the British upper classes. Their inherited wealth and sense of entitlement made him sick to his bones, but he quite liked how they dressed.

Richard snapped out of his reverie as he saw the young man grimace.

'Bloody hell,' he said. He then turned to Richard with an apologetic smile. 'Sorry. My first dead body.'

'I understand. It can be very distressing. But you only need to look at his face. Just tell me if you recognise him.'

'Okay,' the young man said, turning back to look at the victim's face. After a few seconds, he turned back to Richard.

'Sorry. No idea.'

'Are you sure?'

'I think so.'

'Okay. Then can I ask your name?'

'Oh, of course,' the young man said, coming over to shake Richard's hand in a perfect facsimile of Hugh's manners. 'Sorry. Matthew Beaumont. I'm Hugh and Sylvie's son. Lucy's brother.'

'Detective Inspector Richard Poole,' Richard said before internally wincing. He was supposed to be in charge here, not this callow youth. But before he could stamp his authority back on the interview, the light in the doorway was blocked as someone stood on the threshold.

'No way, you have got to be kidding me!' Richard heard the person say in a Caribbean accent, and then in walked what Richard could only call an anomaly.

Whereas Hugh, Sylvie and Matthew were all types of Brits abroad that Richard recognised well – they were patrician, posh, and very much in charge – this young man was barefoot, was wearing a frayed pair of swimming trunks and a filthy T-shirt with a massive logo of a cannabis leaf on the front.

Matthew saw the confusion in Richard's face and smiled in understanding.

'This is my older brother, Tom,' he said, indicating the man in the doorway.

'So it's true,' Tom said. 'A real live dead body. On our land. I can't believe it.'

Richard went to say something, but realised he still couldn't get over how this one member of the family had a Saint-Marie accent.

'The Inspector just wants you to see if you recognise his face,' Matthew said.

'Okay,' Tom said and went and inspected the body.

After a few moments, he did a complicated flick with his right hand that produced a clicking noise.

'A bullet to the heart. That's sick.'

'I agree,' Richard said.

'You do?' Tom asked, surprised.

'Of course.'

'That's sick.'

'What is?'

'It's sick that you think it's sick.'

After a moment's reflection, Richard decided that he and Tom almost certainly had very different working definitions of what the word 'sick' meant.

'Okay,' Tom said, standing up from the body, 'I've never seen this guy before.'

'You haven't?'

'No way.'

'Just like the rest of your family.'

'What's that?' Matthew asked.

'None of you recognise him.'

Matthew frowned as he considered this.

'So how come someone we've never seen before shot himself dead in our shower room?'

Before Richard could answer, Camille stepped into the room.

'Dwayne and Fidel are here.'

'Alright,' Richard said to Tom and Matthew, 'I'll need you to clear the room. Would you tell your family that I'd like to speak to them back at your house in a few minutes?'

Once the room was clear and Dwayne and Fidel had entered with the Crime Scene kit, Richard explained his theory that the unknown man's death wasn't suicide, it was murder. He then tasked Dwayne with working the primary crime scene in the shower room, and he told Fidel to go into the jungle and collect whatever evidence he could find from the clearing where they believed the victim had been hiding.

As for Richard and Camille, they were soon heading up the hill to the Beaumonts' main residence. As they approached, Richard could see that the house was made of the same stone as the rest of the plantation, and its formal dimensions, white sash windows, and shiny black door gave it the look of a Georgian rectory.

Hugh opened the door as they approached.

'Welcome to Beaumont Manor,' he said, and ushered Richard and Camille into the main hall.

Richard realised that the name of the house wasn't misplaced. The main hall was almost pitch black, smelt of furniture polish, and there was a wide wooden staircase that led up to the rooms above. As for why it was so dark, Richard could see that the two sash windows either side of the front door had their shutters firmly shut.

'Sorry about the gloom,' Hugh said, 'but we have to keep our ancestors out of direct sunlight.'

Once Richard's eyes had adjusted to the dark, he could see that the hall was wood-panelled, and every spare inch of wall space was covered in oil paintings of old family members stretching back what looked like hundreds of years. Richard saw glimpses of men in armour, men sitting on horses, and more modern men sitting in front of views of Saint-Marie.

'What a lot of men,' Camille said, and Richard caught the note of sarcasm in her voice.

Hugh, however, didn't, and was clearly proud as punch as he indicated the hall.

'Yes,' he said. 'This whole place is full of history. The floorboards you're standing on are made from the deck of the ship that brought the first Beaumont over to the island. Here, let me introduce you.'

With an enthusiastic grin, Hugh went over to a gilt-framed portrait at the foot of the stairs. Looking at it, Richard could see a narrow-faced man with piercing blue eyes and tightly-curled blonde hair looking straight back at him. The portrait's stare was so intense – so unflinching – that it was somewhat unsettling.

'Great Great Grandfather, the Honourable Thomas Beaumont, the youngest son of Baron Halstead. His older brother inherited the family estate and title, but Thomas, as the younger son, had no role in life, so he did what a lot of younger sons did at the time and decamped to the colonies to seek his fortune. He came to Saint-Marie in 1777, and built the coffee plantation up from scratch.'

'Wow,' Camille said – and Richard again picked up the sarcasm in her voice.

'I know,' Hugh said, having once again taken Camille's comment at face value. 'If you're interested in the history of this place you should talk to Matthew, he's our resident genealogy buff. Anyway, I'm sure you don't have time for all this, let me take you through.'

As he spoke, Hugh escorted Richard and Camille from the gloom of the main hall into a long, sunny corridor, and from there into a large, airy sitting room that was stuffed full of old furniture, family photos in silver frames, and rather startling abstract paintings on the walls in various clashing colours.

Furnishing aside, the immediate impression that Richard got as he entered the room was that the family members had been in the middle of a conversation, and they'd cut it short the moment the Police had walked in. Perhaps it was understandable, Richard thought to himself. After all, a dead body had just been found in one of their outhouses.

Before he addressed the family, Richard noticed that Sylvie was standing with her back to a rather grand marble fireplace – as though she'd been the focus of whatever conversation had been going on – and Matthew and Lucy were sitting next to each other on a sofa. As for Tom, he was sitting in a window seat on his own.

'Thank you all for waiting for us,' Richard said as he and Camille crossed the room to join the family, and Sylvie went to join Hugh as he sat down on an old chesterfield sofa.

'Now, I just have a few questions, it shouldn't take too long.'

'Don't worry,' Hugh said on behalf of his family. 'We'll do whatever we can to help.'

'Thank you. But just to be sure, are you really sure none of you recognised the body of the man we found in your shower room just now?'

'It's all we've been talking about,' Sylvie said. 'And I'm rather relieved to say, we can't even begin to place him.'

'Are you positive?'

'We are,' Sylvie said in a tone that made it clear that she now considered the subject closed.

'I see,' Richard said. 'Then I need to ask where you all were at eleven o'clock this morning.'

'You do?' Hugh asked.

'That's right. Where were you all when the man died?'

'Why does it matter?'

'If you could just answer the question.'

'Okay,' Hugh said. 'I was upstairs in my bedroom. With my laptop. Doing emails and checking up on the world.'

'Was anyone with you?'

'How do you mean?'

'Do you have an alibi?'

This hit home.

'I don't know,' Hugh said. 'Maybe not. I was on my

own. Until Lucy came in and told me someone had just shot themselves in the old drying shed.'

'That's what you call your shower room?' Richard asked. 'The old drying shed?'

'Not any more,' Sylvie said, reminding her husband where the power lay in their relationship. 'I converted it into a shower room a few years ago. Mainly because I was so fed up with the family coming back from the fields covered in filth and mud.'

'Sylvie's right,' Hugh said. 'But since you're asking, I don't think I can prove where I was when that man shot himself. Not categorically.'

'Thank you,' Richard said. 'Then what about the rest of you?'

'Well, that's easy enough,' Sylvie said. 'I was in the kitchen preparing lunch.'

'And can anyone alibi you?'

'Normally Nanny Rosie would be with me, but she's off visiting family on Montserrat for a couple of days.'

'Who's Nanny Rosie?' Camille asked.

'She was the children's nanny when they were growing up, but she's stayed on as our housekeeper since then. Anyway, she's not here, so I was on my own in the kitchen.'

'As for me,' Matthew said, 'I was upstairs in my room at eleven o'clock.'

'Was anyone with you?'

'No. I'm sorry. And like father, I didn't come downstairs

until Lucy arrived saying she'd just found a dead body in the shower room.'

'Very well,' Richard said, and turned to Tom.

'What?' he said, as though he'd only at that moment realised the Police were asking him a question.

'Where were you when the gunshots were fired?'

'I was in the coffee fields.'

'On your own?'

'Sure. I check them every morning regular as clockwork. Me and our crops, eleven o'clock every day. Or thereabouts.'

'Then can you tell me why you didn't return to the main house?'

'I'm sorry?'

'I assume you heard the gunshots? Seeing as you were in the coffee fields?'

'I didn't hear nothing.'

Richard tried not to shudder. What was it with youngsters and their slapdash approach to language? He'd already had to endure Tom using the word 'sick' in a way that made no actual sense, but this was going too far. After all, while it was theoretically possible for someone to hear nothing – or to *not* hear something, of course – it seemed logically impossible for someone to "not hear nothing".

'You didn't hear anything?' Camille said, guessing why her boss now looked as though he'd just sucked on a lemon, and wanting to make sure that the conversation kept moving.

'No way,' Tom said. 'The first I knew anything was up was when Lucy rang me on my mobile. And she told me what had happened. That's when I came back from the fields.'

'I see. Thank you.'

'But I don't understand why you're wasting our time,' Sylvie said. 'That man shot himself, didn't he? So what does it matter where we all were?'

'But that's the thing,' Richard said. 'He didn't shoot himself. He was murdered.'

There was a gasp from Lucy, and Richard could see that the rest of the family were just as shocked.

Sylvie recovered first.

'Don't be ridiculous,' she said.

'Which leads me to my next question,' Richard said, deciding that it was time to steamroller Sylvie. 'Because, according to Lucy, the murder victim has been hanging around the plantation for the last couple of weeks. And we've found some kind of hideout in the jungle that seems to back up her statement. So I need to know, have any of you been aware of a stalker spying on the plantation recently?'

Hugh answered on behalf of the family, but Richard could see how rattled he was.

'I'm sorry, we haven't. I mean, don't get me wrong, it's like I said to you in the shower room. Lucy mentioned to us that she'd seen someone lurking about, but none of the rest of us have seen anyone.'

'So, to be clear,' Richard said to the family, 'not only can none of you identify the murder victim, you're also saying that it was only Lucy who'd even seen him about over the last few weeks?'

Richard looked at the family, and could see that they all agreed with his statement. Very well. Time to move on.

'Then can I ask, do any of you own a handgun?'

There was a sharp intake of breath from Sylvie.

'*What?*'

'It's a simple enough question,' Richard said. 'Do any of you own a handgun?'

'No, of course we don't,' she snapped. 'Why would any of us own a gun?'

It seemed a fair enough answer, but before Richard could ask any follow-up questions, the door opened and Fidel entered the room.

'Sorry to interrupt, sir, but there's something I think you need to see.'

'There is?' Richard said.

'Yes, sir. Although can I ask the family a question first?'

'Of course,' Richard said.

Fidel turned to the room and was suddenly awkward.

'Well, it's just…you see, I was wondering if any of the family own any kind of three-wheeled van at all? Or it could be a three-wheeled motorbike.'

'No,' Hugh said. 'We've got two cars we share between the five of us, but nothing that's got three wheels.'

'Then maybe there's a three-wheeled vehicle on your plantation somewhere?' Fidel asked.

The witnesses were just as sure that there were no three-wheeled vehicles anywhere on the plantation, so Richard thanked the family for their time, and then he and Camille followed Fidel back to the murder scene. On the way, he asked Fidel why he'd wanted to know about three-wheeled vehicles.

'It's probably best if I show you, sir,' Fidel said.

'Very well. How did you and Dwayne got on trying to catch the Commissioner's bootleg rum seller?'

'Well, sir. We spoke to the manager down at the Fort Royal hotel, and he confirmed what the Commissioner told us. There'd been a guy on the roadside trying to sell knocked-off bottles of rum to the guests as they came and went from the hotel.'

'Did you see him?'

'We didn't. He was gone by the time we arrived.'

'Then did you get a description of him?'

'Not in the time we were at the hotel. Camille phoned us and told us you'd found a body, so we dropped everything and came straight here.'

'Quite right,' Richard said, already wishing he could kick the bootleg rum seller into the long grass. But experience told him that once the Commissioner had expressed an interest in a case, he tended to stay involved until the bitter end.

As Richard mulled how best to manage the

Commissioner's expectations, Fidel led them to a group of buildings just beyond the old drying shed.

'Where exactly are we going?' he asked.

'Don't worry, sir. It's just through this building.'

Fidel went through the open door and Richard was instantly hit by the aroma of coffee beans. It was overpowering, Richard thought, as he looked about himself. The room was full of some kind of fabric conveyor belt that led into and out of various old bits of cast iron machinery that were painted dark green. The paint was flaking in places, and there were signs of dark rust on some parts of the machinery.

'What is this?' Richard asked.

'I think this is where they pack the coffee, sir,' Fidel said, indicating a palette tray of empty hessian bags at one end of the assembly line. Richard could see the words 'Premiere Bonifieur blend, Beaumont Plantation, Saint-Marie' printed onto each bag. But before Richard could make much sense of how the machinery might have worked, Fidel was leading across the floor again and taking them through another open door that led out to the bright sunshine and jungle on the other side of the building.

'You searched out here?' Camille asked, impressed.

'Well, it didn't take me too long to gather, bag and log the physical evidence in the jungle clearing, so I thought I'd check the buildings near to the scene of the murder. See if I could find anything.'

'And what exactly is it that you found?' Richard asked.

'That's the thing, sir, I don't know if it's much, but I did find this.'

Fidel pointed down at the dusty ground, and Richard and Camille could see a set of tyre tracks in the dirt. And, as Fidel had suggested to the witnesses, they clearly belonged to a three-wheeled vehicle of some sort.

But if the family said they didn't own any three-wheeled vehicles, then whose vehicle did these tracks belong to?

Richard saw that the tyre tracks continued along the side of the building for about twenty yards, and then they turned and disappeared between two thick bushes. On the further side of the bushes was the main road that serviced the plantation.

Richard realised that if someone had driven a three-wheeled vehicle up to this side of this building, they could have approached from the main road without being seen by anyone who was in the courtyard. It was essentially a private way for a vehicle to access the plantation. And then Richard remembered something else. There'd been a sudden burst of heavy rain when he and Camille had arrived at the plantation at about 11am. So had these tracks been left before or after the downpour?

Getting down on his haunches, he inspected the tyre tracks more closely, and could see that they – and the dirt all around – were pitted with indentations from where the heavy drops of rain had fallen.

'Whatever vehicle was here, it left *before* the downpour

at 11am,' he said. 'I can see that these raindrops fell onto the tyre tracks after they'd been made.'

'Oh,' Fidel said, disappointed.

'However, you're right, Fidel,' Richard said. 'It's interesting, isn't it? There's a three-wheeled vehicle up here recently enough that the tyre tracks are still fresh in the dirt, it didn't arrive or leave by the main entrance, and none of the family drive a three-wheeled vehicle, or know of one operating on the plantation.'

Richard looked at the middle tyre print more closely, and saw a distinctive 'cut' in the mud that repeated every couple of feet or so. Whatever the vehicle was, the rubber of the middle wheel was damaged – which would possibly make identifying the vehicle that little bit easier.

'As long as this remains an unexplained phenomenon, then I want you to get some plaster of Paris from the Crime Scene Kit, and make casts of these tyre prints. In particular, I'd like you to make sure you get a decent cast of this repeating mark on the front wheel.' Here, Richard indicated the repeating 'cut' mark in the middle tyre's print.

'Yes, sir,' Fidel said, thrilled that his lead was important enough to be taken seriously.

'And while you're doing that, Camille and I need to look at the murder scene again, because I think we've got a bit of a problem.'

'We do, sir?' Camille asked.

'I think we do.'

Back at the murder scene, Richard and Camille found Dwayne photographing the body.

'Have you been able to identify the victim yet?' Richard asked.

'Not yet, Chief. Although I think he could be a Brit.'

'You do?'

'He's got some loose change in his pockets, and plenty of it is UK currency.'

'He's got British coins in his pockets?'

'He has, sir.'

Dwayne handed over a small see-through evidence bag to his boss that was full of coins.

'But I also found a receipt in his back pocket you might want to look at.'

Dwayne handed over an evidence bag that contained a cheap till receipt with blue ink so faded that it was hard to read.

'You need to turn it over,' Dwayne suggested.

Richard turned the evidence bag over and could see that on the other side of the receipt, someone had scribbled '11am' in biro.

'It says '11am',' Richard said. 'He was killed just after 11am.'

'Suggesting to me, Chief, that our victim was perhaps here for a pre-arranged meeting.'

'Now that's interesting,' Richard said, and handed the evidence bag to Camille for her to inspect. 'So this murder was possibly premeditated. Have we really got nothing beyond a few British coins to help us work out who this man was?'

'I'm sorry, Chief. Although the victim's got a pretty distinctive scar on the forefinger of his left hand.'

Dwayne crouched down and turned the victim's left hand over, indicating an old scar that ran along the victim's forefinger. It was white, ridged, and a good two inches long.

'I see,' Richard said. 'So, apart from a scar on his left hand, a few British coins, and a cryptic till receipt with "11am" written on it, we don't know who the victim is?'

'That's about it, sir,' Dwayne agreed.

'So what's the problem?' Camille asked, reminding Richard of what he'd said only a few minutes earlier.

'It's this window,' Richard said as he led Dwayne and Camille over to the little metal-framed window on the far wall of the room. 'Or to be more precise, this window, the vent in the ceiling, and that door,' he said, pointing at the ceiling and broken-in door in turn as he spoke.

'Why's that?' Dwayne asked.

'Tell me what you see,' Richard said as he indicated the window.

'Well, Chief,' Dwayne said, buying himself time, 'unless this is a trick question, it's a window.'

'You're right, Dwayne. It's a window. Camille?'

Camille's instincts were already telling her where Richard was going with this. So she got out a pair of evidence gloves, snapped them on, and started checking

out the window frame. She could see that it was fixed
solidly to the stone casement, and the glass was held in
place with old putty that had crumbled in places but had
clearly not been tampered with in any way. But she knew
the real test would be the latch that kept the window
locked shut, and she gently touched it with her fingers. It
didn't move. In fact, she could see that the window's latch
was jammed tightly into the window frame.

What was more, Camille could see that the metal lever
that allowed the window to open and close had an old
butterfly screw on it that was tightly screwed down as
well. Giving the butterfly screw a hard twist to the left,
she unscrewed it enough that she could finally open the
window. She then stuck her head outside. There was an
undisturbed flower bed directly underneath the window
with only a few weeds in, and the rest of the area behind
the shower room was concreted over.

She then closed the window again, reset the catch in
the window frame and re-locked the butterfly screw on
the lever.

'Okay,' she pronounced, 'so the window was locked.
And it can only be locked from the inside.'

'Precisely,' Richard said, pleased that Camille had also
worked it out.

Camille crossed to the centre of the room and looked
up at the ceiling high above them.

'And there's no way in or out of this room through the
roof. Not even with that vent built into the top.'

'Agreed,' Richard said. 'It's far too small.'

Camille led over to the main door.

'And this door is seriously old, isn't it?' she said. 'You couldn't even begin to tamper with the hinges, or get around it or under it in any way.'

'Quite so,' Richard said.

Camille inspected the thick iron bolt that ran across the back of the door. It was about three feet long, and was fixed very firmly inside a solid housing made of iron. And it was obvious that neither the bolt nor housing had been tampered with any more than the hinges of the door had been.

So Camille turned her attention to the door frame. It was just as solid as the door, and the lock worked by sliding the iron bolt across so it slotted into a deep hole that had been drilled directly into the door frame. She could see that the iron bolt had ripped through the wooden frame when Richard had smashed the door open with his sledgehammer.

'As for the iron bolt,' Camille said, 'it was very clearly slid across when you bashed the door open. You can see where the bolt has torn through the wood of the door frame. And that's why we've got a problem, isn't it?'

'Got it in one, Camille,' Richard said returning to the centre room. 'Because this room is entirely made of stone, and there are only three ways a human could have got out of it after the murder – those being through the window on the far side, out through the roof, or through this door. The ceiling is impossible, and both the door and the window were locked from the inside.'

'Oh, I see,' Dwayne said, understanding finally dawning on him. '*That's* the problem!'

'It is, Dwayne,' Richard agreed.

The three Police officers looked at each other.

'That's quite a problem,' Dwayne said on all of their behalves.

'It is, isn't it?' Richard agreed. 'Because, seeing as we found no-one else in here when we broke in, just how did our killer commit murder and then escape from a locked room?'

CHAPTER THREE

When Richard and his team returned to the Police station, he set them to work. Dwayne was tasked with processing the physical evidence. In particular, Richard wanted him to lift whatever fingerprints he could identify on the gun that had very possibly been used to kill the victim – and the two shell casings they'd found near the victim. As for Fidel, he'd stayed at the plantation to create plaster casts of the tyre prints he'd found behind the farm buildings, so he returned to the Police station after every-one else. Once back, he laid out the three chunky blocks of white plaster of Paris on his desk. Each one was about a foot long – and six inches deep, and six inches wide – and the surface of each of the casts was covered in grit and dirt. Fidel set to cleaning them up with a make-up brush. Once that was done, Richard tasked him with trying to use the tyre casts to identify the make and model of the vehicle from a Caribbean-wide database of tyre prints.

As for Richard, seeing as the victim had been found

with British currency in his pocket – and Lucy had said that the man had been lurking up at the plantation for the last few weeks – he decided to pull the border records for all of the Brits who'd arrived at the Saint-Marie airport in the last eight weeks. But when he spoke to the Head of Security at the airport, he discovered that it wasn't quite as simple as that. The man informed Richard that maybe as many as five thousand British tourists had arrived on the island in the previous eight weeks, and while the airport had CCTV footage of everyone as they made their way through passport control, the only way of doing any kind of visual search for the victim would be to sit down and watch every minute of airport CCTV footage from the previous eight weeks.

This was clearly impractical, so Richard asked him to send through the names of every British traveller above the age of fifty who'd arrived on the island in that time, and who'd been travelling on his own. This was because Richard had already guessed – based on the evidence of the tawdry hideout they'd found in the jungle – that their victim had perhaps been operating on his own. In fact, as Richard explained the parameters for the search he wanted carried out, he realised that there would possibly be a few dozen Brits a day who met the criteria. After all, how many fifty-plus British men travelled to a Caribbean holiday destination on their own? And then, once the Head of Security had sent the details over, Richard knew he could either cross-reference the names with whatever hotels were listed on their immigration forms, or – given that he'd now know what flights they'd arrived on – he could just pull the airport CCTV footage for each person's arrival, and see if he could identify the victim visually. And here, Richard knew that their victim's long grey hair and yellow/white beard should make him easy to spot.

In fact, Richard realised, if their victim was indeed from the UK and had arrived at any time in the last eight weeks, it might be possible to work out his identity in the next few hours.

'You're right,' the Head of Security said at the other end of the phone. 'I'd even go so far as to say that you're onto something there.'

'Thank you,' Richard said.

'Although, it'll take longer than a few hours to identify your British traveller.'

'Why? The list won't be very long, will it?'

'Oh it'll barely be a few hundred names. It's just going to take a few days to get the list to you, that's all.'

'I'm sorry?'

'If not longer than a few days. Tell you what,' the man paused as though he were about to do Richard a massive favour. 'I reckon I can get the list of solo Brits to you by the beginning of next week.'

'What?'

'Or soon after.'

'But it's only Thursday now. Surely you've already got this information on your system?'

'Of course. We take everyone's details who arrives on the island. We're a professional outfit.'

'Then it should take all of about thirty seconds to create a search on your system for solo British travellers from the last eight weeks aged fifty years and over, and then you can email me the results. I could start working on this in the next few minutes!'

There was a pause at the other end of the line.

And then the man coughed to clear his throat.

'What's that?' Richard asked.

'Nothing. It's just – well, let me put it like this. I agree, your plan makes perfect sense. It's just we had a bit of an IT problem at the end of last week.'

'You did?'

'So I don't think it will be that easy. But we'll definitely be able to get you the results you want at some point next week. Or the week after.'

'What sort of an IT problem?'

'What's that?'

'You said you had "a bit of an IT problem". So I just wanted to know. What sort of IT problem did you have?'

'Does it matter?'

'It does to me,' Richard said, feeling his blood pressure rising. 'Seeing as I'm trying to run a murder case here.'

'Yes. Well, when you put it like that, that makes a lot of sense.'

'So what was it?'

There was another pause at the other end of the line – and then the man spoke really very quietly indeed.

'An iguana got into a cable duct.'

'What's that?'

'An iguana got into our cable ducts and ate through our network cables.'

'You know, it's funny,' Richard said. 'But I could have sworn that you just told me that an iguana had eaten through your network cables.'

'That's because I did.'

'But how can that have even been possible?' Richard all but shouted into the mouthpiece of his phone. 'I mean, don't you have security precautions in place to stop this sort of thing?'

'Don't use that tone with me, Inspector.'

'Then what tone should I be using? Would you rather I sent you a big bunch of flowers with a card wishing you "condolences at this difficult time"?'

The Head of Security didn't dignify Richard's comment with a response, and Richard found himself exhaling heavily. He'd long ago come to understand – if not accept – that solving cases on a tiny tropical island was always going to be fraught with difficulties. For example, Saint-Marie was too small to have a local Coroner's office where autopsies could be carried out. And there were no Ballistics or Forensics labs either. If Richard ever needed evidence processed by any kind of forensics lab, he generally had to send it to the far larger nearby island of Guadeloupe, and they rarely prioritised Saint-Marie's needs. It's why Richard insisted on as much of the crime scene evidence being dealt with in the office by hand. At least that way, he could have some control over how quickly it was all processed.

But for every 'typical' problem that Richard had to endure in his Police work, he was always staggered by just how many 'atypical' problems he also had to face. Like discovering that he was being thwarted in delivering justice for a murder victim because of an omnivorous iguana.

'Look,' Richard said, 'far be it from me to tell you how to do your job, but if you've got an iguana in your cable ducts, then surely the first step is to remove it? By fair means or foul,' he added darkly.

'Oh don't worry,' the man said brightly, 'we got the iguana out after only a couple of days. It's just that while it was in there, it went pretty much where it liked, and that's when it ate through the network cables. We're still trying to work out exactly which ones. And once we do, we'll have our computers back up and running in no time.'

'So are you even recording who arrives and leaves the island at the moment?'

'Of course. But we've been forced back into utilising the old system of writing every arrival's name down in a ledger by hand, and I don't need to tell you that this has stretched our border control resources almost to breaking point.' Richard knew that when the man said 'border control resources' he was referring to a woman called Janice. 'But I might be able to get some time this weekend to work through the books and pull the names of solo British travellers for you.'

Richard saw his opening at last. 'Then how about I come up to the airport right now and go through the lists myself?'

'I'm afraid that won't be possible.'

'Why not?'

'Janice is using the book.'

Richard took a deep breath to steady himself. Then, as time passed, he realised it hadn't made him feel any better. In fact, it was making him feel very much worse – and significantly hot around the collar – and then he realised that he hadn't breathed out yet, so he quickly expelled the air from his lungs to stop himself from fainting.

'Are you alright?' the Head of Security asked.

'Of course I'm fine,' Richard said, still feeling a touch light-headed. 'But you're saying there's no way I can get the names I need any quicker?'

'Got it in one,' the Head of Security said, glad that Richard was finally 'on side'. 'And I promise you, I'll get you the names at the beginning of next week. Or maybe a few days later – depending on what I'm up to this weekend.'

'Well, let's hope you're not too busy', Richard said before thanking the man for his time and slamming the phone onto its cradle.

Only then did Richard look up and see that his entire team looking at him.

'What's wrong with you lot?' he said tetchily.

'Your face went very red, sir,' Fidel said.

'Are you sure you don't want to take your suit jacket off?' Dwayne asked.

'Camille!' Richard barked, not wanting to get side-tracked again by his team's desire to get him into cooler clothes. 'How are you getting on with identifying our victim?'

'Well, sir,' Camille said, 'no-one's contacted us or any of the other government agencies since this morning to report anyone missing.'

'What about hospitals?'

'None of them has lost any of their patients.'

'Then what about hotels? He must have been staying somewhere at nights.'

'Agreed, sir. But there are no reports of missing guests from hotels, either.'

'So who the hell is he?' Richard asked, his anger driving him up out of his seat. 'I mean, come on, everyone! Theories?'

'Well, sir,' Fidel said, 'he didn't look too wealthy, did he?'

'I'd agree with that.'

'And the empty bottle of vodka we found in the clearing was pretty cheap.'

'Yes. That's true.'

'And, without wishing to be indelicate, sir, he didn't seem in the best condition, did he? Although, I suppose he'd been spending most of his time in a jungle for the last few weeks.'

'Assuming Lucy Beaumont was telling us the truth,' Camille said. 'After all, she's the only member of the family who ever saw the man.'

'Yes,' Richard agreed. 'Assuming she was telling the truth. All of which rather begs the question: what exactly was our victim attempting to achieve up at the Plantation? Was it Lucy he was spying on, or was he up to something else, and it's just one of those things that only Lucy saw him? Actually,' Richard said, a new thought occurring to him. 'While we're on the subject of Lucy, can you fill me in a bit on the family? What do we know about them?'

There was an awkward pause while Camille, Fidel and Dwayne all looked at each other, not sure what to say.

'Oh? Is there a problem?'

'Well, Chief, they're not a very well-liked family on the island,' Dwayne said.

'And why's that?'

'None of the old families who used slaves are much liked, sir.'

This comment caught Richard by surprise. He wasn't so naive as to be unaware of both Britain and France's appalling history of using African slaves to work on their plantations in the Caribbean. However, since Britain had abolished the slave trade in 1807, and slavery itself in

1833 – over 180 years ago – he'd not noticed much in the way of current tensions around the subject.

In fact, as a white Brit who was a guest on Saint-Marie, one of the first things Richard had done when he'd arrived was go to the library in Honoré and ask to borrow a book that would teach him the history of the island, with particular reference to how Saint-Marie had been treated by the British government. It seemed the least he could do as a Brit visiting a former colony. Richard was unsurprised – but nonetheless still chastened – to read about how deprivations, abuse and what could only be called outright kidnap and murder had been the basis of so many families' wealth back in the UK during this period of over one hundred years.

As he looked at his team now and saw how grave and focused they were, he realised how wrong he'd been. The tensions were still there. It's just that they were beneath the surface.

'Go on,' he said.

'Well, Chief,' Dwayne said, 'there are so few families left who go back to the bad old days. But those few who are still here, and are still running the same businesses now as they were then, well, they've got blood on their hands.'

'Yes, I can see that,' Richard said.

Dwayne briefly smiled at his boss's words. For all of Richard's many faults – and there was no doubting that he had *many* faults – his team knew that he treated everyone equally, irrespective of the colour of their skin.

Admittedly, this was mainly because Richard presumed that everyone was going to be a bitter disappointment to him before he'd even met them, but his team had always acknowledged that he was at least colour-blind in his misanthropy.

'So you're saying that the Beaumonts still have enemies on the island?'

'I don't know about that,' Dwayne said. 'But although there's plenty of islanders who work on their plantation when it comes to harvest time, there's very few who are happy working there full time.'

'Yes. We saw that today, didn't we? There was no-one else up at the plantation apart from the family.'

'Exactly.'

'So what do we know about the members of the family?'

Here, Camille got up some handwritten notes from the mess of her desk.

'Okay, so Hugh Beaumont is fifty years old, is solely in charge of the plantation, and from the few enquiries I've made, he's considered a pretty fair boss. Unlike his father William, who he took over from when he died back in 2001.'

'You can say that again,' Dwayne said. 'William was a tyrant.'

'He was?'

'Sure was, Chief. The man was bad news. After Mount Esmée erupted back in 1979 and the coffee fields were wiped out, he drove his workforce to breaking point getting them to clear away the ash, rework the soil and replant the coffee plants. And all along he promised them a serious bonus if they got the fields ready again by the next growing season. When they'd completed the task – and in time – he gave them their bonus, which turned out to be a 10-kilogram bag of coffee each. It was a scandal at the time.'

'Dwayne's right,' Fidel said. 'My mum talks about that winter after the eruption. It was really tough on the whole island. Everyone had to pull together.'

'And William Beaumont took advantage of all of the island's goodwill,' Dwayne said. 'I remember there was an accident one day. One of the pile-drivers that was being used to put in wooden posts for the coffee plants crushed one of the workers, killing him. William didn't even allow anyone from the plantation time off to attend the funeral. It was all about getting the place back up and running again.'

'So William was a nasty piece of work,' Richard said. 'But you're saying he died in 2001, and his son Hugh is less of a tyrant?'

'Got it in one,' Dwayne agreed. 'As far as I know, Hugh runs the place pretty fairly. I've got a few mates who do seasonal work for him. He pays on time. And as long as you work hard, he doesn't mind too much if you arrive a little bit late or leave a bit early.'

'So he's one of the more acceptable Beaumonts? Could we say that about him?'

'More acceptable,' Dwayne agreed, making it clear from the way he leaned on the word 'more' that it was all relative.

'Then what about Sylvie Beaumont, his wife?'

'Well, she's interesting,' Camille said, getting up a Saint-Marie newspaper article from 1991 on her computer monitor. 'She's the same age as Hugh – fifty years old – and her engagement to him made the Saint-Marie *Times* twenty-five years ago. In this article here it says she was originally from Maldon in Essex, and that she met Hugh in a bar on Saint-Marie when she was over here working as a holiday rep for Club Caribbean.'

The Police knew Club Caribbean well. It was full of twenty- to thirty-year olds who came to the island to have 'fun' which, Richard had too often had cause to notice, seemed to involve ingesting vast amounts of liquid before ejecting an equivalent amount again only a few hours later – which hardly seemed 'fun' to him.

'Ha!' Richard said out loud. 'I knew there was something about her accent that didn't ring true.'

'How do you mean?'

'Well, let me put it this way, I don't think the matriarch of Beaumont Manor who we met this morning spoke in quite the same plummy accent when she was a holiday rep from Maldon in Essex.'

'And you should know,' Camille added, 'that she seems to be in the newspapers every month. She's chair of this charity, sits on the board of that marine preserve, you know? She's a do-gooder.'

'A do-gooder who's vain enough to want everyone to see just how much do-gooding she's up to. Very interesting. Good work, Camille. Then what of their children? In particular, can you explain why everyone speaks with a British accent except for Tom?'

'Well, that's easy to explain, sir. Tom speaks with a Saint-Marie accent because he went to Notre Dame School here on Saint-Marie.'

'And Lucy and Matthew didn't?'

'Lucy also went to Notre Dame, but obviously decided not to pick up an island accent. As for Matthew, he was sent to boarding school in the UK. But going back to Tom, he left school with excellent grades, and has just finished an undergraduate course studying Agriculture at the University of Miami.'

'Which is hardly the impression he gave to me this morning.'

'You mean with his cannabis T-shirt and island attitude?'

'Exactly. So why is a bright young man with academic qualifications pretending to be a counter-culture stoner, do you think?'

A silence descended on the room as Richard's team all stopped what they were doing and looked at him.

Eventually, Dwayne spoke.

'Did you just say "counter-culture stoner", Chief?'

'Yes,' Richard said, somewhat irked. 'I'm not entirely out of touch with street argot, you know.'

'No, sir,' Camille said, trying to stifle a laugh.

'What's that, Camille?'

'Oh, nothing sir. Just caught something in my throat.'

Fidel stepped into the breach.

'And sir,' he said. 'You should know. I rang a cousin of mine when we got back to the station. I reckoned Tom would have been at Notre Dame at the same time as him. Anyway, my cousin said that Tom was one of the most popular kids in his year. He was clever, but he didn't make a big deal about it. He played football, but he didn't join any of the teams. He did his own thing. Oh, and he liked to party, and party hard. That was the other thing my cousin said.'

'So he wasn't tainted by the family name?'

'He was a "good guy". That's what my cousin called him.'

'Okay. Thanks for that. Then what about the other two siblings?' Richard said, turning back to face Camille.

'Well, sir,' Camille said, returning to her notes. 'Matthew's the youngest. By some distance. He's eighteen – Tom is twenty-two, and Lucy is twenty-eight – and he came back to the island this summer having left boarding school in the UK.'

'Do you know which boarding school it was?'

'Eton College.'

'He went to Eton, did he?' Richard said, Matthew's easeful manner clicking into place for him. This was because Richard had come across quite a number of

Old Etonians while he'd been at Cambridge, and, to his abiding irritation, every single one of them had been entirely and effortlessly charming. Not that that excused or justified their background of privilege, Richard felt. And nor did it mean that Richard could ever bring himself to trust or like someone who came from such a wealthy background. To his mind, it was simply wrong that so much should be given to so few, and he couldn't help but resent the opportunities that were afforded to this wealthy minority – no matter how charming they always were when you met them in the flesh. As far as Richard was concerned, if private boarding schools like the one Richard had been sent to were 'wrong' – and Richard knew that they were *very* wrong – then schools like Eton were wrong to the power of ten.

'Hang on, though,' Richard said, suddenly realising something. 'You're saying that Matthew – the youngest sibling – was sent to Eton, but Tom – his older brother – went to the local comprehensive school on Saint-Marie?'

'That's right,' Camille said, already knowing where Richard was going with this. 'As was Lucy.'

'There's a story there,' Richard said.

'You could be right, sir,' Camille agreed.

'Then what have we got on Lucy?' Richard asked. 'What do we know about her?'

'Well, sir, she's pretty interesting,' Camille said, picking up another set of notes. 'Because she left Notre Dame school when she was seventeen years old without finishing formal education, and since then she doesn't seem to have done much of anything. She doesn't have a job at the plantation as far as I can tell, she doesn't file tax returns – even though she's twenty-eight years old. But better than that, I found two hits for her on the Police computer.'

'You did?'

'First, she was pulled in for shoplifting when she was twenty years old. She'd been caught stealing a dress from the market in Honoré, but was let off with a caution.'

'And the second time?'

'It was shoplifting again. When she was twenty-three. This time, it was a silver necklace that she was caught stealing from the Caribbean Sands hotel.'

'And was she charged?'

'That's the thing, sir. She wasn't.'

'Why not?'

'I've no idea. Seeing as it was her second offence. But you should know, sir, Charlie Hulme was the arresting officer.'

Charlie Hulme had been the corrupt Detective Inspector who'd preceded Richard's arrival on the island, and Richard could well imagine how the Beaumont family might have leant on him to make sure he didn't press charges.

'Ah, I see,' Richard said. 'But there's a streak of criminality in her, is that what we're saying?'

'That's what it seems like to me.'

'Now that *is* interesting,' Richard agreed, going to look

at the names that he'd written up on the whiteboard that acted as the focus for all of his investigations.

'So, in summary,' he said, 'we've got Hugh Beaumont running the family plantation with a gentle hand on the tiller. He's married to the one-time holiday rep Sylvie, who now thinks herself something of a *grand dame* of the island. And as for their three children, we've got something of an enigma in Lucy, although we know she's been light-fingered in the past; a popular party animal in Tom who just happens to have a heap of qualifications including an Agricultural degree; and the eighteen-year old Matthew, who's only just returned to the island having been educated at one of the most privileged schools in the world. Something of a mixed bag, then.'

'And none of them has a clear alibi for the time of the murder,' Camille added.

'Not so,' Richard corrected. 'None of them has a clear alibi for the time of the murder apart from Lucy. Because, no matter how criminal her past might have been, you and I were with her when the two gunshots were fired, so she's the only member of the family who can't be our killer.'

'And we still don't even know the identity of our victim,' Camille added.

'Or how the killer then escaped from a locked room afterwards,' Richard agreed. 'Or whether the three-wheeled vehicle that was up at the plantation before it rained was part of the murder or not. So we're going to have to redouble our efforts. And I suggest we focus on our victim's identity, because I don't see how we're going to get anywhere with this case until we work out who he was. So, let's snap to it.'

As the afternoon wore on, Richard and his team made steady progress, but none of it seemed to take them any closer to uncovering the identity of the victim.

Richard even realised that he couldn't presume that the victim – if indeed he were a Brit travelling on his own – had even arrived on the island by plane. What if he'd arrived by boat? So he put in a call to the Harbour Master in Honoré and learned that while it would theoretically be possible to get a list of every solo Brit who'd arrived by boat and cleared customs in the last month or so, there were so many bays on Saint-Marie that there was nothing stopping any potential solo sailor from dropping anchor in a quiet cove and illegally accessing the island from there. When Richard asked if the Harbour Master knew of any boats who'd recently arrived unannounced like this, the man had just laughed at how naive the question was.

Richard was left deeply frustrated. If their victim had arrived by plane, it was going to take until the following week to get a list of British arrivals. And if he'd arrived by boat, it would have been possible to sneak onto the island past customs and immigration anyway. How were they going to work out who the victim was?

It was Dwayne who made the first breakthrough.

'Okay, sir, the weapon we found in the victim's hand is a Glock 19,' he reported back to Richard. 'It's not listed on the gun register of the island – meaning it must have been acquired illegally. And although I've been able to lift three partial fingerprints from the handle, they all belong to the victim. As for the rest of the gun, it's been wiped clean. So, whoever carried out this murder must have worn gloves. Or wiped the gun of fingerprints before putting the victim's hand around the handle after he was dead to make it look like suicide. But the fact that the gun has been obtained illegally – and has been wiped of prints, sir – suggests we're dealing with a killer who knew what he or she was doing.'

'I'd agree with you there,' Richard said.

'But the big news is, I've been able to lift a fingerprint from one of the bullet casings we found at the scene. And the fingerprint doesn't belong to the victim.'

'It doesn't?' Richard asked eagerly, heading over to Dwayne's desk.

'It doesn't,' Dwayne said. 'Meaning, the killer may have wiped the gun clean of his fingerprints, but he forgot to wipe the bullets he used. Or didn't know that one of his fingerprints was already on one of the bullet casings.'

'And you're sure the fingerprint on the bullet casing doesn't belong to the victim?' Richard asked.

'One hundred per cent. It belongs to someone else.'

'Then see if you can match it with the exclusion prints we took from the Beaumont family this morning. As a matter of urgency. The fingerprint could belong to our killer.'

'Yes, sir,' Dwayne said.

As Dwayne went to gather the family's exclusion prints to start his comparison, Fidel called over from his desk.

'Sir, I think I've identified the make and model of our three-wheeled vehicle.'

'You have?' Richard asked, thrilled that the case was finally picking up momentum.

'I think so. The dimensions of the axle, wheel width and tyre patterns mark the vehicle out as almost certainly being a "Piaggio Ape 50".'

'And what's one of those when it's at home?' Richard asked.

Fidel pulled up a picture of the vehicle in question, and Richard realised that he knew the type of vehicle well. There were hundreds of the bloody things all over the island: vans that were no more than souped-up three-wheeled mopeds like the tuk-tuks of Thailand, but with a flat wooden loading area at the back for carrying goods instead of space for two passengers. As far as Richard was concerned, he'd spent far too many hours stuck in the Police jeep behind these over-loaded menaces, and his eyes narrowed at the prospect of identifying what this particular vehicle had been doing at a murder scene.

'Right, Fidel,' he said, 'I want you to make this your top priority.'

Fidel was surprised. 'You do, sir?'

'I just said, didn't I? We know this particular Piaggio has a distinctive cut in its front wheel. So I want you to get a list of all the registered Piaggio 50s on the island, and then take that plaster of Paris cast to visit every single one of them until you've identified whose vehicle was up at the murder scene just before our victim was killed.'

'But sir, these sorts of vehicles are bought and sold for cash all the time. I'm not sure all that many are correctly registered up at Government House.'

'I know, Fidel. So maybe this is our chance – finally! – to bring one of these illegal vehicles to justice!'

Richard realised a bit too late that he was possibly coming across a bit too much like a tinpot tyrant, but he didn't much care. As far as he was concerned, these vans were a scourge of the island, and he, through the agency of Fidel, was going to be the sword of truth that finally managed to skewer one of them. Assuming that Fidel could identify the van, of course. And prove that it had indeed been up to no good when it had been up at the plantation. But these were mere details to be worked out once the van was identified.

Richard looked at his team, hoping to see the same sense of missionary zeal in their eyes, but didn't. He could tell from the way that Camille was now cocking her head slightly to one side, that she was maybe considering whether he needed psychiatric help or not.

Luckily for Richard, the awkward silence was broken by the sound of footsteps on the veranda outside. They all turned and saw a little old lady standing on the threshold. She was wearing a purple dress and had tightly-curled grey hair.

'Hello,' she said in a friendly voice.

'Hello,' Dwayne said. 'Can we help you?'

'I don't know, but I hope I can help you,' she said. 'My name is Rosie Lefèvre. I'm the Beaumonts' housekeeper.'

'You are?' Richard was surprised. The tiny old woman in the doorway looked as though a strong breeze could knock her over.

'Then come in, come in,' Camille said.

Camille fussed around Rosie and set her up on a chair in front of Richard's desk. She then got a bottle from the office fridge and poured the old woman a glass of cold water.

'Thank you so much,' Rosie said. 'It's really quite a steep climb up to the Police station from the harbour.'

'It is, isn't it?' Camille agreed.

'Anyway,' Richard said. 'You said you could help us?'

'Well, I don't know about that, but Hugh rang me and told me the terrible news.'

'And when was this exactly?' Richard asked, pulling out his notebook and pencil from his inside jacket pocket.

'Just after I'd arrived on Montserrat.'

'That's right. Sylvie said you'd gone to visit family.'

'I had. Although it's not immediate family. I never had the good fortune to marry. And although I had a brother once, he died many years ago now.' Rosie smiled sadly at the memory. 'Anyway, I've got a cousin on Montserrat I go and stay with for a few days every year.'

'I see. Then can I ask, when did you go to Montserrat?'

'This morning.'

'And what time ferry did you catch from Saint-Marie?'

'I was on the 11am sailing.'

Richard made a note.

'And what time did the ferry dock on Montserrat?'

'At about 12.30. And then Hugh rang me just after I'd cleared Customs. He told me about that man being found in the old drying shed, and I just knew I had to return to Saint-Marie at once. The family needed me. But Hugh also said the man might have been murdered, and no-one had been able to identify the body. So that's why I'm here. To do my civic duty.'

'You'd like to try and identify the victim?'

'Oh yes,' Rosie said, straightening in her chair as she spoke. 'I know I'm old, but that doesn't mean I can't be useful.'

Richard could see a sparkling intelligence behind Rosie's eyes, and he realised that she might have looked frail, but her mind was still perfectly sharp.

'Of course,' Camille said, and then instructed Fidel to choose the least distressing crime scene photos that would nonetheless allow their witness to identify the victim.

'Can I ask,' Richard said, while Fidel gathered the photos together, 'how you came to be working for the Beaumonts? They referred to you as Nanny Rosie.'

'That's right. I first started as a nanny for the family just after Matthew was born. And he was such a kissable little thing. All fat arms, chubby legs and a round belly, you just wanted to scoop him up and squeeze him. Not that I didn't adore the other two of course. But there was such an age gap. Tom was already four when I joined the family, and even then, he was a young man who always knew his mind. When he wanted his tea. What clothes he wanted to wear. You couldn't fight him, he had to get his own way. As for Lucy, well she was at that tricky age, you know? Twelve I suppose she was. Not quite a child, but not quite a teenager either. As tall as a beanpole, and clumsy as you like. Always forgetting things. That's Lucy.' Rosie sighed in pleasure as she considered her life with the Beaumonts. 'I love those children as if they were my own.'

'How lucky for you,' Camille said.

'I know. I've had a good life.'

Fidel came over with three photos of the victim's face that they'd taken at the scene of crime.

'Just so you know,' Fidel said to Rosie. 'You may find these photos distressing. They were taken after the man had been shot.'

Rosie nodded her head.

'I understand.'

Fidel handed over the three black and white photos and Rosie looked at the top photo in silence. However, Richard could see that she didn't recognise the victim's face. Rosie then very carefully moved on to the second photo – again without any apparent recognition – and then she studied the third. After this, she made sure the stack of photos was squared off neatly before returning them to Fidel and turning to speak to Richard.

'I'm sorry, but I don't recognise his face.'

'You don't?'

'No. How frustrating.'

Richard was bitterly disappointed. After all, if the family didn't recognise the victim – and now Rosie didn't, either – then who would?

'But while we have you,' Camille said perching on the edge of Richard's desk – somewhat proprietorially he found himself thinking – 'it's clear you know the Beaumont family well.'

Rosie smiled. 'Oh yes.'

'You like them?'

'Of course.'

'You've told us something of what the family were like in the past, but can you tell us something about what they're like now?'

'How do you mean?'

'How do they get on? Are they a happy family?'

'Well, yes. I mean, they have their ups and downs. We all do.'

'For example?'

Rosie's brow furrowed as she tried to work out what she should say.

'Anything you tell us will be treated in the strictest of confidence.'

'I understand. Of course. Well, since you're asking, they

are a happy family. It's just…well, I'm not sure that Sylvie has ever been – what's the word? – well, maternal, really.'

'She's not?'

'Not that it matters. The children have always had me. But she thinks too much about herself if you ask me.'

'Even though she does so much charity work?' Richard asked.

'Her charity work always seems to be about her more than it is about the people she's trying to help,' Rosie said.

'Do you think she's capable of murder?' Richard asked, and Rosie was shocked.

'No, of course not!'

'Only, it's possible that one of the Beaumont family is the person who did this.'

Rosie was shocked.

'Is that a joke?'

'I'm sorry, it isn't. Which is why we'd like to know if you think any of the family might be capable of murder.'

'Of course not. None of them could do anything so horrible. It's simply impossible to imagine.'

Richard saw Rosie frown as a thought occurred to her.

'What's that?' Richard asked.

'What's what?' Rosie said, but Richard and Camille could see that Rosie was now flustered.

'What were you thinking?'

'Oh, it was nothing.'

'It really would help us a lot,' Camille said, 'if you told

us whatever is on your mind. Even if you think it's got nothing to do with the case.'

Rosie took a moment to compose herself. Richard once again noticed the intelligence in the old woman's eyes, and he got a sudden insight that Rosie was one of those older people who could remember *everything* from her life.

'Well, I suppose I shouldn't be surprised it occurred to me. Considering what we're talking about. Not that it has anything to do with the case. Just like you said.'

'We'd still like to hear it,' Richard said.

'Well, it was just a memory that popped into my head. You know how that can happen? You just remember something suddenly?'

'Of course,' Camille said.

'And it was from when the children were much younger. Matthew had just had his fifth birthday, so Tom must have been nine and Lucy was seventeen I think. Anyway. I came across Tom in the garden. As I say, he must have been about nine years old. He was crouching on the ground and looking at something on the grass. As I got nearer, he tried to hide what he was looking at.'

'And what was it?'

'Well, I'm sorry to say that it was a dead bird. I don't know how it got there. Maybe it had died from natural causes. But Tom was holding a knife in his hand. A pocket knife, I think. But he'd used it to cut the bird open. And I know young boys can be a little wild, but he hadn't just cut into the poor creature, he'd spread all its... organs...

out to the bird's side. It was like some kind of ritual thing.'
Rosie took a sip of water, and Richard could see that the
memory still upset her. 'Of course, he denied that he'd had
anything to do with the dead bird. He said he'd found it
on the grass like that. But I sent him to his room at once.
I was so angry with what he'd done. It took me a long
time to get over that. But then, perhaps the children were
more damaged by their past than we gave them credit—'

Rosie stopped talking mid-sentence as she was struck
by a sudden realisation.

'What do you mean, "their past"?' Richard asked.

'My word, is it possible?' Rosie said, more to herself
than to anyone else, and Richard and Camille could
see that her mind was awhirl as she tried to marshal her
thoughts. After a moment longer of indecision, she looked
at Richard.

'You're saying the man who was murdered this morning couldn't be identified?'

'That's right,' Richard said.

'Then can you tell me, did he have any identifying
features?'

Richard and Camille's interest sharpened.

'What makes you say that?'

'Was there perhaps a scar on his left hand? On his first
finger?'

'There was.'

'Then can I see those photos again? And a photo of the
scar if you've got it?'

'Fidel, bring over all the crime scene photos.'

Fidel had already scooped them up and was heading over.

'Ms Lefèvre, you might not like what you see,' he said, but Rosie had already grabbed the photos and started shuffling through them until she found the photo that Dwayne had taken of the long scar on the forefinger of the victim's left hand.

'Good heavens,' she murmured to herself, 'is it you?'

She then shuffled through the photos again until she was looking at the first photo she'd been shown of the victim's face.

'You know what, it could be,' she said to herself.

'It could be who?' Richard asked, unable to hide the impatience in his voice.

'Someone I've not seen in twenty years. That's why I didn't recognise him. I just haven't thought about him for decades...' Rosie trailed off as she seemed to look inside herself, and Richard saw that she was coming to a decision.

'Please!' Richard implored. 'If you could just tell us who it is!'

Rosie looked from Richard to Camille. And then she looked from Camille back to Richard again, and Richard had to use all of his self-control not to shout at the woman to just bloody well tell him who the man was.

'Very well,' Rosie said. 'I think the man in the photos is Freddie Beaumont.'

'And who's he?' Richard asked.

'Lucy, Tom and Matthew's father.'

This wasn't quite what Richard and Camille had expected to hear.

'I'm sorry?'

'I think the man who was shot dead this morning is Lucy, Tom and Matthew's father.'

'But we've met their father,' Richard said, confused. 'His name's Hugh. Hugh and Sylvie are the children's parents.'

'Ah,' Rosie said, and Richard could see how uncomfortable the old woman was discussing such private matters. 'That's not quite true. Hugh and Sylvie are actually the children's uncle and aunt. It's Hugh's brother Freddie who's their biological father. And he was the most terrible drunk. A desperate and violent drunk. That's why Hugh and Sylvie ended up adopting his children.'

Rosie held up the photo of the victim's face.

'But that's who I think this dead man is. It's Freddie Beaumont. The children's real father.'

CHAPTER FOUR

Richard and Camille returned to the Beaumont Plantation with Rosie. As the three of them approached the
manor house, Lucy came out and greeted Rosie with a
big hug.

'Are you alright?' she asked.

'I'm fine,' Rosie replied. 'Don't you worry about me.'

'Thank you so much for bringing Rosie back,' Lucy
said to Richard.

Richard explained how their visit wasn't entirely social,
and a few minutes later, he'd once again gathered the
whole family in the sitting room. But this time, Richard
noticed that Rosie placed herself in between Lucy and
Matthew as they sat together on the sofa. She was holding
their hands tightly.

But just as interesting as Rosie's solidarity with Lucy
and Matthew was the fact that Tom was once again sitting in the window seat on his own. Richard could see

that Tom maybe didn't quite 'fit in' with his two other siblings. But then, Tom was the middle child of the three siblings, and Richard knew that it was typical for oldest and youngest siblings to form a bond that excluded the middle child.

Richard found himself wondering, were Tom's studied attempts to appear 'different' – be it his island accent, or his stoner attitude – really just his way of finessing the fact that his other two siblings didn't want to spend their time with him anyway? As Richard was considering this, he remembered the story that Rosie had told of Tom ritually slaughtering a bird when he was nine years old. Yes, Richard thought to himself. He wanted to find out more about Tom.

'So why did you want to talk to us?' Sylvie asked from her position on the sofa, and Richard turned and smiled at her.

'First, can I just check something? Are you really saying that none of you recognise the man who was murdered in your shower room this morning?' he asked.

As he spoke, Camille laid out photographs of the victim on the coffee table for them all to see.

The family looked again, but shook their heads.

'No, I'm sorry,' Hugh said, taking his gold-rimmed spectacles off as he looked at Richard. 'We really don't know who that man is or, I promise you, we'd have told you this morning.'

'That's interesting,' Richard said. 'Because we now

believe that the man who was murdered was Freddie Beaumont.'

Richard saw Rosie squeeze Matthew and Lucy's hands even tighter as if she was trying to keep them from running away.

'It was *Freddie*?' Hugh said, unable to process what Richard had just said.

'We're sorry to tell you so bluntly,' Camille said, throwing a dismayed look in her boss's direction, 'but it does seem strange that the only person who recognised him was Rosie, when she's the only person here who's not actually related to him.'

Hugh picked up one of the photos again and looked at it for a long while.

'Is this really what he looks like now?' he asked Rosie, almost like a little boy lost.

'I didn't recognise his face, either,' she said kindly. 'It was the scar on his left finger. That's what made me realise.'

'What scar?' Hugh asked.

Richard was surprised. How on earth did a nanny know about a scar on Freddie's hand, when his own brother didn't?

'I think it's time you told us about your brother,' he said to Hugh.

Hugh exhaled, overwhelmed by the task he'd been set.

'Of course,' he said. 'But where to begin?'

'At the beginning?' Camille offered.

'No. I'll start at the end if you don't mind. But are you saying the man was Freddie?'

'Do you really not recognise him?'

'If I'm being honest, now you say it's him, I can perhaps see it could be. But you have to understand, I've not seen him in over twenty years. None of us have. And I would never have imagined he could end up looking so...' Here, Hugh looked at the photo again and groped around until he found the right word. 'Ravaged,' he eventually said. 'That's what he looks like. Like he's been ravaged by time.'

Hugh handed the photo to his wife, but she only had eyes for her husband.

'He's dead?' Sylvie said, as though it was only now striking her.

Hugh looked back at the Police.

'Sorry,' he said. 'It's just a bit of a shock to realise that this is how it ended for him. You see, if you've got someone in your family like Freddie, you're always wondering how it's going to end. Because you know it's not going to end well for him. He was so destructive...'

Hugh trailed off, and then Richard saw him focus on what he had to do.

'Alright,' Hugh said. 'Let me tell you about my brother, Freddie. He was my only sibling. He was four years older than me, and I don't remember a day of my life when he wasn't in trouble. He was always breaking things. Or stealing things. Or having tantrums. It's like he didn't have a moral compass, or a shred of compassion about how his actions affected others. And he *never* cared about consequences. He used to drive Mother and Father crazy.'

'This would be your father, William?' Richard asked.

'That's right. And my mother, Jean. She died when Freddie was seventeen. I was thirteen. But I genuinely think that raising Freddie was what put her in an early grave. And I know that Father never really recovered after Mother's death, either. For the next twenty or so years – until he died – Father just seemed to get more and more cranky and withdrawn.' Hugh sighed as he recollected this two-decade sweep of time. 'Anyway, when I was growing up, Freddie was nasty as hell to me. He bullied me. Mind you, he bullied everyone. Screaming and shouting until he'd get his way. Then there was a brief respite when he was sent off to boarding school.'

'In the UK?'

'That's right. All the men of the family have been educated at Eton for the last 300 years, so that's where Freddie went when he was thirteen. But while things settled down while he was away, he was still back here during the holidays. And he didn't get any better as he became a teenager. He became so much worse. I know he'd been smoking – on and off – since he was about ten years old, but he now started drinking as well. He'd get workers on the plantation to buy him bottles of spirits that he'd drink on his own before going out with a gun to shoot the local wildlife. And he'd shoot anything.

Parrots. Lizards. Anything that moved. He was obsessed with guns. But we didn't know the half of it.

'When he was seventeen, he beat up another boy at Eton and put him in hospital. This was soon after Mother died, so perhaps there were mitigating circumstances, but the school had had enough of him and he was expelled. I'd only just started at Eton myself. And it wasn't easy for me when I arrived, I can tell you. Freddie was so roundly reviled that I was also cast as a trouble-maker from the start. It took me years to convince the school that I wasn't.

'Anyway, after he was expelled, everyone expected Freddie to return to Saint-Marie and get on with his life here, but he never even got on the plane. You see, we used to own a small house just off the Fulham Road in London, and he went there instead. He holed up and refused to come back. God knows what he got up to, but it was 1980, and London was a rough place back then. The country was falling apart, the steelworkers were striking, and as far as we could tell, Freddie fell in with a pretty hateful group of rich kids in Chelsea.

'I did visit him at the house once. Father said I had to go up to Fulham and try to convince Freddie to come back home to Saint-Marie. I was just this gauche thirteen-year-old boy up on a day trip from school, and Freddie introduced me to all of his friends, including this girl called Lady Helen Moncrieff. She was seventeen years old – just like Freddie – and to my thirteen-year old's eyes, she was quite the most beautiful girl I'd ever seen in my life. But so fragile. That's the word I'd use to describe her. When she spoke, it was barely in a whisper. In time, we'd all learn that she'd been addicted to Valium since she was fourteen years old. God knows what horrors she was taking painkillers for. None of us ever met her father, the Earl of Arlington. Or any of her family, for that matter. We later found out she'd been cut off without a penny long before she met Freddie. Anyway, I'm getting ahead of myself.' Hugh pushed his glasses up on his nose and took a deep breath, ordering his thoughts before pressing on. 'But no-one knows what Helen saw in Freddie. I mean, he was seventeen years old, he'd been expelled from school and had no prospects, as he was the first to admit. But Helen fell in love with him and was absolutely under his spell from that moment on.'

As Hugh paused again, Richard realised that he seemed to be telling the story of Freddie and Lady Helen to Lucy, Tom and Matthew, as much as he was telling it to the Police. It was clearly something that had been told many times before. Something they gathered around to hear.

'But the more time Helen spent with Freddie, the more he became abusive towards her. And not just verbally. There was this time — when I was fifteen — and she came down to Eton to take me out for lunch. It was the only time I saw her alert and clear-eyed. She said she wanted to say goodbye to me. She couldn't take any more of living with Freddie. He was a mean drunk, she said. And a cheat. And a thief. And he pushed pills on her, that was the other thing she said. He wanted to control her. And she didn't say it in so many words, but I guessed that he was also hitting her. I was so angry. So angry with what my own brother was doing to this beautiful woman. But I was also relieved. Because Helen said she was finally going to escape Freddie's clutches. She was going to pack her bags and leave. She should have done it years ago, she told me.

'Then, two weeks later, Helen and Freddie turned up roaring drunk at my house at school. Helen told me she'd found out a couple of days before that she was pregnant, and she and Freddie had just got married at Chelsea registry office. I couldn't believe it. Only a fortnight before, she'd been telling me how she was going to escape from Freddie, and now here she was, married to him. I felt so betrayed.'

'And the baby was lost,' Lucy said in a whisper.

Hugh looked at Lucy.

'And the baby was lost. That's right.' A moment of deep sadness passed between Hugh and Lucy, and then he turned back to the Police and carried on his story. 'After my father found out that Freddie had married Helen, he went crazy. Mainly because Freddie – his eldest son – had married without his permission. Even if the woman he'd married was the daughter of an Earl. Because William was also a terrible snob. Social standing was paramount to him, although he was the first to say that it didn't much matter how noble you were, if you were a "Pill Head" like Helen. That's what he always called her. "The Pill Head".

Anyway, he finally booted Freddie out of the house in Fulham and let it to another family through a local estate agents. Freddie and Helen moved to a flat in Notting Hill, and it's from this moment forwards that our knowledge of them becomes patchy. Freddie got a job for a while at a Bond Street auctioneers, but he got sacked from that. For thieving, I understand. He then became an estate agent for a spell, but that didn't last, either. And within a few years, I'd left school and was back in the Caribbean.

'So life fell into a pattern. I ran the plantation with my father. I met Sylvie, I got married. And, from time to time, we'd get slurred phone calls from Freddie, begging for money. He'd make up all these improbable stories of how his life was in danger. From gangsters sometimes. Or from the neighbours, or the Police. Or he'd suddenly claim that he had a mystery illness that required immediate treatment. But it was always about trying to trick more cash out of us. And he was *always* drunk. After a while, we got used to hanging up on him when he said he was at death's door, or was about to kill himself. He'd always seem to survive, and be back to make another begging phone call a month or two later. And then, in 1987, Helen gave birth to Lucy. As I'm sure Rosie has told you – because Lucy, Tom and Matthew aren't our natural children. They're our adopted children.'

Richard noticed how proudly Hugh said this, and was once again impressed with Hugh's natural command of any situation, whether it was confronting a dead corpse in a shower room or announcing to the Police that his children were actually his nephews and niece.

'Anyway, from the moment that Lucy was born, William became obsessed with getting his only grand-daughter out to the safety of Saint-Marie. But Freddie had become seriously bitter by now. He was jealous of me for running the plantation, even though he didn't want to run it himself. And he always complained that we were cutting him out of our lives even though we were desperate for him to relocate to Saint-Marie with Helen and Lucy. It was tragic, really. And it caused us so much pain. And then Tom was born, in 1995. And the mind boggles at how Freddie and Helen got through those years. I know at one stage father paid off all of their debts and gave them money to buy four single tickets to Saint-Marie. So they could finally come home here. But the money was just spent, and no aeroplane tickets were ever bought. And I think this happened more than once – with Freddie promising to bring his family out here if father paid off his debts – but he never did.'

'And what was Helen's role in all of this?' Camille asked.

'We don't really know,' Hugh said. 'Because Freddie moved his family to Maze Hill in South East London in 1997. To a tiny two-up two-down. And for a spell we completely lost sight of them. They just vanished off the radar.

'But things came to a crisis when father received a

desperate phone call from Helen in 1999. She said she'd just given birth to her third child – Matthew – and she said she couldn't take any more of life with Freddie. And there was no way she'd be able to raise three children. According to my father, she was pretty incoherent when he spoke to her that time – from drugs or alcohol, he couldn't tell. But the point was, Helen told Father that she was going to walk out on her new-born baby. She was going to walk out on all of her children. Just to get away from Freddie.'

A silence fell on the room that none of the witnesses wanted to break.

'What happened?' Camille asked.

'Well,' Hugh said, 'Father put out the word on Saint-Marie that day. He needed a trained nanny he could hire immediately to go to London to save his grandchildren. By that evening, he'd found Rosie, and she was on a plane to Heathrow.'

'Is that so?' Camille asked Rosie.

'That's right,' she said. 'I left for the UK the same day I was hired.'

'And what happened when you arrived?'

'In London?' Rosie said, clearly uncomfortable at the idea of having to talk about the past in front of the children. 'Well, after I got there, I took a taxi to Freddie's house, and I have to admit that what I found deeply shocked me. They were a family living in squalor. I can't pretend otherwise. There was food rotting in the fridge, nothing had been cleaned for months, and everywhere you looked there were empty wine bottles, dirt, filth and cigarette ash. It was just horrible. As for Helen, she looked like a ghost. And she had a big bruise by her left eye. And bruises up her left arm. And she didn't even seem stable on her feet. I wondered at the time if she was stoned on something. Or drunk. I never found out, because the moment she realised that I was the nanny who'd been sent by her father-in-law to look after her children, she handed me her new-born baby, and told me his name was Matthew. She then said that she was going to visit her family, and walked out of the door.'

'She said she was going to visit her family?' Camille asked.

'That's what she told me. She was going to visit her family, and then she walked out. I had no idea when she'd be back. But with her gone, the immediate problem became Freddie. When I found him, he was upstairs in a drunken stupor surrounded by bottles in his bedroom. The room stank. He stank. It was so very shocking to realise that this was a member of the Beaumont family. But I got Lucy and Tom in from playing outside in the street, and I told them that I was now in charge. I got them clean. I got baby Matthew clean. William had sent me over with an amount of money, so I was able to buy new nappies and take the children out to a local restaurant. I wasn't sure when they'd last eaten a decent meal. Then I managed to get them to bed, and still Freddie was upstairs, fast asleep.

'The next day I got the two older children to school in the cleanest clothes I could find, and I was looking after Matthew when Freddie came down the stairs. And if he looked at me for more than two seconds I'd be surprised. He didn't care that I was there to help look after his children. He didn't seem to care that his wife had walked out the day before and hadn't yet come back. He just put on a coat, told me he was going out, and then left. So I went to a payphone in the street, rang William and reported what I'd found. He told me to take the children to the airport, and bring them back to Saint-Marie as soon as possible. I wasn't sure if it was a good idea until Freddie got back from the pub that night.

'He was drunk. And that's when he got the scar on his left hand. Because it was as though this was the first time he'd realised I was in his house. And he got really angry. He started smashing empty wine bottles against the wall. There was glass everywhere. I was terrified. So I called the Police, but that just made him even angrier. And it was then that he went to grab a broken bottle, and he got that deep cut all along the length of his index finger. There was blood everywhere, so I told him to sit still, and I used an old cloth to staunch the blood while I called for an ambulance. Luckily for Freddie, I was a trained nurse. And also luckily for him, the ambulance arrived before the Police did. So he'd already gone to hospital when the Police got round to asking me if I wanted to press charges against him. And because I knew I would need Freddie's co-operation to take his children out to Saint-Marie, I decided that I wouldn't.

'Freddie returned to the house the next morning, his left hand wrapped up in a bandage. He told me he'd be scarred for life. I told him I was taking his children to visit his grandparents in Saint-Marie. He asked for a fifty pound note to tide him over. I gave him one, and he left for the pub. And that was it, the last time I saw Freddie Beaumont. I arrived on Saint-Marie with Lucy, Tom and baby Matthew in my arms the following morning.'

'And what about Lady Helen?' Camille asked. 'What happened to her?'

'We don't know. Nobody's seen her from that day to this.'

'They haven't?' Richard asked, surprised.

'I tried to contact her family at the time,' Hugh said. 'Seeing as the last thing she said to Rosie was that she was going to visit her family, but the Earl and the Countess of Arlington didn't seem to care what had happened to their daughter. All they'd tell me was that she hadn't gone anywhere near them. And if she did turn up, she wouldn't be welcome.'

'And she really hasn't been seen since then?' Camille asked.

'She hasn't,' Hugh said.

Camille looked at Richard and knew that he was thinking the same thing. It seemed highly unlikely that a mother would walk out on her children and never make any attempt to contact them again. Especially now that they were all grown up, and had been out of the clutches of her alcoholic husband for decades. But then, Camille found herself wondering, if Lady Helen had really been destroyed by a marital life of abuse, maybe walking out forever was the only way of preserving whatever remaining sanity she had.

'So what happened after you got the children to Saint-Marie?' Richard asked.

'Well that's the thing,' Sylvie said, before Rosie could continue with her story. 'When the children got here, they were wild – just like Rosie is saying. Although not Matthew, of course. He was only a baby. But Lucy and Tom were out of control. They wet their beds at night. They couldn't sleep. It took months for them even to look any of us in the eye.'

Richard noticed Rosie squeeze Matthew and Lucy's hands a bit tighter in support.

'By the end of the year,' Hugh said, trying to soften the impact of his wife's words, 'we'd reached a rapprochement of sorts. Matthew was six months old. Lucy and Tom were putting on a bit of weight and getting a bit of sunshine into their skin as well. They were healing. Physically perhaps more than psychologically, but they were still healing.

'All this was about the same time that my father was diagnosed with cancer. It was hardly unexpected. He was 84. But as he declined, he tried to get his affairs in order, and he came up with a plan. You see, Sylvie and I had never had any children ourselves. We'd not been blessed that way. And here were three children who needed a mother and father who could give them the love they needed. It was only natural that Sylvie and I started to think about adoption. So we approached Father and asked for his blessing and help in getting Freddie to let us formally adopt his children.

'Father thought it was a great idea right from the start. So his lawyers contacted Freddie in the UK. And they offered him twenty thousand pounds to cover his costs if he would let us adopt his children. It was an outright bribe, frankly, and Freddie rang us up the moment he received the letter and said that he accepted the deal. By the beginning of the following year, we'd adopted Lucy, Tom and Matthew, and it was the best thing that ever happened to us, wasn't it?'

Hugh had asked this last question of his wife, although it took her a moment to realise that she was being spoken to.

'Of course,' she said brightly. 'And we kept Nanny Rosie on as well. We had to. She was part of the family by now.'

Richard noticed Hugh's brow furrow.

'And then Father died,' Hugh said.

'And?' Richard asked, waiting for Hugh to continue.

'He left his entire estate to Freddie,' Sylvie said bitterly.

'He did?' Richard asked, surprised.

'Not quite, darling,' Hugh said, but it was clear that he was only trying to correct his wife on a technicality.

'You see,' Hugh said to Richard, 'our family can trace ourselves back to a Duke who came over to England with William the Conqueror. Which means our family tree stretches back the best part of a thousand years. And in all that time, the estate has always been inherited by the first-born child. Whether the first-born child was the best choice or not. So, as father saw it, he couldn't possibly leave his estate to me. I was only his second-born son.'

'And you're still defending him!' Sylvie said in exasperation.

'He had no choice,' Hugh said evenly. 'The estate can only be passed on through primogeniture. So he did the next best thing he could. He put the estate into trust for the duration of Freddie's life – which made sure that Freddie could never get his hands on even a cent of the family money. And he made me sole Trustee of that estate. That way I was still in charge. Still in control.'

'Then hold on,' Richard said, realising something. 'What happens now?'

'How do you mean?' Hugh asked.

'Because if you're saying that the estate was in trust while Freddie was alive, what happens to it now that he's died?'

Richard could see that this point hadn't occurred to the family before. They looked at each other, trying to work it out. Perhaps unsurprisingly, Hugh got there first.

'Lucy inherits.'

Everyone turned and looked at Lucy, and all Richard could see was confusion in her eyes.

'What's that?'

'You inherit,' Hugh said, and Richard could see that Hugh was trying to work out the ramifications of this as he spoke. 'You've just inherited everything.'

'I have?'

'Yes. I mean, there were a few conditions in father's will, but my memory is that they weren't much. We'll need to check with the family solicitor.'

'What do you mean, there were conditions?' Richard asked.

'Well, just the standard stuff,' Hugh said. 'You know, that the estate could only be inherited by someone who was of sound mind and body, over the age of twenty-one, not serving a prison sentence, that sort of thing. As I say, I'm sure Lucy qualifies. Lucy, I think you've just inherited the Beaumont estate.'

Richard thought he noticed a moment of understanding pass between Hugh and Lucy, but it was so fleeting that, just as he saw it, it seemed already to have gone.

'Bloody hell,' Lucy said, as the full weight of what Hugh said hit her. And then she giggled to herself, the laughter erupting out of her before she could stop it.

'I'm so sorry,' she said to the Police, although she didn't appear to be sorry at all. 'But is it true? Is Freddie really dead?'

'It would appear so,' Richard said.

'And how does that make you feel?' Camille asked.

'I don't know,' Lucy said, but with a sense of wonder as she contemplated the new realities of her life. 'Because I've wished that man dead my whole life. Every day. And now he's really gone?'

'You've wished him dead?' Richard asked sharply.

'Oh yes. And so would you if you'd seen how he treated my mother. Before she walked out on us all. That man deserved to die.'

'She doesn't mean that,' Rosie said.

'I do,' Lucy said. 'And if I'd known that it was him in the shower room this morning, I'd have happily killed him myself.'

Lucy was looking hyper-excited – her eyes shining – and Richard was reminded of her skittish manner when she'd first come into the Police station. She'd been pumped up and jittery then, and she was looking similarly wild now. But was it because of the surprise of learning that she'd just inherited the family estate, or was it really because she loved imagining Freddie dead? Either way, it seemed a pretty bold move to admit to the Police that she'd happily kill her biological father, considering that it was her biological father who'd been killed that morning.

The door opened, and Dwayne entered looking like a cat who'd not only got the cream, but had also got his hands on the cow who supplied the cream.

Richard went over and had a quick word with him. After a few moments, he returned to the group.

'Lucy?' he asked. 'Did you just admit that you wanted to kill your biological father, Freddie Beaumont?'

Lucy realised what she was being asked. But she couldn't very well deny what she'd so freely said only moments earlier.

'I suppose so. Why?'

'We recovered two bullet casings from the murder scene this morning. And there was a fingerprint on one of them. A fingerprint that didn't belong to the victim.'

'So?' Lucy asked.

'So, Police Office Myers here has been comparing that fingerprint against the exclusion prints we took from all of you this morning, and he's found a match. So can you tell me why your fingerprint is on the casing to one of the bullets that killed Freddie Beaumont this morning?'

Comprehension came much more slowly to Lucy than it did to the rest of the family.

'What is this?' Hugh asked. 'You must have made a mistake.'

'I haven't, Mr Beaumont,' Dwayne said. 'There were seven points of comparison. The print on the bullet casing comes from your daughter's right middle finger.'

'Can you tell me why that is?' Richard asked Lucy.

'I don't know,' Lucy said, but everyone could see that she was panicking.

'I think you do,' Richard said.

'It's a mistake. Father's right. You must have made a mistake.'

'Very well,' Richard said. 'You can tell us now, or we can take you down to the station, charge you with murder, and you can tell us then.'

'But I've got nothing to do with this!'

'Then start telling us the truth,' Richard said.

Lucy didn't say anything. Not for a few seconds. And then she spoke.

'I own a gun,' she whispered.

'What?' Rosie asked, looking at Lucy in amazement.

'You own a *gun*?' Hugh said, just as stunned.

'And yet I remember standing here only this morning,' Richard said, 'and asking if any of you owned a gun, and you all said that you didn't. Yourself included, Lucy.'

Lucy nodded, not entirely trusting her voice.

'So why did you lie?'

'Because…'

'Yes?'

Lucy took a deep breath.

'Because I think it was my gun that was used this morning. I mean, I don't know for sure, but when we broke into the shower room and I saw that dead body there, I was so shocked. And then when I saw that the gun he was holding looked a lot like mine, I didn't know what to think. It was like my mind just shut down.'

'But you recognised that it was your gun?'

'No way. I just saw that it looked similar. I *thought* it could be mine. That's all.'

'Then can you tell me – just for the record – what type of gun do you own?'

'It's a Glock 19,' Lucy said.

'Which is exactly the same make and model of handgun that was used to kill your biological father.'

'But it can't have been my gun!' Lucy said, desperately. 'Even if it was the same make. I mean, there must be loads of those sorts of guns on the island.'

'Of course,' Richard said, as if he agreed entirely with the point Lucy was making. 'But it should be easy enough for us to find out one way or another. Now that we know you also own a Glock 19. You just have to take us to it, and when we see that it's still safely in your possession, we'll know that it can't have been the gun that was used to kill your father this morning. Won't we?'

Everyone was looking at Lucy, and they could all see the fear in her eyes.

CHAPTER FIVE

Lucy showed Richard, Camille and Dwayne into her bedroom, where she said she kept her handgun. When they got there, Richard could see that it wasn't so much a bedroom as a self-contained flat that was crammed into a bedroom. There was a desk with a computer on it next to an old microwave; a bureau with jars of sauces and pasta piled up next to a single electric hob; and clothes strewn everywhere. Richard noticed that even Dwayne thought the place was untidy, and that was saying something.

But what most caught Richard's attention was the strong smell of coffee that filled the room. Looking at the foot of Lucy's bed, he saw an old trunk with a mess of coffee-making equipment on it. There was an old hand-cranked bean-grinding machine, a battered French Press cafetiere, and an ancient tin caddy with 'Premier Grade Bonifieur Coffee' written in swirling gold print on the side.

Lucy was oblivious to the mess as she opened the doors

to her wardrobe, revealing clothes jammed onto hangers and shelves, and a large domestic safe sitting on the floor.

'I keep my gun in this safe,' she said, stepping aside so the Police could see. 'And you'll see, it'll still be there. I haven't taken it out in years.'

Richard saw that the lock was controlled by an electronic keypad.

'You keep your gun in here?'

The dismissive tone in Richard's voice puzzled Lucy. 'Yes. Why?'

'Well, it's hardly secure.'

'What are you talking about? It's a safe. Safes are totally secure.'

'Ha!' Richard said dismissively. 'I reckon that safe would take all of five minutes to crack.'

Dwayne and Camille looked at their boss, surprised that he was choosing this precise moment to brag about his safe-cracking skills. For Richard's part, he got onto his hands and knees and started a visual inspection of the keypad.

'Now that's very interesting,' he said. 'Dwayne, go to the Police jeep, would you, and get the Crime Scene Kit. I want you to dust this keypad for fingerprints.'

'Okay, Chief.'

With a shrug to Camille, Dwayne left the room, and Richard got back to his feet.

'Who else knows that you keep a gun in this safe?' he asked.

'What's that?' Lucy said, and Richard wondered if she was trying to buy herself time.

He repeated the question more forcefully.

'Well, no-one I suppose,' Lucy said, and Richard once again got the distinct impression that she wasn't telling the truth.

'Who else knows about your gun?' he asked for a third time. 'And please stop lying to us.'

'Oh, Tom knows,' Lucy suddenly said as if it had only just occurred to her.

'He does?' Camille asked.

'I suppose so. You see, it was Tom who helped me get it a few years ago. From one of his contacts on the island. It's not exactly a legal firearm – if you know what I mean. So yes, Tom knows. But that's it. It's not something I've advertised to the others.'

'And why exactly did you get it?'

'I'm a young woman. I don't always feel safe.'

'You take it out of the house with you?'

'I never even take it out of the safe.'

'And you're saying it's in there now?'

'Of course. I mean, I've not taken it out. Not that I've checked. Which was pretty stupid of me, I now realise.'

'It was. Especially for someone who's already got a Police record.'

Lucy blanched. 'You know about that?'

'Of course.'

'That was just… I wasn't very happy at the time. I'd

left school and I didn't know what to do with my life. I fell in with a bad crowd.'

'The first time you were caught shoplifting? Or the second?' Richard asked.

'Look, that was all in the past. It's got nothing to do with my life now. I've moved on.'

'Have you?' Richard asked. 'Because, from our enquiries, we've not exactly been able to establish what it is that you currently do.'

'But I do loads,' Lucy said, now very definitely looking embarrassed. 'I mean, I help around the house. You know, when Rosie needs it. And I help on the plantation. When I can.'

'So how do you get by financially?'

'Well, I don't spend much money. As you can see from my room. And father gives me a small allowance. Or handouts when I need them.'

Richard could see how Lucy was trying to appear bright and fulfilled by her life, but he believed that the squalor in her room belied her words. Lucy was a woman who wasn't on top of things – who wasn't happy – and who felt she needed to keep a gun for protection. So why was that?

'Very well,' Richard said. 'Can you tell me, when did you last open your safe?'

'It was a few days ago.'

'Exactly how many days ago did you last open your safe?'

Lucy thought for a moment.

'It was three days ago.'

'And why did you open it?'

'I was putting something into it.'

'Which was?'

'A document from the house's library. Just an old document Tom had found and asked me to put in there for safekeeping.'

Richard and Camille shared a glance. This was now the second time that Tom's name had come up in relation to Lucy's gun and safe.

'Then tell me,' Richard continued, 'did you perhaps see the gun in the safe when you opened it up three days ago?'

'I don't know. I think so. I wasn't really looking for it. I was just putting a document in there for safekeeping.'

'I see. Then can I ask about your inheritance?' he asked.

'What's that?'

'Only, I can't help noticing that you've just inherited the whole plantation.'

'Don't we need to open the safe?'

'Not until my officer has returned with the Crime Scene Kit and he's had a look at that keypad. So can you tell me how you feel now that you've inherited everything?'

'I don't know how I feel,' Lucy said.

'Then what do you plan to do with your inheritance?'

'How do you mean?'

'Considering the fact that you don't even currently have

a job. What will you do now that all of the profits from the family business will be yours to spend as you like?'

Lucy laughed.

'What?' Richard asked.

'You think there are profits?'

'There aren't?'

'No way. We've been running at a loss for decades. As you noticed when you pointed out there were no other workers currently on the plantation.'

'Yes, but you told us that was because it was the wrong time in the growing season.'

'That's just what we tell people. But it's not even close to the truth. Even in the "off" season, you still need people to keep weeds out of the fields, clean the machinery and repair the drying racks, that sort of thing.'

Richard remembered how the machinery he'd seen in the coffee packing area of the plantation had looked battered and rusty.

'But I thought the Beaumonts were one of the richest families on the island?'

'We used to be. But that's not been the case for decades. So even if I've inherited the business, that doesn't really mean I've inherited any money.'

'But surely the land must be worth something?' Richard asked.

Richard could see that he'd struck a nerve with this comment.

'How do you mean?'

'Even if the estate isn't turning a profit, this house must be worth a fair few bob on its own. And you own all of these acres of land. There's got to be someone out there who'd buy it from you. You could turn a tidy profit if you sold up.'

'Maybe. But we've not been able to sell the land while the estate remained a trust. Those were the terms of grandfather William's will. So we've just muddled along, and whenever we really run out of cash, we sell another family heirloom.'

'An heirloom?'

'Well, like the house we used to own in Fulham. Father sold it about ten years ago. And that cash kept us going for ages. But I think the money from that sale ran out quite a few years ago. You'll have to ask father. I don't really get involved in the business side of things.'

Richard remembered the look that he'd seen pass between Hugh and Lucy when they both realised that she was about to inherit the plantation.

'But now that you've inherited, the trust is dissolved, and you can sell the plantation, can't you?' he asked.

'I suppose so. If that's what Father's saying. I'd need to check.'

'And would you?'

'Sell?'

Dwayne entered with the Crime Scene Kit, went over to the safe to start processing it, and Lucy took advantage of the interruption to go and look out of the window.

'I've wanted to sell this place my whole life,' she said, and Richard could how tense Lucy was. She was like a spring that had been wound up so tightly that it could suddenly snap. Or explode.

'What's more,' she continued, 'I think it's our duty to sell. My family has been a blight on this island since the first day we arrived here. Our wealth was created using slaves as a work force. It's shameful. The least we can do is sell the plantation, leave the island, and make sure that all traces of the Beaumont family are finally wiped out from Saint-Marie.'

'You really think that?' Camille asked.

Lucy looked squarely at Camille as she answered.

'I do.'

Camille didn't quite know what to say to that, but she was spared from answering by Dwayne.

'Okay, Chief, you need to see this safe.'

'I don't think I do,' Richard said smugly.

'But I think you do.'

'I don't, Dwayne, because I imagine you're about to tell me that you can't find a single fingerprint on any of the keys on the keypad.'

Dwayne was amazed. 'How did you know that?'

'Because it's like I said. Anyone can break into a keypad safe.'

'But I don't understand,' Lucy said. 'I opened the safe only the other day. My fingerprints should be all over the keypad.'

'Ah, and that's what makes breaking into one of these safes so very easy,' Richard said. 'You see, simple logic says that to get into a keypad safe, all you need to do is wipe the keypad clean of fingerprints when the owner's not about. You then wait until the owner next opens the safe, and then all you have to do is sneak up to the safe afterwards and use some graphite powder and a brush to reveal the numbers on the keypad that the owner pressed to open it up. Because only four digits will have fingerprints on them. The four digits of the code that were used to open the safe. And in one fell swoop you've reduced the number of possible combinations you'd need to break into the safe from ten thousand – which is all of the different ways you can combine ten digits – down to a mere twenty-four, which is the maximum number of ways you can combine four numbers. And I reckon it would take about two or three minutes to try out the twenty-four possible combinations.'

Dwayne turned to Camille.

'Did you understand any of that?'

'I think so,' she said, before turning to her boss.

'Are you saying that you think someone's recently broken into Lucy's safe?'

'I think that's exactly what I'm saying.'

'So why aren't there any fingerprints on it now?'

'Because, after you've broken into a safe, it would be only natural to wipe the whole thing clean afterwards. To get rid of the graphite powder that you'd previously used to reveal the owner's fingerprints on the keypad.'

'I think you could be right, Chief,' Dwayne said. 'I think the keypad was wiped clean afterwards with a blue cloth.'

'You do?' Richard said eagerly, heading over to Dwayne.

'I do. There's a tiny thread of blue cloth snagged on the safe's hinge just here, sir.'

Dwayne handed a magnifying glass to his boss. Richard bent down to inspect the hinge of the safe, and he was gratified to see that Dwayne was right. There was a thin strand of bright blue thread – only half a centimetre long, and barely observable to the naked eye – caught in the hinge of the safe. It had very possibly got trapped there when the person who'd broken into the safe had tried to clean up afterwards.

Using a pair of tweezers, Dwayne picked the thread up and deposited it inside a clear cellophane evidence bag.

'Good work, Dwayne. Maybe we'll be able to identify the cloth that the piece of thread came from.'

'Thanks, Chief,' Dwayne said, beaming at the compliment.

'Now, Lucy, could you tell us the combination of the safe?'

Lucy told Richard her four-digit code, and he borrowed the tweezers from Dwayne so he could press the numbers on the keypad without leaving any of his fingerprints behind. An LED light just above the keypad lit up green as the electronic lock inside the safe pulled back. Richard then very carefully opened the door, and he, Dwayne, Camille and Lucy looked inside. There was a hundred or so dollars in cash, Lucy's passport, and a few other personal documents.

There was no handgun.

'It's not there,' Lucy said in sudden shock. 'The gun… it's gone! Someone's taken my gun!'

Lucy's reaction was so melodramatic that all three Police officers separately wondered if maybe she was protesting too much.

'And you're sure it was in the safe?'

'Of course it was! I've had a Glock 19 and a box of bullets in there for years.' A thought suddenly occurred to Lucy, and she said, 'Yes, what about the box of bullets? Is that still there?'

Richard looked through the safe to see if he could find a box of bullets. He couldn't, but he soon realised that the gun and the bullets weren't the only things that were missing.

'There aren't any bullets in here – boxed or otherwise – but I also don't think I can see the document that Tom asked you to put in here, either.'

'What's that?' Lucy asked.

'You said your brother Tom asked you to store an old document in your safe three days ago. That's why you opened it up. But all I can see in here are modern-looking documents. Where's the document he asked you to store?'

As Richard said this, he stepped back so that Lucy could see into the safe for herself. After a few moments, Lucy stood up again. She looked utterly baffled.

'I'm sorry,' she said. 'It's not there.'

'Are you sure?'

'Yes. The gun's gone. And the bullets. But so is the document.'

The three Police Officers looked at each other.

'Then can you tell us what was in this document?' Richard asked.

'I don't know,' Lucy said, trying to remember. 'It was just an old handwritten document. I didn't really look at it. I think it was a list of names. But I can't imagine for a second why anyone would want to take it.'

'Okay, then I'm going to ask you something, and I want you to think very carefully before you answer. You've already told us that Tom knew that you kept a gun in your safe. Is that right?'

Lucy nodded.

'And it was also Tom who told you to put an old document in your safe three days ago?'

Lucy nodded again.

'Then, if Tom knew that your biological father Freddie Beaumont was on the plantation, would he have wanted to kill him?'

Lucy was shocked by the question.

'Of course not. Why would he want to do that?'

'I don't know. You tell us.'

'But it's impossible. Tom was only four years old when we left the UK. He had no idea how evil that man was.'

'And was he really evil?' Camille asked.

Richard saw Lucy's jaw tighten.

'Yes,' she replied.

'But in what way was he "evil"?' he asked.

'Where do you want me to start? He was manipulative. He was selfish. He was jealous. He lied. He stole. He was emotionally abusive. Physically abusive. And he was drunk the whole time. How long have you got?'

'He was physically abusive?' Camille asked.

'Never to me. I was only small. But he hit my mother the whole time. When he lost control. But I'd be in bed – in the middle of the night – and I'd hear her crying in the room next door. Just crying and crying. Can you imagine what that was like? Or there was the time I saw him smash a kitchen cupboard door into the side of her head. Just like that. In the middle of the day, and for no reason at all. He was just drunk and angry, and he wanted to cause her pain. We all lived in fear of him. In total fear. And Mother just took it. For as long as she could. So yes. That man was evil. But then, it's not like it's the first time our family has thrown up a nasty piece of work.'

'It isn't?'

'You ask the rest of the family about "Mad Jack".'

'And who's he?'

'One of the younger sons of Thomas Beaumont, the guy who founded the plantation. And he was evil. Just like Freddie was. So yes. We've got bad genes, if you ask me. I reckon that whatever madness drove "Mad Jack" also drove my biological father.'

'Very well,' Richard said, wanting to move the interview on. 'Then if not Tom, who else in your family might have wanted Freddie dead?'

'No-one.'

'Really?'

'Of course not. You've got to understand, we haven't seen my biological father in decades. He hasn't even come up in conversation for years. He's not part of our lives.'

'So no-one else has a grudge against him?'

'No.'

'It's just you that still hates him?'

'That's right. Just me. Not that it matters what I think of him.'

'And why's that?'

'Because I was with you when he was killed. Thank God. So it doesn't much matter that it was maybe my gun that was used to shoot him – or that I still hate him, even after all these years – I couldn't have been the person who pulled the trigger, could I?'

Richard was surprised at the clarity with which Lucy had expressed herself, but he had to admit that she had a point. If Lucy were ever to stand trial for the murder of Freddie Beaumont, her defence lawyer would be able to put both Richard and Camille in the dock, and they'd have to admit that they were in the middle of a jungle clearing with Lucy at the precise moment that Freddie had been shot dead.

So, seeing as Lucy couldn't be the murderer, who else could it have been?

It was pretty obvious to Richard that they needed to talk to Tom as a matter of some urgency. So, leaving Dwayne to finish processing the safe, Richard and Camille thanked Lucy for her time and headed back down the staircase to find her brother. On the way, Richard paused by the portrait of the Honourable Thomas Beaumont, the plantation's founder. Richard found himself marvelling at how cold and dead the man's eyes were. It was as though he was looking out from his picture, weighing Richard's worth and finding it wanting.

'So what do you think of Lucy?' Camille whispered to her boss.

'I don't know. I thought she was pretty erratic at first, but now I'm not so sure. She explained how she couldn't be the killer pretty succinctly, didn't she?'

'She did.'

'And I just don't think you'd so freely admit to hating the deceased if you really were the killer.'

'Unless it's a double bluff.'

Richard indicated the portraits of Thomas Beaumont and his many descendants on the walls. 'And I'll tell you something else Lucy was right about. An old family like this doesn't get stinking rich without there being blood on their hands. And looking at the honourable Thomas here, I can well believe he was capable of spilling blood.'

Camille agreed, and she quietly smiled to herself at Richard's ability to get so indignant about all injustice – no matter how many hundreds of years ago it might have happened. And as she looked at her boss, she saw how the little duck tail of hair at the back of his neck was wet with sweat. Dwayne was right, she thought to herself. They had to get Richard into more appropriate clothing. If he continued wearing woollen suits in the Caribbean, he'd eventually be out on a shout one day and drop down dead from heat exhaustion. But how to get her boss to understand that he had to change his wardrobe? That was the question.

Tom entered the hallway and saw Richard and Camille looking at the portrait.

'Oh,' he said. 'It's you.'

'Indeed,' Richard said. 'But more importantly, it's you.'

'What do you mean by that?'

'Could we have a word?'

Tom absorbed this information before replying.

'Okay,' he said. 'You'd better follow me,'

Tom led through the hallway, along a blissfully cool corridor with stone flagstones, and into an office at the back of the house.

As Richard and Camille entered the room, Tom went and sat behind a desk that was placed squarely in front of windows that perfectly framed the summit of Mount

Esmée behind. It was quite a powerful image, Richard found himself noting.

As for the rest of the room, it seemed a pretty typical farm office. A pile of muddy boots lay in a heap by an old stable door that led outside. There was a decades-old map of the plantation that was covered in Post-it notes and handwritten annotations. And all of the many shelves and metal filing cabinets in the room were covered in a mess of paperwork, manuals, books and magazines. Richard got the impression that this was a busy and active place of work.

'Is this your office?' Richard asked, seeing how proprietorially Tom was sitting behind the desk.

'No way, man,' Tom said with a laugh. 'But when Dad's not here, I get to pretend.'

'And is he often not here?'

Tom smiled. 'There's a lot of work outdoors on a plantation like this. And when Dad's not at work, he's out in the fields doing his painting. So I get a pretty free run of his office.'

'He paints, does he?' Camille asked.

'Sure does. You know, oils and pastels. And landscapes – that's what he loves painting the most. Getting out under the big sky, he calls it. And he's good. He had an exhibition at the Pascal gallery last year.'

Richard shook his head. The phrase 'the Pascal gallery' didn't mean anything to him, but he could see that Camille was impressed. Very well. So Hugh was a fair-to-middling painter.

Richard picked up a spreadsheet of figures from the desk and looked at it.

'So, what are you currently working on?'

'Pretty much everything.'

'How do you mean?'

'Well, since I graduated last year, I've been trying to understand how the plantation works. You know, dive into the balance sheets, try and get my head around the different variable and fixed costs, capital investment plans – that sort of thing.'

'I see,' Richard said. 'You studied agriculture at Miami University, is that right?'

'Sure did,' Tom said, proudly.

'And what was that like?'

'It was tough. But rewarding. I learned a lot.'

'And now you're trying to return the plantation to profit?'

'How do you mean?'

'Lucy just told us how the plantation hasn't made any money for years.'

Tom looked guarded.

'She did, did she?'

'She did.'

'Well, it's hardly a secret. And you're right. We haven't really turned a decent profit since the great eruption of 1979. So that's why I'm going through everything. I'm trying to see if I can turn the business around.'

'And can you?'

'Maybe. Don't know yet. But it's going to take a bit of a push. We've got to drag the whole production line into the 21st century.'

'You sound pretty committed.'

'Hey,' Tom said with a warning note in his voice. 'Just because I don't take myself too seriously, doesn't mean I'm not serious about my work. Okay? Anyhow, I don't reckon you wanted to talk to me about business plans.'

'No. Of course not. But we do want to know what the document was that you asked Lucy to store in her safe three days ago.'

'What's that?'

'Did you ask your sister to look after a document for you three days ago?'

'Yeah. So?'

'And did you tell her to put it in her safe?'

'What's this got to do with anything?'

'Did you ask her to store it in her safe?'

'Sure. So what?'

'Then perhaps you can tell us what this document was?'

'Are you serious? My biological father gets shot dead in an outhouse and all you want to know about is what document I gave my sister three days ago?'

'That's it in a nutshell,' Richard said with a smile.

'Alright. If you must know, it was a list of the first slaves that Thomas Beaumont brought to the island. But that's all it was. Just a hand-written list. From about two hundred years ago.'

'And why did the document need putting in a safe?'

'Okay,' Tom said, and Richard could see that he was thinking less and less of the Police with each passing second. Very well, Richard thought to himself, let him feel superior – that's when witnesses made mistakes.

'So, I've been having a clear-out of this office,' Tom continued. 'I mean, I know it doesn't look like it, but you should have seen this place before. There used to be a load more old books and ledgers everywhere. And Rosie and Matthew have been helping as well. In fact, Matthew's been badgering me to get all our historical documents into one place for years. So he can write a definitive history of the family. That's what floats his boat. But Rosie's always been interested in the history of the plantation as well. So that's what we've been doing these last few months. Trying to bring order to the chaos – that's what Rosie calls it. Bringing order to chaos. And it's been kind of rewarding. You know, finding all these old documents and records, and seeing how this place used to be run.

'Anyway, I was going through this old ledger from 1803 and that's when this slip of paper fell out. I could tell it was old from how yellow it was. And how it was torn at the edges. But I could also see that it was written in Thomas Beaumont's own hand, and dated 1777, a month after his ship first arrived on Saint-Marie. Matthew got really excited. The Honourable Thomas Beaumont was the first Englishman to bring slaves to Saint-Marie, so this was basically a record of the first families from Africa to be brought to the island. He said we had to get it to the Saint-Marie museum. And in the meantime it had better be stored somewhere secure, like Lucy's safe.'

'So that's why you asked Lucy to store the paper in her safe? Because it was of historical importance?'

'Sure did. Now can I ask you a question?'

'Of course.'

'Who cares?'

'Lucy's safe is also where she kept her handgun.'

'It is?'

'As well you know, because it was you who got her the gun.'

After a moment, Tom shrugged his shoulders.

'Okay. So I spoke to a few mates a few years back. They got hold of a gun for her. She keeps it in her safe. So what?'

'We think it was her gun that was used to kill Freddie Beaumont.'

Tom's eyes widened in surprise.

'You're kidding me,' he said.

'When we went to get it from her safe, we discovered that it was missing. Which makes it all rather coincidental, don't you think? That the only other person in the family who knew about the existence of Lucy's gun was also the same person who asked her to access her safe three days before the murder.'

'But that's all it can be. A coincidence.'

Richard didn't believe in coincidences – not where murder was concerned – so he decided to go off on a stroll around the room and let Tom sweat for a bit. Stopping at a photo on the wall, Richard threw a sideways glance at Tom and saw how unsettled he was by Richard's sudden silence. So Richard studied the photo some more. It showed fifty or so young boys wearing school uniform and standing on raised benches in front of an ivy clad wall. The faded handwriting underneath the picture said that it was a photograph of 'Manor House 1983', and the cut-out paper crest that was glued to the top of the picture made it clear that the boys were all in the same house at Eton College.

'Is this a photo of Freddie?' Richard asked, as if it was the most natural question in the world.

'What's that?' Tom asked, confused by the sudden change of subject.

'This school photo here. Is your biological father one of the boys?'

'No, Freddie had left when that was taken. But father's there if you look in the bottom left of the picture.'

Richard looked, and thought he could see a young, eighteen-year old Hugh Beaumont, with shaggy hair, staring back out at him from the front row.

'Yes. I think I can see him. Which reminds me, Hugh said that every male member of the family has been educated at Eton for the last three hundred years.'

'That's right.'

'But not you.'

'Sure.'

'So why was that?'

'I didn't want to go to boarding school.'

'Why not?'

'I just didn't want to. Okay? So when I was about ten or eleven years old, I told father I wanted to stay on the island with my friends. And he agreed. He even told me he was proud of me. I'd be the first male member of the Beaumont family who'd break the cycle. So, instead of going to some posh school on the other side of the world, I got to spend my secondary school years with my mates. Surfing at the weekends. Partying the rest of the time. Man, have you any idea what it's like being a teenager on a Caribbean island?'

Richard of course didn't, but he could see a smile slip onto Camille's face as she remembered her teenage years. Yes, well, the less he knew about Camille's teenage years the better, Richard thought to himself.

'I see,' Richard said. 'And, of course, I don't suppose your parents could have afforded to send you to boarding school. Not if the plantation's been losing money since the great eruption of 1979.'

'That was also part of it. For sure.'

'So how did you feel when they sent Matthew to Eton?'

'What's that?'

'Because it must have cost hundreds of thousands of pounds to educate him. Hundreds of thousands of pounds I can't help noticing that your parents didn't spend on you.'

'Yeah, but I didn't want to go. Matthew did. And if

he's never wanted to do anything original in his life, I can hardly blame him for that, can I?'

'Do you really believe that?'

'Of course. Or I wouldn't have said.'

'But how did your parents afford the fees?'

'It wasn't so hard. Dad sold a painting.'

'One of his own?'

Tom laughed. Not entirely kindly, Richard noticed.

'No way. One of the family heirlooms. Some old oil painting by some important dead guy. It fetched three hundred thousand pounds. And that's the money that sent Matthew to Eton.'

'Which is interesting,' Richard said, 'because you're now saying that while you spent three years studying Agriculture at Miami University learning how to save the family business, your parents were spending hundreds of thousands of pounds giving your brother an education that was not only denied to you, but which could have been used to save the family business.'

'That's not how I saw it. Have you even been listening?'

'Then tell me about the bird,' Richard said, deciding that he wanted to keep Tom off balance.

'What?' Tom asked.

'Nanny Rosie told us that she found you dissecting a dead bird when you were nine years old.'

Tom went very still.

'I just wondered if you had anything to say about that?'

Tom placed his hands on the table, and Richard could see that he was trying to control his temper.

'It's not true.'

'So Rosie is lying?'

'No. It's just she didn't know what had happened. And she still doesn't know.'

'So what really happened?'

'I'll tell you once – and then that's it. Okay? I was in the garden when I was a kid. That much is true. And I saw something on the ground by the sand pit we used to have over on the east side of the house. So I got closer and I saw it was a bird. I didn't know what sort. But it was already dead. And all its entrails had been pulled out and were on the grass to the side of the bird. Like the bird was having an operation. Looking at it made me feel physically sick. I couldn't work out who could have done that to it. But I saw Lucy's knife on the grass next to the dead bird. You know, her pocket knife. Anyway, I picked it up, and was holding it, and that's when I saw Nanny Rosie emerging from a bush nearby. When she saw me holding the knife, she went crazy. Shouting at me for cutting the bird up, even though I kept telling her I was innocent.'

'She didn't believe you?'

'No, she took her belt off, smacked me real hard with it, and sent me to my room without any supper.'

'She smacked you?'

'Don't be put off by how old and frail she is now. When

she was younger, she had a violent streak in her. She ruled this house with an iron fist.'

'I see,' Richard said, trying to absorb what he'd just learned. 'So it wasn't you who killed the bird?'

'I just said, didn't I?'

'Then who do you think it was?'

'I don't care. It wasn't me, that's all that matters. Okay?'

Richard decided that it was time to get back to the apparent coincidence of Tom asking Lucy to store a document in her safe three days before the murder, so he returned to Tom's desk – but as he did so, he glanced into the metal waste paper basket to the side of the room and noticed that there was something black and charred at the bottom of it.

To Camille and Tom's surprise, Richard got down on his hands and knees and looked inside the bin. He could see that were three or four black pieces of burnt paper.

Richard picked up the little metal bin and took it very carefully over to Tom's desk.

'Mr Beaumont, have you set fire to a piece of paper in this bin?' Richard asked.

'What's that?'

'It's just I was about to ask you about the piece of paper you told Lucy to store in her safe, when I noticed that someone seems to have burnt a piece of paper in this bin here. It's fallen into a few pieces.'

'I don't know what you're talking about.'

'You don't?'

'No.'

'In which case, can you tell me how big the document was that you gave to Lucy?'

'I don't know. It was sort of A4 in length, but it was a bit thinner. It was a long strip of paper with a load of names written down it.'

'I see,' Richard said, and returned his attention to the charred paper in the bottom of the bin. There were four separate pieces, and they all appeared to be quite narrow.

'I think you need to tell us what's really going on.'

'I don't know what you're talking about.'

'The fact that there's a document that seems to have gone missing from Lucy's safe. And here's a document that someone seems to have burnt in your office bin. On the same day, I hasten to add, that your biological father was killed by a handgun that we think was also taken from your sister's safe.'

'Look,' Tom said, 'what does it matter? It's obvious the man killed himself.'

'What's that?' Richard asked. He'd been waiting for the moment that someone tried to push him into believing that Freddie's murder was suicide. After all, Richard had already guessed that the killer's plan had been to make the scene look like death by suicide. So, did the fact that Tom was now mentioning this mean that he was maybe their killer?

'Only I can't see how it could have been murder,' Tom said.

'Why's that?'

'Well, it's kind of obvious. Lucy told me how you had to break down the door to the shower room, didn't you? And how there wasn't anyone else in the room when you opened it up. So doesn't it just make more sense that Freddie went into the shower room, locked the door and then shot himself? I've no idea why, but maybe it sort of makes a warped kind of sense. He comes back to the family home to end his life.'

'And how do you think he managed to get hold of Lucy's gun?' Richard asked sceptically.

'I've no idea.'

'Or do you think it's likely that a man who was, in effect, a complete stranger to you all would have known that your sister kept a gun in her safe, and would then have been able to get into the house to get it?'

Richard looked at Tom, and there was perhaps a moment of indecision, but then Tom just shrugged again, trying to make it look as though he wasn't bothered one way or another. Okay, Richard thought to himself, if that was the way Tom wanted to play it.

Richard despatched Camille to get Dwayne and the Crime Scene Kit again. He knew that if he could get the pieces of burnt paper safely back to the station, then he'd maybe have a chance of forensically revealing what was written on them before they were burnt. It wouldn't be easy, but it was a possibility.

Within the hour, Richard had carefully sandwiched

each piece of charred paper between glass plates, and he was standing with Camille by the Police jeep while Dwayne loaded the new evidence and the Crime Scene Kit into the back of it.

'So what do you think of Tom, sir?' Camille asked her boss.

'I don't get him,' Richard said, pulling his handkerchief out of his top pocket and wiping the sweat from his face and back of his neck. 'He goes to all this effort to look all laid back, but it turns out he's doing a forensic audit of the family business.'

'I know what you mean, sir. I think there's a streak of vanity in him that isn't healthy.'

'You do?'

'Because he wants to be everyone's friend. Doesn't he? That's why he wears those clothes and speaks like he does. But he also thinks he can single-handedly turn the business around. Even though no-one else has. Not if the plantation's been losing money since 1979. So, his father's failed. And his grandfather, for that matter. But Tom thinks he's the guy who can be the family's saviour.'

'You've got a point there, Camille,' Richard said, impressed − not for the first time − with his partner's insight into a witness's psychology. And the more he thought about it, the more he decided that Camille was very possibly right. He had even felt it for himself during the interview. Tom tried to pretend that he was humble and low status, but there'd been a strong streak of pride in the way he'd answered the Police's questions.

And there was no doubting – in Richard's mind at least – that this was a murder that was carried out by someone who was supremely arrogant. After all, the killer had shot Freddie dead inside a room that could only be locked down from the inside, and yet he or she had then managed to escape from the locked room by the time the Police had broken in. It was almost as if the killer were challenging the Police to have the wit to solve the murder – which was pretty much a textbook definition display of arrogance, Richard thought to himself.

So was Tom their killer?

Richard turned to look back at Beaumont Manor and was surprised to see a figure standing at an upstairs window looking down on them all.

It was Sylvie.

But as Richard looked at her, Sylvie turned from the window and vanished from view.

CHAPTER SIX

Rather than go back to the Police station with the pieces of burnt paper, Richard got Camille to stop off at a photography supply shop so he could buy a packet of photographic paper, some plastic trays and all the necessary chemicals for developing photos. They then went back to his shack on the beach where he pulled an old blanket out of a wooden chest and rootled around in a drawer until he'd found a red lightbulb. This wasn't the first time he'd used his home as a makeshift photographer's studio for a murder case.

Richard had learned the technique he was about to use from an old FBI handbook from 1929 that he'd found in a dusty pile of books in a store room at the back of the Honoré Police Station. Dwayne had suggested that they take all of the old books down to the beach, cover them in petrol, make a bonfire and then throw a big party, but Richard had insisted on bringing them back to his shack so he could see if any of them were of any interest. And, in fact, these ancient Police manuals had proved hugely useful, if only because they all came from a pre-digital age, so whatever forensic techniques they described were generally ones that Richard found he could replicate even with Saint-Marie's limited resources.

First, he knew he needed to create a darkroom, so he used the blanket to block off the light to the area beside his fridge in the house's little kitchen annex. With the red lightbulb screwed into a table lamp placed at his feet – so he could have illumination in a wavelength the photographic paper didn't pick up – Richard got out the first burnt piece of paper that he'd safely transported between two glass plates. He took off the rubber bands that had been keeping the plates firmly fixed to each other. He then put the plates down on a little shelf and oh-so-carefully lifted the first glass plate up, trying not to disturb the fragile charred paper that was now open to the air again. Richard then placed an A4-size piece of undeveloped photographic paper over the charred fragment and put the glass plate back on top of the paper so that the photographic paper would be held firmly in place. He then turned the whole contraption over, removed the other glass plate, put a second piece of photographic paper over this side of the burnt paper and then replaced the glass plate. He then wrapped rubber bands around the glass plates to keep them secure.

Richard had created a sandwich with the burnt piece of paper now fixed tightly between two A4 pieces of photographic paper – that were themselves held in place by two glass plates and rubber bands. He then put the sandwiched evidence inside a thick black plastic bag that he knew would stop all light from penetrating. And, once he'd fixed another set of elastic bands around the whole thing to make sure the black bag was firmly wrapped around the glass plates, he then repeated the process for the remaining three pieces of burnt paper.

After forty-five minutes of painstaking work in the sweltering heat of his makeshift studio, Richard emerged, covered in sweat, but with a sense of great satisfaction. According to his old FBI manual, if a document had handwriting on it before it was burnt, then the charred pieces of paper would still carry the faintest of indentations where the pen nib had pressed into the paper. And it should be possible to get a photographic imprint from these faintest of indentations. All you had to do was fix undeveloped photographic paper to both sides of the fragment of burnt paper – it had to be fixed to both sides as it wasn't possible for the naked eye to tell which side of the fragment was the side that had writing on it – and then you left it all in a place where there was no light, for example inside a heavy black plastic bag.

The theory said that the photographic paper would, over time, develop a 'ghost image' of whatever faint indentations had been on the paper before it was burnt.

The only problem with the whole technique was the fact that the manual made it clear that the photographic paper had to be left to develop for at least a fortnight, and there was no guarantee it would even work by the end of the process. After all, as Richard had privately admitted to himself, there was actually no proof yet that there had even been anything written on the paper in the first place. But his instincts said that if the piece of paper had been burnt, then it must have been burnt for a reason, and the most obvious reason was because it contained information that implicated one of the suspects in some kind of wrong-doing. The pieces of paper might even reveal the identity of the murderer.

There was only one way of finding out. And that was for Richard to wait patiently for two weeks until the photographic paper had worked its magic on the evidence. And luckily for Richard, he knew that waiting patiently was very much his long suit.

★★★

Over the next few days, Richard tried to press his team forwards with the case, but it was difficult to make significant headway.

At first, Fidel had written Rosie Lefèvre's name on the whiteboard as a possible suspect, but when they checked the times of her trip to Montserrat on the morning of the murder, they discovered that her alibi held up. Customs at Honoré Port didn't actually check passports when passengers left the island – of course they didn't, Richard found himself thinking – so they didn't have any records prov-ing her journey out. But when they got hold of Rosie's credit card statement, they were able to piece together her movements that day. On the morning of the murder, she bought a return ticket at 9.30am for the 11am ferry to Montserrat. Montserrat customs were then able to send through a CCTV screengrab of Rosie clearing customs at 12.30pm, which was when the 11am ferry had docked.

When Dwayne followed up by going down to the Customs Shed at the harbour, he found the man who'd sold Rosie her ticket on the morning of the murder. What was more, the man distinctly remembered serving Rosie because, after she'd headed off to catch her ferry, he realised that she'd left her credit card on the counter top. Rosie returned that afternoon after the ferry had got back from Montserrat, apologised for having left her credit card behind by mistake, and thanked him for looking after it.

But if Rosie could be ruled out, then that left Freddie's immediate family as the most credible suspects. And the mystery three-wheeled vehicle driver, of course. Fidel still hadn't been able to find the vehicle that had been up at the plantation on the morning of the murder.

Although Richard was trying to keep his team focused on the immediate Beaumont family, he soon discovered that Camille was also trying to work out what had hap-pened to Lady Helen after she'd walked out on her family. Camille was puzzled by Lady Helen's last words to Rosie, that she was going to visit her family. What exactly had she meant by that?

'Well, that's obvious,' Richard said. 'She must have meant her parents. Or siblings. Or cousins, even. You, know, Camille. Family.'

'I know, sir,' Camille said, 'but how can we work out who all of those people are?'

'Well that shouldn't be too hard seeing as she's the daughter of an Earl,' Richard said, going to Camille's computer and firing up her web browser. 'You see, our country's obsession with nobility means that there are all sorts of lunatics out there running websites that detail the genealogy of the British aristocracy – alive or dead – going back hundreds of years.'

'There are?' Camille asked sceptically.

Richard typed 'Lady Helen Moncrieff' into an internet search engine, and within seconds he'd found a number of websites that listed all of the dozens of members of her immediate family. Camille was amazed that all of this private information was freely available online, but it meant that she had the names she was looking for. And, once she had the names, it didn't take too long for her to get the contact details of Helen's immediate and not-so-immediate family.

First she tried phoning Helen's parents at their house just outside Dorchester in Dorset, but she seemed to be unable to get through to them. The phone was always picked up by a man called Stephen who claimed to be the family butler. After considerable confusion on Camille's part, it eventually became clear to her that the reason why Stephen claimed to be the family butler was in fact because the family did indeed have a butler, and his name was Stephen.

And while Stephen always said he'd pass on Camille's message to the Earl and Countess that she wanted to talk to them about their daughter, Lady Helen, no-one ever called her back. In the end, Camille had to explain that if neither the Earl nor the Countess contacted her, she'd be forced to get in touch with the local Police and get an Officer to come to the house to take a formal statement.

The Earl himself rang Camille that afternoon, but it was an entirely fruitless conversation. At Richard's insistence, Camille had put the call on speakerphone so they could all listen in, and they all heard the Earl explain in wine-soaked tones that he was very sorry but there really was very little he could say that could possibly help the Police. He had four children, Helen was the youngest, and she'd always been 'not quite right in the head'. The Earl was entirely matter-of-fact as he ran through the list of Helen's suspensions, rustications and eventual expulsions from various private schools throughout her childhood. And he remained just as brusque as he then went on to explain how he'd had to cut his daughter off without a penny long before she hooked up with 'that nasty piece of work, Freddie Beaumont'.

As for what had happened to Helen following her disappearance, the Earl explained that he and his wife had lost touch with her even before her third child Matthew was born. Furthermore, it was only in 2003, when Freddie got in touch to ask for some cash, that he and the Countess discovered that their daughter had vanished four years beforehand. The Earl explained that he obviously refused to give Freddie any money, but he'd also felt at the time that there wasn't much he or his wife could do if Helen had decided to disappear herself. And the Earl was adamant that his daughter hadn't been in touch with him or his wife – or anyone else in the family, as far as he was aware – from that day to the present.

Following this conversation, Camille decided that the Earl was so horrible that it was highly unlikely Helen had been referring to him when she said she was going to visit 'family'. It must have been someone else she was referring to. So Camille printed out the personal details of Lady Helen's three older siblings and decided to contact them next.

As for the rest of the team, Richard kept Fidel scouring the roads and byways of Saint-Marie looking for the three-wheeled van with the cut in the front wheel that had been up at the plantation on the morning of the murder, and he tasked Dwayne with pulling whatever financial information he could get on the family. In particular, seeing as Lucy said that the business was losing money, Richard wanted to see the company accounts for the plantation.

Dwayne soon discovered that the family hadn't been lying when they said that the plantation was steadily losing money. The registered accounts for the business showed that the plantation was making losses of between twenty and thirty thousand dollars a year, and had been for a number of years. Dwayne could also see that there were sporadic injections of cash every year or so.

But what caught Dwayne's eye was the list of salaries that he was able to uncover. Lucy and Tom were both on an income of a thousand dollars a month. Although this didn't seem like very much money, Dwayne was soon able to see from their bank statements that they didn't contribute to the upkeep of the house in any way, and didn't pay any bills either, so it was pretty much cash that they could put straight into their pockets. And although Matthew wasn't on the payroll – which was understandable since he'd only left school two months before – Dwayne could see that both Hugh and Sylvie paid themselves a salary of forty thousand dollars a year.

In the context of a business that lost tens of thousands of dollars a year, this eighty thousand dollars-a-year combined salary seemed highly irregular to say the least.

And the issue didn't get any clearer when Dwayne checked over Hugh and Sylvie's bank statements. Hugh seemed to live within his means – and even had a savings account with quite a few thousand dollars in it – but Sylvie was a heavy spender, and had a number of credit cards on the go with near-to-maximum levels of debt on them. What was more, she sometimes took cash out on one card to pay off the minimum payment on another, a practice that showed that Sylvie was not a woman who was in control of her finances.

When Dwayne had reported his findings back to his boss, Richard had been fascinated. Not so much about the fact that Sylvie was a spender when her husband Hugh wasn't, but because it was now clear that Hugh never baled her out. That suggested that she either kept her financial affairs a secret from her husband, or that Hugh didn't approve of how Sylvie spent her money and refused to help her when she got into trouble. Either way, it was a pretty clear indication – in Richard's mind at least – that Hugh and Sylvie's relationship wasn't quite as functional as they'd maybe liked to make out.

As for Richard, now that he knew the identity of the victim, he was kept busy trying to piece together Freddie Beaumont's life in the UK. In particular, Richard wanted to work out where Freddie had been living before he came out to the Caribbean. Unfortunately, Hugh said that the family didn't have a current address for Freddie as they'd lost touch with him in about 2003. And when Richard tried to contact Freddie's last known address, he discovered that he wasn't known there. However, Richard felt that the name 'Freddie Beaumont' was just unusual enough to give him a fighting chance of pinning down his whereabouts. Especially if Freddie had been living in the London area.

Richard soon discovered that the name 'F Beaumont' appeared fifty-three times in the London phonebook, but there were only three instances of the name in South East London, which was the area of London where Freddie had last been known to be living.

When Richard phoned the second 'F Beaumont', a young man picked up the phone. He said that although he wasn't Freddie, he was the warden for the almshouses that were run by St. Alfege church in Greenwich, where Freddie Beaumont lived. When Richard described Freddie's physical appearance, the warden confirmed that the description not only fitted the Freddie Beaumont who lived in the almshouse, but he also knew that Freddie had relatives who lived on Saint-Marie. What was more, Freddie hadn't been seen for over three weeks.

It was the positive identification that Richard had been hoping for, but he could also tell that there was something the warden wasn't quite telling him. It was as though the man was reluctant to talk to the Police. After a bit of pushing from Richard, the warden admitted that Freddie wasn't much liked in the almshouse. He was moody, introverted, and prone to sudden bursts of violent temper. In fact, Freddie was on a written warning from the warden. One more complaint and he was out.

Richard thanked the man for his time and next contacted the local Police station in Greenwich. Once he'd explained that he was heading up a murder case, he was told that a couple of officers would go to the almshouse and search Freddie's room for clues that might explain what he was doing back on Saint-Marie.

Richard was still waiting to hear back from the Greenwich Police when he decided to make his daily phone call to the Head of Security at Saint-Marie airport. And, just as had happened on every day since they'd first identified the victim's name, the Head of Security explained that although he now knew that he had only to look for the name 'Freddie Beaumont' in the Immigration records, he and Janice still hadn't quite found the time to go through the ledgers.

It was while Richard was chuntering to himself about the impossibility of trying to run a murder case on a tiny island, that Fidel chose to return to the station from another day of trying to identify the owners of Piaggio 50s from the official records.

'What do you mean you still haven't found it?' Richard said, almost before Fidel had finished his verbal report.

'I'm sorry, sir, but I'm trying my best.'

'But you've been working on this one lead for days. Why haven't you found our van driver?'

Not for the first time, Fidel explained that he had to visit each Piaggio 50 owner in person. And of the thirty-seven owners he'd so far paid calls on, eight had sold their vans on to other people without filling in the relevant paperwork. And when he'd pinned down exactly who these eight people were – and then visited *them* – he'd discovered that three of them had already sold their vans on to other people, again without filling in any of the correct paperwork.

'But I don't understand,' Richard said. 'If these vans aren't legally registered then how can they have insurance?'

Fidel explained that, as far as he could tell, none of these drivers had any kind of insurance, and Richard's apoplexy went through the roof.

'Then why don't you arrest them all for driving illegal vehicles?'

Fidel felt that he was too junior to explain to his boss how the island worked, so Dwayne stepped in on Fidel's behalf.

'Because,' Dwayne said carefully, 'if we arrested everyone who had dodgy vehicle papers on the island, we'd never be doing anything else.'

'Yes, but if they're breaking the law, they're breaking the law, Dwayne. It's our job to bring them to justice. I mean, I don't want this to come as a surprise to any of you, but we *are* the Police. Or maybe we aren't.' Richard looked from Dwayne to Fidel, and then back again. 'Nope. We're the Police. So if we aren't upholding the laws, then who is?'

'Chief,' Dwayne said, 'you have got to calm down.'

'Calm down? Why am I the one in the wrong?'

'Because there's breaking the law and then there's breaking the law.'

'*What?*'

'There's breaking the law,' Dwayne said, knowingly. 'And then there's breaking the law.'

'Yes. But they're both breaking the law.'

'Who's breaking the law?' an urbane voice asked, and everyone looked over to see Commissioner Selwyn Patterson standing in the doorway with a deadly smile on his face.

For a brief moment, Richard considered snitching on his team, but then he had a sudden insight that the Commissioner – who pretty much knew everything about everything – would no doubt be perfectly aware that not all the vehicles on the island were licensed.

'Don't worry, sir,' Richard said through gritted teeth. 'Just a little training exercise. How can we help you?'

'Well,' Selwyn said, 'I just wanted to know how the case was going?'

'The case?' Richard said, trying to work out what to say. 'Well, we've identified the victim as being Hugh Beaumont's brother, Freddie. And the killer could well be someone in his immediate family.'

Selwyn looked at Richard, nonplussed.

'What are you talking about?'

'The Beaumont case.'

'But I was referring to our bootleg rum pedlar.'

It was Richard's turn to be nonplussed. 'You are, sir?'

'Of course. If a family up in the hills choose to take pot shots at each other, that doesn't affect our standing in the tourist community. But I now hear that our counterfeit rum seller has moved on from the Fort Royal hotel and is selling his fourth-rate product on the roadside by the La Toubana hotel. And if I can find that out, I'd have hoped that my island's premier investigative team might have done the same.'

Richard was stunned by the implied criticism.

'Yes, sir, but we've been quite busy trying to run a murder case.'

'And I'm a busy man, too, Inspector,' Selwyn said. 'But I make sure I meet all my commitments.'

Richard knew that the Commissioner's commitments mostly consisted of attending drinks parties. However, as much as Richard would have liked to point this fact out to his boss, he didn't want to be sacked just yet. Not while there were illegal Piaggio van drivers out there on the island who needed apprehending.

'Then I'll assign my best officer to the case. We'll get your man.'

Selwyn's smile broadened.

'Good.'

He then turned and ambled off, leaving a somewhat flummoxed Police team behind.

'Just for the record,' Dwayne said before Richard could issue any orders, 'I don't think that I'm your best officer. I mean, don't me wrong, Chief. I'm a good officer, but I'm not your *best*. So if you need to send someone to follow this up, I don't think it should be me.'

'I'd agree with you there,' Richard said, 'but I can't

spare Camille from the Beaumont case. And I'm not releasing Fidel from finding his three-wheeled van. Not while I have strength in my body. So, unfortunately for both of us, that leaves you to work the bootleg rum case.'

Dwayne's shoulders slumped.

'And just for clarity's sake, I think that our bootleg rum seller is breaking one of the laws we *should* be arresting people for.'

Dwayne sighed as he picked up his Police cap.

'Okay, Chief. I'll see what I can do.'

Once Dwayne had left, Richard turfed Fidel back out onto the streets to continue looking for the unidentified three-wheeled van, which left Richard and Camille to work the Beaumont case. However, within the hour, Dwayne returned to the Police station. He was holding a cardboard box in his hands.

'What are you doing back here so soon?' Richard asked. 'Wasn't the bootlegger at the hotel?'

'He was there alright, Chief.'

'And he was selling illegal bottles of rum?'

'He was. Look. I managed to get some of his stock.' As Dwayne said this, he pulled a bottle of counterfeit rum from the cardboard box.

'But I don't understand. If he was there, and he was selling bootleg rum, then why haven't you arrested him?'

'Well, Chief, it wasn't that simple.'

'It wasn't? What do you mean?'

'Okay, so I got down to the Toubana hotel, and I spoke

to the doorman and he said that the bootleg guy was on the other side of the hotel. You know, at their second entrance road. The one that comes in from the hills. Anyway, I decided I had to approach with caution.'

'Of course. That goes without saying.'

'So I got back onto the Police bike and drove around to the other side of the hotel. But don't worry, I made sure I parked up and dismounted so I could approach our bootleg rum seller on foot. Clandestinely. You know.'

'I do.'

'And you should have seen me! I mean, I'm not dressed for undercover work' – here, Dwayne indicated his sky blue Police shirt and jet black trousers – 'but there was a line of palm trees along the road, and I reckoned I could use them as cover to get as close as I could to the guy before I made the arrest. Because I could definitely see a man by the entrance to the hotel with a blue rucksack at his feet. And he had a load of rum bottles laid out on the dust by the roadside.'

'What did he look like?'

'Our rum seller? He's Caucasian, but I reckon he's been out in the Caribbean a long time. He's got that dark tan. And he was wearing old shorts, a vest and flip flops. Oh, and he had blond dreadlocks that went half way down his back as well. You know the type.'

Richard did. The island was covered in hippy back-packers who were so keen to express their individuality that they all wore exactly the same clothes, the same leather bracelets, and they all seemed to wear the same red bandanas over their hair. These were generally the people, Richard knew, who'd left their homes to travel the world to 'find themselves' – a concept that Richard found laughable. After all, they didn't need to go to the other side of the world to 'find themselves'. All they had to do was stay at home and look in a mirror, and they'd be able to see that they dressed like idiots, looked like idiots, and this was, in fact, because they *were* idiots.

'So what happened?' Camille asked.

'Well, all was going well,' Dwayne said. 'I got to within three palm trees of our rum seller. I'd silently got my handcuffs off my belt, and I was ready to close and make my arrest. But just as I took my first step out from behind the palm tree, a soft-topped sports car came out of the hotel. It didn't stop to buy any rum from our guy, but it slowed to a stop when it saw me.'

'It did?' Richard asked.

'It did.'

'And why was that, Dwayne?'

'Well, Chief, because the driver recognised me.'

'And who was the driver?'

'A young Danish tourist called Anne-Sofie.'

'Really?'

'That's right.'

'But if she's a tourist, how on earth did she know you?'

'Well that's the thing, Chief. I'd already met her earlier this week.'

'So?' Richard said, not really understanding where Dwayne was going with his story.

'You know what I mean?' Dwayne said with a slow wink. 'I'd already "met" her earlier in the week.'

'Yes, you said that, Dwayne. I'm not entirely stupid.'

'I think,' Camille said, 'Dwayne's suggesting he maybe met this young woman in a romantic setting, sir.'

'Oh, I see!' Richard said, understanding coming to him in a flush of red-cheeked embarrassment. 'Right. Of course. I see.'

'And, from the look on Dwayne's face right now,' Camille continued, her eyes narrowing, 'I think there's every chance that he and this young woman didn't part amicably.'

'What are you talking about?' Dwayne said, his pride dented by Camille's accusation.

'So what was it this time?' Camille asked. 'Did you leave her the next morning without saying goodbye?'

'Hey! I always say goodbye. I was brought up properly.'

'Then maybe she found out she wasn't the only person you're currently seeing?'

'And that's way out of line. I've *never* been caught seeing more than one woman at a time.'

'Then let's see, what does that leave?'

'Nothing,' Dwayne said, trying to move the conversation on. 'I've no idea why she was so cross with me.'

'Then how about this? The following morning, you said goodbye, but you also said you'd ring her, and you never did.'

Dwayne looked at Camille as though she were a magician who'd just guessed the number he was thinking of.

'How did you know?' he asked, shocked.

'Hang on,' Richard said, finally beginning to untangle Dwayne's narrative. 'Although I already feel I've heard more details about your private life than is strictly necessary, am I right in saying that this woman's been waiting for a phone call from you ever since your... encounter with her earlier in the week?'

'I was going to ring her, as I told her just now. I just hadn't got round to it yet.'

'But either way, when she saw you on your undercover operation, she stopped her car and wanted a word with you.'

'She wanted more than a word with me, Chief. And that's when our bootleg rum man looked over and saw me standing in the middle of the road in my Police uniform. And before I could do anything, he grabbed up what bottles he could, stuffed them into his rucksack and set off like a rocket.'

'So you gave chase?'

'You bet I did. And you should have seen me, Chief. I was after that guy like a hammerhead shark bearing down on its prey... Like a cheetah bringing down an impala... Like—'

'Like someone who didn't catch up?' Camille asked.

Dwayne frowned.

'He had a head start on me.'

'You let him go?'

'No way. It's just he had a head start on me. That's all.'

'Even though he was wearing flip flops?' Richard asked.

'What's that?'

'When you described our rum seller earlier on, you said he was wearing shorts, a vest, and flip flops.'

'Oh. That's right. He was.'

'And now I think about it, you also said he picked up his rucksack before he left as well.'

'You make it sound like I wasn't trying.'

'Dwayne, you let a man who was wearing flip flops and carrying a heavy rucksack full of rum outrun you.'

Dwayne looked briefly uncomfortable, but then his face brightened as he reached into the cardboard box he'd been carrying and pulled out a couple of bottles of rum.

'But I was able to pick up the bottles he left behind. And look at the label. Because I'm telling you, the Commissioner's right. These are all fake.'

Dwayne handed the bottle to Richard and he saw that the cheaply-printed label proclaimed that it was 'Caribbean Calypso Rum'.

'And I tasted it as well – strictly in the line of duty of course – and it's some seriously bad stuff, I can tell you. The Commissioner's right. It'll be giving the island a bad name.'

Before Richard could decide what to do next, Camille's computer 'chimed'. She went over to her desk and saw that an email had just arrived.

'Sir?' she said. 'The autopsy report on Freddie Beaumont has just come through.'

'It has?' Richard asked, all thoughts of the illegal rum seller vanishing as he went over to join Camille at her desk.

'Yes, sir,' Camille said as she scrolled through the document, trying to pick out the salient details. 'And it's saying the victim was shot with two 9mm bullets that were fired by the same gun.'

'The gun we found at the scene?'

'That's what it says here. The striation and firing pin marks on the bullets they removed from the victim's body match the marks they were able to observe on the test rounds they fired from the Glock 19 we found at the scene.'

'So it really was Lucy's gun that was used to kill Freddie?'

'It was. One of the bullets penetrated the victim's wrist, causing severe fracturing to both the ulna and radius. The other bullet penetrated the victim's chest in the left fourth intercostal space close to the sternum bone, penetrating the right ventricle of the heart.'

'Which is pretty much the definition of a killing shot.'

'But there's something else you should see, because the report is also saying that the victim was suffering from Hepatocellular carcinoma, whatever that is.'

'It's cancer of the liver.'

'It is?'

'So Freddie Beaumont had cancer of the liver when he died?'

'The coroner writes that it was at quite an advanced stage.'

Richard called over to Dwayne.

'Dwayne, find out who Freddie's doctor is, would you? It's probably someone practising in Greenwich in London, but speak to the warden of the almshouse where he stayed, he should know who looked after Freddie.'

'On it, Chief.'

Richard's desk phone started ringing, and he went over to answer it. To his surprise, he recognised the voice at once. It belonged to his nemesis, the Head of Airport Security. And to Richard's surprise, the man told Richard that he'd finally managed to check through the immigration ledger, and he'd found a record of a 'Freddie Beaumont' clearing customs at the airport on the fifth of the month, nearly four weeks before. Even better than that, now that the Head of Security knew the day and the flight number for Freddie's arrival, he'd been able to dig out the Immigration Landing Card that Freddie had filled in before he'd been allowed through customs.

'You've got Freddie Beaumont's Landing Card?' Richard asked, excitedly.

'It's in front of me right now,' the Head of Security said.

Richard had always felt that the Saint-Marie Customs' insistence that every visitor fill in a form declaring that they weren't transporting any illegal plants, gold bullion, prohibited cheese, and so on, was a complete waste of time. After all, if someone really were illegally transporting any of the items on the prohibited list, they'd hardly be tricked into revealing their secret by a piece of paper.

But, for once, the island's somewhat old-fashioned approach to admin worked in Richard's favour. Freddie had filled in his Landing Card perfectly – including the address of the hotel he was staying at while he was on Saint-Marie.

Richard didn't immediately recognise the hotel's name, but he knew who would. So, thanking the Head of Security for finally coming through for him, Richard ended the call and excitedly showed the address to Dwayne and Camille.

'This is apparently where Freddie Beaumont was staying,' he said. 'Do you know it?'

Dwayne and Camille said that they knew the hotel well. It was a low-rent bed and breakfast at the other end of town. So Richard and Camille took the jeep over to the guest house and, once they'd woken the owner up, they were shown into a box room at the back of the dilapidated building.

It was swelteringly hot in the tiny room, the paint on the walls was mouldy in places, and there was only one bare lightbulb in an old pendant hanging from the ceiling.

As to why the owner hadn't yet reported Freddie missing, he explained that Freddie had paid for his room in cash, in advance, so he didn't much care whether the room was used or not. In fact, he said with a leering grin, as far as he was concerned, it was better that the room wasn't used.

Richard sent the owner back downstairs, and he and Camille started to search the room.

They soon found an old green canvas bag that had a few changes of clothes in it. And in the rickety bedside table, Richard found two crisp fifty Euro notes, a scattering of loose change – including British coins – and Freddie's passport. There was also a load of old grocery packaging in the plastic bin in the corner of the room. Maybe Freddie had spent each night at the hotel, and each day up at the plantation, Richard thought to himself.

Camille was making a cursory search of the single bed when her hand felt something underneath the pillow. Lifting the pillow up, she revealed a small bundle of envelopes tied up with string.

'Okay, sir, I think I've found something,' she said, picking up the package and untying the string. Looking at the first envelope, she could see that the date stamp on the front was too faded to see, so she passed it to Richard while she looked at the contents of the other envelopes.

Richard could tell from how dry the paper was that it was old, and the letter inside seemed to confirm this fact.

The letter was dated 15th June 2011. It was written in a faded blue ink, and from the handwriting, Richard guessed that it had been written by a child.

It started 'Dear Freddie'.

Scanning the letter, Richard could see that it was

written by a young boy on the occasion of his fourteenth birthday at the end of his first year at Eton College. As Richard read about Oppidans and Collegers – of Dames and Beaks – he could feel this young person's sense of abandonment burning through every line. Richard turned the page to see who'd written the letter and saw that it was signed 'Matthew', and in brackets it said '14 today!!!'.

Richard did the maths in his head. Seeing as Matthew had only just left school that summer, that meant that he was eighteen years old now. And this letter suggested that he'd been in touch with Freddie five years ago.

'Sir,' Camille said, 'there are five letters in total.'

'One for each year Matthew was at Eton,' Richard said, already understanding.

'And they're always sent on the same date, sir. The 15th of June.'

'Matthew's birthday. He wrote to his biological father on his birthday every year he was at secondary school.'

'And Freddie kept every letter, sir. And brought them out to the Caribbean with him.'

'Show me the most recent letter,' Richard said. 'What does it say?'

Camille opened the envelope at the bottom of the pile, and Richard saw that it had been printed out on a laser printer.

Manor House
Eton School
Windsor
SL4 6DX

Freddie Beaumont
St. Alfege Almshouse
Greenwich
London SE10 9XE

15th June

Dear Freddie

I'm writing this to you from my study as I head into my last week at Eton. And I know you don't want to read this, but I thought I'd write to you anyway and let you know how my last year at school has gone.

And the truth is that it seems to have passed like all the other years. Not to be too down on it. I mean, it's still 'the best school in the world', and it's not like I'm actively unhappy, but I still don't get this place. The beaks keep telling us to be exceptional. To change the world. To use our privilege 'for good' (whatever that means). But what if you're not exceptional in any way? What if you're not bright? Or not rich? Or not well-connected, or part of any of the smart sets? Where does it leave someone who's just... average? Anyway, I'm sure I'll work it out. All I know is, I can't wait to get this tie off from around my neck. And then let the future begin!

I'll sign off the same way I do every year – although I feel I can do it with proper authority now that I'm actually eighteen years old. I still don't know what 'crimes' you committed in the past, and, after all this time, I'm not sure I care. But if you ever want to get in touch, I'll always be here.

Always.

Your son,

Matthew

Richard looked up from the letter.

'He wrote this only two months ago.'

'And in it,' Camille said, pointing to the last paragraph on the page, 'he asks Freddie to get in touch with him.'

'And he never told us. Matthew never told us that he's been in touch with his biological father for years.'

'So why's he kept that a secret?'

'Indeed. And if he's been lying to us about that, what else has he been lying to us about?'

'I suggest we find out, sir.'

'I agree. But let's see precisely what's in these letters first.'

Richard turned back to the first letter and started reading it again. And as he did so, the church clock on the far side of the town marked the hour, striking its heavy bell three times.

CHAPTER SEVEN

Richard and Camille found Matthew sitting on the house's veranda reading a travel guide to India.

'Oh hello,' Matthew said, looking up from his book.

'Could we have a word?' Richard asked.

'Of course. How can I help?'

Richard reached into his jacket pocket and pulled out a bundle of cellophane evidence bags that he handed to Matthew. Each see-through bag contained one of Matthew's letters.

'Where the hell did you get these?' he asked.

'Your biological father brought them to the Caribbean with him,' Richard said.

'What?'

'We found those letters in Freddie's room. Under his pillow.'

'He kept them?' Matthew said in wonder.

'He didn't just keep them, he brought them with him to the island.'

Matthew was briefly speechless.

'Sorry,' he eventually said, refocusing his attention on the Police. 'It's just a bit of a shock. Knowing that they meant something to him after all.'

'You didn't know?'

'I didn't,' Matthew said quietly, and then Richard saw the young man mentally pull himself together.

'Anyway,' he said. 'How can I help you?'

'Can you confirm that you wrote these letters to Freddie Beaumont?'

'I can.'

'And you wrote to him every year on your birthday?'

'I did.'

'And why was that?'

'Well,' Matthew said, considering how best to start his story. 'When I arrived as a thirteen-year old at Eton, we were told we always had to do the "right thing". So, at the end of that first year, I got it into my head that I should write to my biological father. You know, that while the rest of the family had written him off, the honourable thing to do would be to open up a line of communication with him. After all, he was my biological father.'

'You felt it was your duty?'

'That's it exactly. So, every time Freddie ignored one of my letters, or sent back a cursory reply that just fobbed me off, I knew that a good Etonian would just stiffen his resolve and keep on plugging away. You don't give up. You persevere.'

'I see,' Richard said. 'So why did you lie to us?'

'What?'

'You didn't tell us you'd been in touch with Freddie over the last five years.'

'I didn't lie to you. I just didn't tell you.'

'But why not? You must have realised we'd want to know.'

'I didn't. I mean, I wrote to Freddie once a year on the occasion of my birthday. But that was it. I never met him. Or had any other contact with him. It was just those five letters. So when you told me that the person who'd died in our shower room was Freddie…? I was saddened, don't get me wrong – I realised there'd never be any kind of reconciliation with him now – but I didn't for one minute see what my letters to him could have to do with his death.'

'Did you invite Freddie Beaumont to Saint-Marie?'

'No. You can see for yourself. Seeing as you've got the letters I wrote to him. I never once asked him to come to the Caribbean.'

'And why exactly should we believe you?'

Matthew was nonplussed.

'Because I'm telling the truth.'

'But what's to say you didn't make any other contact with him? For example, did you ever phone him?'

'No. I wouldn't have dared make any other contact with him. Not with how he replied to my letters.'

'Why? How did he reply to you?'

'I'll show you his replies if you like. I've got them in my room upstairs.'

'Thank you,' Camille said. 'We'd very much like to see whatever letters Freddie wrote to you.'

As Matthew led Richard and Camille into the gloom of the main hall, Richard saw all of the family portraits and remembered how Lucy had said that she believed Freddie's dangerous behaviour was inherited from one of the family's badly-behaved ancestors. He also remembered that Tom had said that Matthew was the family historian who was trying to write a definitive history of the Beaumonts.

'Just one moment,' Richard said as they reached the bottom of the stairs. 'Do you mind me asking? Lucy told us that Freddie was cut from the same genetic cloth as one of your ancestors.'

Matthew looked at Richard, surprised. But then, Richard noticed, so did Camille.

'I'm sorry?' Matthew asked.

'Lucy said that there was some old relative… that's it, he was called "Mad Jack", I think. But she said that whatever madness drove him had also been inherited by your biological father.'

'You want to know about "Mad Jack"?' Matthew asked.

'I do,' Richard said.

'And you want to know about him *now*?' Camille asked her boss.

Richard ignored his subordinate. As far as he was concerned, he had to try to understand every single aspect of the case, no matter how trivial it might seem. You could never pre-judge what was important or what wasn't. Everything was important. Until proven otherwise, of course.

'I do, Camille,' Richard said before turning to face Matthew. 'What can you tell us about him?'

'What do you want to know?'

'Why did Lucy think that "Mad Jack" was like Freddie?'

'Well, by all accounts he wasn't interested in working or getting stuck in. He just wanted to drink and fight. I suppose that's what Lucy means when she says Freddie was like him. Although, by all accounts, Jack was so much worse.'

'He was?'

Richard could see that Matthew was reluctant to tell the story. It clearly offended his sense of honour. The same honour, Richard thought to himself, that had perhaps made Matthew write to his biological father once a year for the past five years.

'Alright,' Matthew said with a sigh, realising that Richard wasn't going to drop the subject. 'Way back in the eighteenth century, when this place was first built, the plantation slaves lived in wooden dormitories further down the mountain. Jack was a frequent visitor, I'm ashamed to say, because he felt he had *droit du seigneur* over the women. Apparently, he'd get steaming drunk, go down to the dormitories, steal a woman, rape her, and then throw her back into the dormitory. He was a disgusting and depraved monster. But all this is as nothing compared to what he did on the fifth of February 1798.

'According to the court records we've got in the family archives, Jack was particularly drunk that night, and he went into a dormitory and tried to rape a young girl. She was only twelve years old. That's the sort of person he was. He was pure evil. Unhinged. But the girl's father – a man called Arnauld D'Or – attacked Jack. They got into a fight and Jack shot Arnauld dead. Just murdered him there and then. Jack then told the other slaves in the dormitory that if they spoke a word of what they'd just seen to anyone else, he'd make sure they all hanged. And then he staggered back up the mountain to this house.

'But later on, Jack realised that there were now multiple witnesses who'd seen him kill Arnauld in cold blood. And, as far as we can tell, he returned to the dormitory in the middle of the night and set fire to it. The dormitory was dry as tinder, it went up in seconds, and everyone inside was burnt to death. He murdered them all. Just so they wouldn't ever testify against him.'

'That actually happened?' Richard asked, amazed.

Matthew had the good grace to favour Camille as he replied.

'To our family's eternal shame,' he said. 'It did.'

'But if everyone died,' Richard said, unable to stop his policeman's mind from spotting a logical hole in a person's testimony, 'how do you know any of this?'

'One man got away,' Matthew said. 'An old guy named

Gabriel. And the next morning he walked all the way to the Governor's House on foot, and told him that Jack Beaumont had shot Arnauld dead and then set fire to the dormitory, killing twenty-three others. When the authorities investigated, they found that one of the corpses in the burnt dormitory did indeed have a pistol bullet inside him. There was a sensation on the island. Jack was tried for the death of twenty-four people.'

'And that's why Lucy thinks that Freddie is like "Mad Jack"?' Camille asked. 'She thinks he's a murderer?'

'Of course not,' Matthew said. 'But Freddie's unhinged. And unstable. I'm sure that's all she means.'

'I see,' Richard said. 'So what happened to "Mad Jack" when he was brought to trial?'

'Just before the trial was due to start, Jack made sure that the pistol that he'd used to kill Arnauld was found in a wooden chest that belonged to his accuser, Gabriel. Jack also bribed other witnesses to say that they'd seen Gabriel shoot Arnauld dead with the pistol, and that it was Gabriel who later set fire to the dormitory. And before too long it was Gabriel who was hanging from a gibbet, killed by the Crown for a multiple murder he didn't commit, while Jack remained scot-free. So yes. No matter what Freddie did in his lifetime, Lucy's wrong when she says that he's anything like Jack. The man was a murderer. Now, can we get on?'

Matthew led them up the stairs to his bedroom, and Richard decided that there was something about

Matthew's calm self-assurance that didn't quite ring true. After all, he'd just found out that his biological father had cared about the letters he'd written to him, and now here he was – only minutes later – happy to explain the family history as though he were a guide in a stately home. Where was Matthew's angst? Or his teenage confusion and doubt? It had to be inside him somewhere. And, as Richard continued to mull Matthew's character, he started wondering if his easeful manner was in any way fake. Something Matthew put on in the same way that he might put on a suit. Or a school uniform, Richard thought wryly to himself. After all, Matthew was still just a teenager, really, and Richard couldn't help feeling that there had to be a mess of teenage emotions somewhere under the surface. But how to access them?

When they entered Matthew's bedroom, Richard was surprised to see how simply decorated it was. In fact, as he scanned the room, he saw no posters on the wall, no photos of friends anywhere – it seemed entirely devoid of personality. Even more surprisingly, considering Matthew's age, there weren't even any of the touches of non-conformist conformity that Richard remembered so well from his teenage years, where all of his friends could be relied upon to have the same Che Guevara posters on their bedroom walls and 'Keep Music Live' stickers on their cellos.

Richard went over to a bookshelf and pulled down a 'How To' guide to applying to university. Seeing the array of Post-it notes sticking out of various pages, Richard remembered something he'd read in Matthew's last letter to Freddie, and he decided that it was time to test Matthew's composure.

'Tell me, how did you get on in your A-levels?'

'What's that?'

'Only, I imagine you've got your A-level results by now.'

'That's right. I have.'

Richard could see that Matthew had dodged the question.

'Tell me, what did you get as your results?'

'I got a B and two Cs,' Matthew said, trying not to look brittle, and failing.

'Oh. I see,' Richard said, and put the guidebook to universities back on the bookshelf.

'Precisely,' Matthew said, understanding the point that Richard was making perfectly well.

'So what are your plans?'

'I don't know. Maybe a bit of travelling. Then I don't know what.'

'But no university for you?'

'Maybe. Although I'm not sure who'll have me with those sorts of grades.'

'Yes, I see your problem,' Richard said. 'After all, they're a fair set of results for a normal person, but not for someone who's had hundreds of thousands of pounds lavished on their education. No wonder you told Freddie in your last letter that you didn't feel bright enough for Eton.'

'Your point being?'

'Or rich enough. You said that to him as well.'

'Okay. So there were plenty of rich kids at my school.'

'And well-connected kids, that's what you also said.'

'What is this?'

'You thought you were just an also-ran, didn't you? Or "average", that's what you called yourself.'

'For heaven's sake!' Matthew said. 'Does it all have to be about my bloody school? I went to Eton, okay? And while I was there, I admit it, I didn't feel like I fitted in. I wasn't clever enough. Or interesting enough. I was just normal. Is that what you want me to say? That I felt inadequate every second I was there? Okay, then I will. But I also made some good friends, and had some good times as well. It was just a boarding school. It's not who I am, and I'm out of it now. Happy now?'

Richard smiled to himself. Good. *This* was the Matthew who'd written to Freddie each year. Someone who wasn't sure of his place in the world. Someone who didn't even have a relationship with his biological father.

'Anyway,' Matthew said sulkily, 'we didn't come up here to talk about my career prospects. Did we?'

'Of course not. So if you've got Freddie's letters to hand…?'

Matthew opened the drawer to his bedside table and pulled out a bundle of cheap-looking envelopes.

'Don't get excited,' he said. 'He only wrote three times.'

Matthew handed the letters to Richard and went over to the window to wait.

Looking at the date stamps on the envelopes, Richard could see that the three letters had been sent over the last five years. The oldest was easy to identify. It was the most dirty around the seams. Richard pulled the letter out.

It was a single sheet of A4 paper, and there was just the briefest of messages scrawled onto it in a cheap biro. It said:

Don't contact me again.

Richard turned the page over, but there was no writing on the other side. That was it. Just four words. And no signature.

Richard opened the second letter. This one was written in the same hand, but was barely any longer. It said:

I don't care that you're not happy. Don't write to me.

As for the third letter, Richard could see that the date stamp on the envelope said that it had been sent on the 17th of June, just two days after Matthew had last written to him.

'He replied quickly enough this year,' Richard said.

Matthew didn't say anything. Richard could see that he was still feeling bruised.

Richard took the letter from the envelope. It said:

Stop writing to me.

I've got cancer. So this time next year I won't even be alive.

But seeing as you've always wanted my advice, I'll give you some now. Don't screw up your life like I screwed up mine. You can have that for free.

Freddie.

Richard looked up from the letter.

'He told you he had cancer?'

Matthew shrugged. He still wasn't that interested in cooperating.

'And you knew this two months ago?'

'So?'

Richard held up the piece of paper. 'Who else knew?'

'How do you mean?'

'Who, apart from you, knew that Matthew had cancer?'

'No-one.'

Richard could see that Matthew was still sulking.

'I don't believe you. Someone as honourable as you wouldn't have been able to keep this information to himself. I'm sure you must have told someone. So who did you tell?'

Matthew exhaled before replying.

'Alright. I told Father.'

'You told Hugh?'

'You're right. I felt I had to tell him. After all, he's Freddie's brother. And the head of the family.'

'I'm sure you did the right thing,' Camille said. 'But what did Hugh say to you when you told him?'

'Well, he was pretty angry if I'm honest. Mainly because I'd been writing to Freddie for all of these years behind his back. And also because I told him we should get Freddie out to the Caribbean. So he'd have a chance of a reconciliation before he died. But Father wasn't having any of it. He said that the letter was a fraud, I wasn't to make any further contact with Freddie.'

'How did he think it was a fraud?'

'He said it was a typical Freddie trick. The letter was the bait to make us get back in touch with him. And then he'd try and get more money out of us. Or try to manipulate us somehow.'

'Hugh didn't believe that Freddie was dying?'

'He didn't. Even though that's what Freddie said in his letter.'

'And what did you think?'

'Well, I didn't know what to think. I mean, I have to defer to Father on this. He knew Freddie. And Father was insistent. I had to stop being so naïve. He made me promise that I wouldn't contact Freddie again, and he told me he didn't want me even mentioning his name again. I've rarely seen him so angry, if I'm honest.'

'So what did you do?'

'I did as I was told. I just dropped it. I mean, Freddie had told me not to get in touch in his letter anyway. Now father was saying the same thing.'

'You didn't contact Freddie again?'

'Not since that last letter I wrote him.'

Before Richard could ask another question, they all heard a loud sneeze from the other side of Matthew's door. Richard barely had time to look over at Camille before she'd covered the distance to the door and flung it open to see the quickly-retreating back of Lucy as she headed towards the main staircase.

'Lucy, wait!' Camille called out – and now Richard saw Lucy stop at the top of the stairs and turn back to face the Police.

'Yes?' she said.

'Thank you for your time, Matthew,' Camille shot over her shoulder as she headed out into the corridor, Richard following in his partner's wake.

'Can I help you?' Lucy said.

'That very much depends,' Richard said, 'on whether you tell us why you were eavesdropping on our conversation with your brother.'

'I wasn't.'

'Then how come we heard you sneeze by the door, and yet when we opened it, you were very distinctly scurrying away?'

'I wasn't scurrying,' Lucy said as she nervously tucked a strand of stray hair behind her ear.

'So what were you doing?'

'I was heading to my car. Alright?'

Richard could see the guilt in Lucy's face. She was lying.

'Or to be more precise,' Lucy continued, trying to hide her nerves with words, 'I was leaving my bedroom and heading to my car when I heard voices coming from Matthew's bedroom. So I stopped to find out who it was. That's hardly a crime, is it? But as soon as I realised he was talking to the Police, I knew I shouldn't be eavesdropping. So that's when I left. But I sneezed as I went. That's all. And that's when you opened the door. It was just bad timing. But I was already leaving.'

'So you were outside the door for only a matter of seconds,' Richard asked. 'Is that what you're saying?'

'That's it exactly.'

'Then can you tell us where you're going to in your car?'

'I'm sorry?'

'Where are you going in your car?'

Lucy's smile tightened, and Richard could see that she was failing to think of an answer fast enough.

'Oh you know… into town.'

'Where exactly?'

'Oh. Well. Around. Do I have to tell you everything?'

'No, of course not,' Camille said kindly. 'But do you mind if we walk with you to your car?

Richard didn't know what Camille was up to, but he knew his partner well enough to know that she was up to something.

'Yes,' he agreed. 'We've got a few questions, so how about we accompany you to your car?'

On the way through the house, Richard tried to ask Lucy if she'd got any further with her plans for the plantation since she'd inherited it, but she just gave vague answers about making sure that she didn't rush into any decisions too hastily. So, as it was fresh in his mind, Richard asked her about "Mad Jack", and Lucy shut down that conversation even more quickly. In fact, having heard from the family that both "Mad Jack" and Freddie were unhinged, Richard found himself wondering if maybe Lucy had inherited elements of the trait as well. She was being erratic, evasive, and she was clearly up to something – not that he could work out how to get her to tell them what it was.

'Just before you go,' Camille said as they reached an open-backed truck parked to the side of the house. 'Can I give you something?'

'That depends on what it is,' Lucy said, and Richard got the impression that Lucy was feeling a lot of pressure. But – again – why?

'Are you alright?' he asked her.

'I'm fine,' Lucy said. 'Just fine,' she said again, to make it clear just how fine she was. 'What is it you wanted to give me?'

'Hold on,' Camille said as she started searching for something in her handbag. But whatever she was looking for wasn't immediately to hand, so she put her handbag up on the metal side of the back of the truck. She fumbled around again and then she turned back to Lucy holding a business card.

'Sorry that took so long,' Camille said with a smile, 'but this is my card. If you think of anything that might be of relevance to the case, no matter how small you think it is, please don't hesitate to get in touch.'

'Okay,' Lucy said, taking the card and clearly wondering why Camille had chosen this exact moment to give it to her. 'I will.'

Lucy got into the cab of the truck, turned the engine on and drove off.

'She's lying to us,' Richard said. 'She's going somewhere she doesn't want to tell us about.'

'I agree.'

'If only we could tail her. Find out where she's going.'

'But we can.'

'Not down those hairpin roads. She'll see us in her rear view mirror if we try to follow her in the Police jeep.'

'But she'll only see us if we try to catch up with her.'

'Of course, Camille. But how will we know where she's going if we don't catch up with her?'

'Well it's funny you should say that, sir, but I think that when I had my handbag on the side of her truck, my mobile phone fell out and got lost in the old sacks in the back.'

'What's that?'

'I think I dropped my phone into the back of Lucy's truck by mistake.'

'But why on earth would you do that?'

'No reason, sir. It was just a mistake. Like I've been saying. But now I'm thinking about it, it would only be natural that I would now borrow your phone and go to a website where I can enter my details and track the GPS signal of my phone.'

'You can do that?' Richard asked, surprised.

'I can. And this website should be able to show me exactly where my phone is on a map in real time. And if that means that we'll also know where Lucy's truck is, well, that's just an unexpected bonus.'

'Hang on,' Richard said, finally understanding what Camille was saying. 'Is this even remotely legal?'

'What?'

'What you've described.'

'Of course it's legal.'

'But you can't just bug a suspect's car without a warrant.'

'I've not bugged her vehicle.'

'But you're tracking it.'

'I'm not! I'm tracking my phone that just *happens* to be in the back of a suspect's truck.'

'I can't let you do this.'

'But this is just a commonsense way of getting my phone back.'

Richard was in a quandary. He desperately wanted to follow Lucy's truck to find out where she was going, but there was no way he could break the rules and bug a suspect without first securing a warrant.

Seeing her boss's indecision, Camille sighed.

'Look, I'll tell any disciplinary tribunal that I didn't tell you what I was doing before I did it. And that you were reluctant to pursue.'

'You would?' Richard asked, impressed that his partner would go out on a limb for him like this.

'I would,' Camille said, bitterly disappointed – though not in any way surprised – that her partner wouldn't go out on any kind of a limb for her.

'Then, seeing as it'll be entirely your fault,' Richard said with a broad smile, 'let's go and retrieve your phone.'

Camille got up a webpage on Richard's phone, logged into her own phone's account, and used the 'Find My Phone' feature to show its position on a map. Richard could see a flashing blue dot wending its way down the hairpin turns of the mountain.

'This is amazing,' he said.

'Thank you, sir. I suggest I drive. You keep an eye on that blue dot, and let's find out where Lucy wouldn't tell us she was going.'

'You mean, let's go and get your phone.'

'Of course sir. That's what I meant to say. Let's go and get my phone.'

Half an hour later, Richard and Camille were driving through the outskirts of Gosier, the capital city of Saint-Marie. And whereas the rest of the island was picturesquely rundown – almost genteelly so – Gosier had a definite edge of modern-day urban decay about it. So, although the narrow streets were built on a grid system, the town's houses, shops, and few public squares were now many decades into a steep decline. Roofs were missing tiles, balconies hung skew-whiff from walls, and hardy buddleias grew directly out of cracks in the walls. Everywhere you went in Gosier, you were faced with rusting satellite dishes, a mess of cables strung in haphazard fashion between the buildings, and a very pungent smell of decay.

Gosier was also where Government House was, but it was situated to the western end of the town where there were street cafés, wider, palm tree-lined boulevards to stroll along, and a crumbling old castle that overlooked the sea. It was this section of the town that the tourists flocked to. It was also where the Commissioner had his office, at the top of the main Saint-Marie Police Building.

However, Richard could see that the blue dot of Camille's phone wasn't heading into the western part of the town. Instead, it was moving inexorably towards the far-rougher area of the old harbour – which was basically the most rundown part of the town. Richard had been wondering for quite some time what Lucy was doing in an area so semi-criminal, when he realised that the blue dot had stopped moving.

'Okay, her truck has stopped in the old car park to the side of the fish market.'

'It has?' Camille asked, just as surprised as Richard. 'Then let's go and see if we can find her.'

Camille drove up to the old harbour and parked by a rusty derrick that rather improbably had a bush growing out of its main hinge. At this time of day – after the fish market had closed – the area was unsettlingly deserted, Richard saw. There were just a couple of fishermen further along the wharf using a hose to clean out a pile of empty plastic crates. They looked over as Richard and Camille got out of the Police jeep. It wasn't a friendly stare.

Richard and Camille could see that Lucy's truck was parked on its own, so they went over to it and Camille fished out her mobile phone from the hessian sacks in the back.

'Well, I'm happy I didn't lose that,' she said, to complete her fiction. 'But now we're here, I wonder where Lucy is?'

Richard couldn't help noticing that the fishermen were still staring at them.

'How about we get back in the jeep,' he said, 'and just drive around?'

Camille noticed Richard's sideways glance at the fishermen.

'Are you frightened, sir?'

'No. Of course not.'

'Then I know,' Camille said, an idea suddenly coming to her. 'Let's go and talk to those fishermen.'

'*What?*'

'I suggest we go and talk to those two fishermen. See if they saw where Lucy went.'

'You mean those fishermen over there?' Richard said,

and only then did he realise that he was pointing at the two men at the exact same moment that they were already looking at him. The men responded to Richard's interest by starting to walk towards him, oozing menace.

'Oh no worries,' Camille said. 'Looks like they're coming to talk to us.'

'Right, that's it,' Richard said to his partner. 'I'm your superior officer, and I'm ordering you to get back into the jeep so we can carry out a vehicular sweep of the area.'

Camille barely managed to stifle her laugh as she followed an already-departing Richard over to the Police jeep.

'Okay, sir,' she said as she climbed into the driver's seat. 'Seeing as you're so sure that this is the best course of action.'

'Yes, well I am,' Richard said, irked – not for the first time – by how Camille so often seemed to have the superior status in their conversations even though he was her commanding officer.

As the two burly fishermen closed in, Camille reversed the Police jeep and calmly drove out of the car park. She then started driving up and down the nearby streets. The buildings here tended to be only one storey high, and there were plenty of structures that were derelict or even reduced to rubble. It didn't make sense to Richard or Camille that Lucy would have anything to do with anyone in this part of town, so where was she and what was she doing here?

After twenty minutes of fruitless searching, Richard decided that Lucy could really be anywhere by now. And there was little point running an observation on her truck back at the car park. After all, if they asked her where she'd been when she eventually returned to it, she could just fob them off with a lie. So Richard and Camille drove back to the Police station.

When they entered, they discovered Dwayne hard at work behind his desk. Richard asked him whether he'd been able to get hold of Freddie's doctor in London.

'Sure did, Chief,' Dwayne said, 'and she told me that Freddie was a long-standing alcoholic and heavy smoker who only rarely visited her, and was resentful when he did. But Freddie collapsed earlier in the year, and when he was taken to hospital they carried out a number of tests that revealed that he had advanced cancer of the liver.'

'So he really was dying?' Camille asked.

'The doctor said she didn't expect him to survive the year,' Dwayne said. 'Especially seeing as he was refusing to be treated.'

'He was?'

'That's what she told me. He wouldn't accept chemo-therapy or any of the other treatments on offer. And even when the doctor gave him pills to help slow the cancer, he didn't bother taking them. "It's like he had a death wish", that's what she said. Her words, not mine. Not that it would have made much of a difference, according to the doctor. His cancer was pretty advanced when they found it.'

'Which is interesting, isn't it?' Richard said. 'Because I think our killer almost certainly didn't know that Freddie had cancer.'

'You think so?'

'After all, why would anyone risk a twenty-five-year sentence for murder if they knew that Freddie would be dead soon anyway?'

'Good point,' Dwayne agreed. 'So who knew that Freddie had cancer?'

'Well,' Camille said. 'According to Matthew, the only two people who knew that Freddie was dying were him and Hugh. So are we saying we should strike them off our list of suspects?'

'Not so fast,' Richard said, 'but it's something we should bear in mind.' Richard turned back to face Dwayne. 'What else have you got?'

'Well, sir,' Dwayne said, picking up a pile of printouts, 'the Greenwich Police have also been in touch to say they've finished searching Freddie's room in his almshouse. And they've emailed over a whole load of photos of his room – and scans of his personal papers, bank statements and so on. They're here, sir.'

'Thank you,' Richard said as Dwayne handed over the pile of printouts.

Richard remembered how Matthew had said that he'd only been in touch with Freddie once a year, and then only by letter. But was he telling the truth? That's what they needed to find out.

'Did the Greenwich Police find any letters from Matthew Beaumont?'

'They didn't find any personal letters from anyone.'

'I see. Then did they send over Freddie's phone records?'

'He doesn't have a mobile phone. But they sent over a printout of the phone records for the main landline for the almshouse.'

'They did?' Richard said, impressed by the diligence of the Greenwich Police as he started looking through the printouts in his hand.

'Are you looking to see if Matthew has been in touch with him?' Camille asked.

'I am,' Richard said, as he pulled the almshouse's phone records from the pile of paper and spread them out on Dwayne's desk.

He saw it almost at once.

There was one phone call to the almshouse that was marked 'INTERNATIONAL' – and when Richard looked more closely, he could see that the number that had rung into the almshouse had a Saint-Marie dialling code.

'Look,' Richard said. 'On the fifth of August, someone phoned the almshouse from a Saint-Marie phone number at 18:37, UK time. The phonecall lasted nine minutes. I think it's fair to presume that the recipient of that call was Freddie Beaumont.'

'But if it was 18.37, UK time,' Camille said, 'what time is that on Saint-Marie?'

'11.37am,' Richard said as he took the printout over to his desk and typed the Saint-Marie number into a reverse directory on his computer.

He was surprised by what he discovered.

'Okay,' he said. 'The Saint-Marie phone number that called the almshouse that day belongs to the public phone box just opposite Catherine's bar.'

'It does?' Camille said.

'But this is a major breakthrough,' Richard said, 'because it means that we now know that *someone* rang Freddie Beaumont in the UK on the 5th of August from a public phone box on Saint-Marie at 11.37am our time. Three weeks before he was murdered. And spoke to him for nine minutes.'

'So how can we work out who made the call?' Camille asked.

'Well,' Richard said, heading over to the list of suspects on the whiteboard. 'I think we can safely assume it must have been one of the family, can't we? So I suggest we go through the Beaumonts' bank statements, emails, messages and so on for the 5th of August and see if we can prove that any of them were near Catherine's bar at 11.37am. But let's all start with Matthew. Since he's the person we already know has been secretly in contact with Freddie for the last five years, I bet you he's the person who made the phone call.'

'I agree, sir.' Camille said.

Unfortunately for Richard and his team, it soon became

apparent that there was no paper trail that put Matthew anywhere near the payphone in Honoré on the 5th of August. So Richard suggested they widen their search to include all of the Beaumonts.

'By the way, where's Fidel?' Richard asked Dwayne later that afternoon, apparently apropos of nothing.

Dwayne recognised that his boss was frustrated at their lack of progress and was looking for someone to kick, so he tried to be as neutral as possible.

'He's still looking for the three-wheeled vehicle, sir,' he said.

'He is?' Richard said in irritation. 'Why can't he find it?'

'He's doing his best, sir.'

'You reckon?'

'Sir,' Camille called over from her desk. 'I think I've found something.'

'You have?'

'Maybe. I'm looking at Hugh Beaumont's credit card statement, and he doesn't spend any money anywhere near Honoré on the 5th of August, but he does make a transaction that day. A quite significant transaction.'

'What is it?'

'He spent six hundred and ninety-nine dollars with Saint-Marie Airlines. At 12.45pm.'

'He did?'

'I mean, it could just be a coincidence, but I'm also looking at his diary' – as she said this, Camille held up some printouts of Hugh's diary – 'and as far as I can see, he's not flown anywhere since the 5th of August. And nor does his diary list any flights coming up. Not as far as I can tell.'

'Then ring the airline, would you?' Richard said. 'I agree. The fact that Hugh bought an airline ticket within an hour of our mystery phone call to the UK is definitely worth looking into.'

As Camille made the call, Richard went back to the whiteboard to try and make sense of the names and information that was written there. One of these people had killed Freddie in the shower room. Richard was sure of it. But who was it?

Richard was still deep in thought when he heard Camille end her phone call.

'Oh okay, thanks for your help,' she said, putting the phone back down into its cradle. 'Sir, we were right to look into the 5th of August, because the airline desk has just confirmed that Hugh Beaumont bought a return ticket from London Heathrow to Saint-Marie, on the fifth.'

'He did?'

'But the flight wasn't booked in his name. It was booked in the name of Freddie Beaumont.'

Richard and Dwayne were stunned.

'It was *Hugh* who paid for Freddie to come out to the Caribbean?' Dwayne asked.

Richard picked up a board marker and angrily drew rings around Hugh Beaumont's name on the white board.

'Even though Hugh told us that he'd not been in touch with Freddie for years,' he said. 'And let's not forget that it was also Hugh who told Matthew that Freddie was a fraudster, and no-one should contact him under any circumstances.'

'He's been playing us from the start,' Camille said.

'He has, hasn't he?' Richard said, putting the lid back on the board marker with a satisfying pop. 'In which case, I suggest we go and interview him and find out why.'

CHAPTER EIGHT

While Richard and Camille went to the plantation to interview Hugh, Richard sent Dwayne down to the old harbour area in Gosier. It still annoyed him that they'd not been able to work out what Lucy had been doing there, and he knew that if anyone could winkle out any gossip from the ne'er-do-wells who hung around the fish market, it would be Dwayne.

Dwayne had readily agreed. After all, an afternoon spent sharing gossip in the waterfront bars of Gosier was very much his idea of an afternoon well spent.

As for Richard and Camille, once they'd arrived at the plantation, they found Hugh at the far end of one of his coffee fields standing by an easel and canvas. He was so engrossed in what he was doing that he didn't hear the Police arrive, and when Camille called out 'Mr Beaumont?', he spun around, a look of fury in his eyes.

'What the hell—' he said before realising it was the Police who'd interrupted him, and Richard saw how quickly Hugh composed himself, adopting his usual 'man in charge' manner again.

'Sorry about that,' Hugh said with a self-deprecating smile. 'I don't like being interrupted when I'm working.'

But Richard had seen that briefest spark of anger. And Richard also couldn't help noticing how quickly Hugh had hidden it. Just like Matthew seemed to have a bruised psyche hiding under his glossy exterior, maybe there was anger inside Hugh that he was just as careful to keep well-hidden?

Whilst Richard was storing this thought away for later consideration, he looked at the picture on the easel that Hugh was painting and was surprised by what he saw. The painting was mostly pink and yellow swirls where the sky might have been, and the rolling fields of coffee plants were represented in the painting by thick red and black streaks that had been applied with a palette knife. It was only because Richard could see the view that Hugh was painting that he was able to correlate the crazed swirls and stabs on the canvas with the real world setting at all.

And it was as Richard was looking at the painting that he realised that all of the abstract paintings that he'd seen in the family's sitting room must have been painted by Hugh as well.

God, Richard thought to himself, Hugh was *terrible* at painting.

After all, here was a majestic view of the coffee fields as they rolled down to the Caribbean Sea, but he hadn't even managed to make the sky blue, or the fields green.

'Don't worry,' Hugh said, correctly interpreting Richard's silence. 'The colours I choose make sense to me. Anyway,' he continued, wiping the excess paint from his knife with an old cloth, 'I guess you're not here to talk about my art.'

'I don't know,' Camille said, surprising Richard. After all, Richard tended to agree with Hugh that they weren't there to talk about his painting. Especially now that he'd seen the quality of his painting.

'Tom told us that you had an exhibition at the Pascal gallery last year.'

'I did,' Hugh said, unable to keep the pride out of his voice.

'What was that like?'

'It was…' Hugh tried to think of the correct word. 'Transformative,' he eventually said.

'It was?'

'Mainly because so many of the pictures sold,' he added with a smile, not wanting to come across as too full-of-himself. 'But I've been painting all my life. It's what I loved doing at school. When everyone else was out playing rugby, or cricket – hitting things or people with balls, anyway – I'd lose myself in the art department, drawing and painting. And I carried on painting, even after I left school and took over the plantation here. It's what I'd do at the weekends. Or on holidays. I always have my paints with me. But I'm strictly an amateur. The exhibition last year was very much a first for me, and it was Sylvie who put me up to it. She's on the board of the gallery. She spoke to Pascal three years ago, so I had two years' notice. But even so, it was exhausting getting together enough paintings I was happy with.'

'You took the challenge seriously?'

'More seriously than anything I've ever done before. Which is why I say it was transformative for me. You see, no-one laughed. Or said my paintings were rubbish. And, as I say, I even sold a few of them. And now I'm taking commissions. This painting here is for the Saint-Marie Country Club. Anyway, how can I help you?'

'Well, that's easy enough. We want to know why you didn't tell us that you knew your brother Freddie was dying.'

Hugh paused as he placed his now-clean knife into a wooden box he had on a little fold-up table to his side.

'What's that?'

'You knew that your brother was dying.'

'I did?' Hugh said, but Richard could see that he was trying to buy himself time.

'Or was Matthew lying to us when he said he'd shown you the letter that Freddie had written to him?'

'Oh you know about that, do you?' Hugh said in a failed attempt to appear unflustered.

'And we also know that you then told Matthew that you thought Freddie wasn't dying. In fact, Matthew suggested that you lost your temper with him and said that Freddie's letter was just another ruse to get more money from the family. And that Matthew was to cease all contact with Freddie. Is that true?'

Hugh decided to look at his painting, and Richard was about to tell him to answer the question when Camille touched her hand to his arm. Richard flinched, but got the message. He was to keep quiet. After a few more moments of introspection, Hugh spoke as though to nobody.

'Alright. That's what happened. I admit it.'

'You told Matthew to cease all contact with Freddie?'

'I did.'

'So why did you then buy flights for Freddie to come out to Saint-Marie yourself?'

It was as if Hugh had been slapped in the face.

'How…?' he eventually mumbled. 'How do you know all this?'

'Never mind how we know, but do you admit it? Was it you who bought tickets for Freddie to come out to the Caribbean?'

Hugh was panicking now – and Richard decided to push harder.

'Which means that it was also you who rang Freddie from the public payphone in Honoré that morning as well. Seeing as it was you who then bought the flights only an hour later.'

'I don't know how you know…' Hugh said, before trailing off.

'It was you who rang Freddie from just outside Catherine's bar?' Camille asked.

'It was,' Hugh said, unable to think how else he could answer the question.

'And it was you who then bought your brother a return flight from London to Saint-Marie?'

'It was.'

'So why didn't you tell us any of this?' Camille asked, as if she were a friend who was only trying to understand Hugh better.

'Because it isn't that simple.'

'Why not?'

'Because, although I've not seen my brother for the last twenty years, there's not a day I don't think of him. Because I see his children. *My* children. And I know how great they are. And I think how damned selfish Freddie's been his whole life. All he's ever thought about is himself. Never anyone else. And never his own kids, who he gave up for adoption at the first opportunity.'

'And it makes you angry?' Richard said, fishing.

Hugh sighed. 'No. Not any more. I mean, don't get me wrong. It used to. Do either of you have children?'

'No,' Richard said, and Camille shook her head.

'Well, each year your child's alive, your love for them just seems to grow. It's overwhelming. Just how precious they become to you. You know you'd sacrifice anything for them in a heartbeat. *Anything.* And what I've never understood is, how did Freddie never feel any of this for his children? So yes, it used to make me angry. The way he just abandoned them. But as the years passed, I realised

I was just grateful to have Lucy, Tom and Matthew in my life. I was the lucky one.'

Hugh's words briefly reminded Richard of how Nanny Rosie had said that while Hugh was a good parent, Sylvie didn't – as she put it – have 'a maternal bone in her body'.

'And does Sylvie feel the same way as you?' Richard asked.

'Of course. We were never fortunate enough to have children of our own. Our kids have been a blessing to us. A blessing.'

'So how does this explain why you lied to us?' Richard asked.

'I suppose all I'm saying is, I've got quite a complicated relationship with my brother. So when I saw his body in the shower room like that... shot dead... I didn't know what to do.'

'So you're now admitting that you recognised him?' Richard, unable to keep the irritation out of his voice.

Hugh licked his lips, and Richard got a sense that he was weighing up a decision. And, as the silence grew, Richard had a sudden premonition: Hugh was about to tell another lie.

'I wasn't entirely sure I recognised him,' Hugh said. 'Remember, I hadn't seen Freddie in the last twenty years. And although I admit that I spoke to him on the phone a few weeks ago, I still didn't know for sure that he'd used the flights I'd sent to him.'

'You didn't?'

'I didn't. I haven't had any contact with Freddie since I phoned him.'

Richard found himself wondering: was this the lie – that Hugh hadn't seen Freddie since the phone call? Or was he lying about something else? What wasn't in doubt – to Richard's mind at least – was that Hugh still wasn't telling them the whole truth.

'And anyway,' Hugh said, finding confidence as he continued his story, 'he didn't look anything like he did twenty years ago. The man I saw on the tiles of the shower room was sallow, ill, a tramp. That's who I thought it was initially. Just some old guy who'd wandered up onto the plantation and shot himself.'

'Until you looked closer.'

'Yes,' Hugh finally admitted. 'Until I looked closer, and then I knew.'

'So why didn't you tell us there and then that you knew it was your brother?'

'I'm sorry. I should have done, but I was so shocked. I was reeling.'

'You hid it well.'

'That's the public school training. You can hide any emotion,' Hugh said with a rueful smile. 'But I realised that I was perhaps the only person in the whole family who'd recognise that the bearded tramp who'd just died in the shower room was actually Freddie. And I have to admit that I'm a proud man. I didn't want the family name dragged through the mud. So I thought that all I had to do was say nothing, and there was every chance that no-one would even discover his real identity. The children would be spared from discovering that they'd just seen their biological father shot dead.'

'So you're saying that you kept quiet because you wanted to protect the family name?'

'And the children. Although it wasn't that well thought through. It was a snap decision I made there and then. But once I'd told you that I didn't recognise him, I felt I couldn't change my story.'

'I don't believe you.'

'What?'

'Because I can perhaps imagine you keeping quiet in the heat of the moment. But after we then returned to the house – days later – and revealed that the victim was your own brother? Why did you continue to lie to us that you hadn't worked this out for yourself? What are you hiding?'

Hugh was surprised by the question, and Richard's instincts were telling him that Hugh was still lying to them.

'I've already said. I was worried about the scandal. I didn't want the children upset. And once you worked out that the dead person was indeed Freddie, I didn't see the point of coming forward and revealing that I'd known all along.'

'Because we'd see how suspicious your actions had been?' Richard asked.

'Look,' Hugh said, trying to move the conversation on.

'I admit it. Matthew showed me the letter that Freddie had written to him. Saying he had cancer. And I told Matthew to drop it, and that it was just another one of Freddie's tricks to get money out of us. And you're right, I got pretty angry with Matthew and told him not to contact Freddie again. But after Matthew left, I found myself wondering, what if Freddie was "The Boy Who Cried Wolf"!", and this was the one time he was telling the truth? I mean, don't get me wrong, I still didn't think that he had terminal cancer, but what started to gnaw at me was the thought, what if I was wrong? Because if I was, then I'd just banned Matthew from seeing his biological father before he died.

'After a few more days, I realised that I should do what Matthew wanted me to do. So I went into Honoré and phoned the number I had for Freddie's almshouse from a public payphone. I didn't dare ring him from the house. I couldn't risk being overheard.'

'Who did you tell that you were ringing Freddie?'

'No-one.'

'Not even your wife?'

'No. Not even Sylvie. This was between me and Freddie. I didn't want anyone else hurt or confused. Especially seeing as I didn't know what Freddie would say to me. But anyway, I rang Freddie's almshouse from Honoré and found myself talking to someone who went and got him, and then there he was. After two decades, I was talking to my brother on the phone.'

'And what was it like?' Camille asked.

'The first thing he said to me was, "What do you want?", so he hardly made it easy for me. But I told him that I'd read his letter to Matthew, and I asked him if he was really dying. He told me that he was.'

'Did you believe him?'

'No. Not if I'm brutally honest, but I'd already decided that I had to do the honourable thing. So I said that maybe we should all see him. He just laughed and told me that it was all a bit late for that. I tried to ignore his attitude, which was pretty bitter and needling. Remember, he was still my older brother and he wanted me to know it. But I just pushed on and asked him if he'd get on a plane and come out here to visit us. He said I'd have to organise the flight. So I told him I'd do that. He then said it would have to be flexible dates, he didn't know when he'd be able to come out. I agreed to that as well. But I was getting angry now. I mean, I was the person who'd raised his children for the last twenty years. In the end, he still hadn't even asked me about them once by the time he hung up on me.

'It was a frustrating experience to say the least. But I said I'd sort out a ticket for him, so that's what I did. I went to the airport that morning, paid for a flight in his name, and then, realising I might as well be hung for a goose as for a gander, I changed some money into sterling, put it into an envelope along with the flight tickets, and posted it all to Freddie in the UK. And then... nothing. Can you believe it? I heard nothing. No indication that he'd received the money, no indication he'd even used the flight or arrived on the island.

'And I began to suspect that Freddie had done it again. He'd tricked me. Just like when he was seventeen and got our father to send him money to buy flights to come back to Saint-Marie. And like every time since then that he'd got money out of us under the pretext of coming out to the Caribbean. So he wasn't dying this time. He didn't have cancer. He'd just taken my cash again and no doubt spent it on booze. As he'd always done. But this was also why I was so shocked to see him dead on the floor of the shower room. I genuinely didn't know he was on the island. I thought he'd stayed in London to drink away the cash I'd sent him.'

'Hugh Beaumont, did you kill your brother?'

'What? No! Look, I didn't like Freddie, I'll admit that to anyone. I'll even admit that there have been times over the years when I've thought I'd rather he was dead, but the first time I saw him in twenty years was when he was already dead and on the shower room floor.'

Richard looked at the sincerity shining from Hugh, but his gut was still telling him that Hugh was 'playing' the Police somehow. But what was it that Hugh wasn't being entirely truthful about? Richard wanted time to let his thoughts percolate, so he thanked Hugh for his time, and he and Camille left the plantation owner to his painting.

While walking back to the Police jeep, Camille could see that her boss was deep in thought.

'What did you make of Hugh?' she asked, as they approached the main house.

'I don't know. But I've got a feeling he's still holding out on us.'

'I know what you mean,' Camille said, and then she stopped dead in her tracks. 'You do?' she asked.

'I do. Although it's just an instinct, really. A gut instinct that says he's still lying to us – or not being entirely truthful – about something.'

Richard realised that Camille was looking at him in wonder.

'What?' he asked, unsettled.

'Are you saying that you've got a *gut instinct* that he's lying?'

'Yes,' Richard said. 'Why's that so interesting?'

'So you've formed an opinion about a suspect that's not based on cold logic? Or an actual piece of physical evidence?'

Richard sniffed.

'So? What of it?'

'Well, that's a first,' she said in delight, before noticing Rosie Lefèvre sweeping the house's veranda with a broom, and heading off towards her.

'What are you talking about?' Richard asked, neither understanding the point his partner was making, nor why she'd changed direction and was now heading towards Rosie.

Camille stopped briefly, turned, and fixed her boss with a devilish grin.

'I just think that's a big deal.'

'Why? Stop being so cryptic.'

'Because, sir, that suggests to me that, for the first time since I've known you, you're going on your instinct about a suspect. A *hunch*.'

Richard was thunderstruck. Was it true? Had he really just formed his opinion of Hugh based on something as unprofessional as a hunch?

'But that's impossible,' he said. 'I'm sure there was physical evidence that informed my opinion, even if it was just the shifty look in his eyes.'

'Fair enough, sir, but I still call that a hunch,' Camille said, heading off towards Rosie again.

'Well, you'd be wrong to,' Richard huffed as he caught up with his partner and fell into step. 'Anyway, where are you going?'

'There's a couple of questions I want to ask Rosie. If that's alright with you, sir?'

'Okay,' Richard said, if only to close the conversation down – because, as he and Camille approached the veranda, he found his mind racing. Was Camille right? Had he really just formed his opinion of a suspect based on a hunch, rather than using objective facts or physical evidence? Was he...? The idea sent a chill through him, but Richard made himself finish the thought: was he... loosening up? It wasn't possible, Richard told himself. He didn't 'do' change, that was one of the immutable truths of his life. But as he and Camille stepped up onto the veranda, he found it hard to shake the uneasy feeling that something inside himself had maybe just shifted. Like a continental shelf. Or an iceberg calving.

'Good afternoon!' Rosie called out as she saw the Police approach.

'Good afternoon, Rosie,' Camille said, looking at the broom in the frail old woman's hand.

'Oh don't worry about me,' Rosie said, smiling. 'It's the work that keeps me fit.'

'So you still enjoy working?' Camille asked, impressed.

'Of course. I've always loved my job.'

'Really?' Richard asked, finally emerging from his introspective jag. After all, as far as he was concerned, no-one ever truly enjoyed their job.

Rosie laughed.

'You know,' she said, 'centuries ago, my family worked as coffee pickers on this plantation. They weren't allowed into the house. Can you imagine that? They weren't even allowed to address the owner by name. They had no rights. But that was then. And look at me now. I get to run the whole house and call the Beaumont family my friends. That's how much times have changed.'

'Sorry,' Camille said, feeling that she had to apologise for her boss's evergreen lack of sensitivity. 'But I just wanted to know a bit more about your trip to London when you met Lady Helen.'

Rosie was surprised.

'You do? It was such a long time ago.'

'I know, but you told us that Lady Helen walked out on her family on the same day that you arrived. Is that right?'

'That's right.'

'And she said that she was going to visit her family?'

'Those were her exact words. I arrived. She checked that I was a professional nanny who'd been sent by her father-in-law William from Saint-Marie, and once she knew that the children would be safe, she walked out.'

'But she must have said something else to you.'

'How do you mean?'

'When she left. You see, I think something happened to her. I don't know what, but I've spoken to her parents, and they say Lady Helen didn't stay with them either before or after Matthew was born. And when I spoke to Lady Helen's siblings and cousins – and Aunts and Uncles – they all said the same thing. None of them had seen her for months before Matthew was born, and not one of them ever saw her afterwards, either. So what I'm trying to work out is, what did Helen mean when she said she was going to visit her family when she never went to see any of her family?'

'Oh,' Rosie said, finally understanding. 'I see.'

'So what else do you remember when she walked out?'

'I'm sorry, I'm not sure I remember anything that can help. Not after all this time. I just remember that she was sitting on an old sofa surrounded by the most terrible mess. And she was smoking a cigarette, that's right. She was smoking, and I could see that her hand was trembling.

Then she stubbed her cigarette out and asked for twenty pounds.'

'She did?' Camille asked, pouncing on this new fact.

'She did. She asked for twenty pounds. It was such an odd request that I just gave it to her.'

'Then what happened?'

'Well, she got up, told me to look after her children, said she was going to visit her family, and then she walked out of the house. That's all I can remember.'

'Did you notice if she had any luggage with her?' Richard asked, now just as intrigued as Camille.

Rosie thought hard before answering.

'No. She didn't.'

'Then did she have a handbag?' Camille asked.

'No.'

'Or any kind of bag on her at all?'

Rosie shook her head again. 'I don't think so.'

'Are you sure?'

'Oh yes. I'm pretty sure. I've got a good memory.'

'Then can you maybe remember what she was wearing?'

'It was summer. Let me think. Yes, she was wearing a summer dress. It was bright red actually. With little white dots on. You know, like a dress from the 1950s. It was very pretty. And white shoes. That was it. A red dress with white dots on, and white shoes.'

'And she had no other luggage or bags with her when she walked out of the door?'

'You're right,' Rosie said, as she realised how odd this was. 'She just had the clothes she stood up in, and no luggage or bags with her at all.'

Camille looked at her boss and knew that he was thinking the same thing.

If Lady Helen had no luggage with her, then where was she really going that day?

Camille was now a woman on a mission. As she explained to Richard on the drive back to the Police station, Helen's statement that she was going to visit her family just didn't ring true: no woman leaves home forever without a handbag or money. Rosie had just given her twenty pounds, but that was hardly enough to begin a new life.

'And you're sure she didn't go to visit her family?' Richard asked as they entered the Police station together.

'One hundred per cent,' Camille said, going to her desk and turning her computer on. 'Every member of Helen's family I've been able to talk to says that she hasn't been seen from that day to this. So where did she go?'

'Well,' Richard said, turning to look at the whiteboard of names, 'what if she had an accomplice?'

'How do you mean?'

'Only, you're right. You can't leave for a new life wearing only the clothes on your back. You need documents. Other clothes. Money. So, what if Helen had already given her luggage, money and passport and so on to a third party she could trust, and the twenty pounds was all she needed to get to that person?'

'Yes, that's a possibility, isn't it?'

'Because if someone else was involved in her escape, she could have ended up anywhere in the world. And seeing as you've not been able to find her anywhere within the UK, maybe we have to conclude that she left it?'

'You think she might have skipped the country?'

'It's a possibility.'

'Good idea,' Camille said, getting up Matthew's original statement on the computer screen. 'Rosie went over to get the children just after Matthew was born. And Matthew was born on 15th June 1999, so how about I contact UK Border Control and see if they have a record of a Helen Beaumont leaving the country at any time after the 15th June 1999?'

'Also get them to look under the name of Helen Moncrieff,' Richard suggested. 'It's possible she kept her family name.'

'Okay, I'll see what I can find.'

While Camille got on with her enquiries, Richard stayed at the whiteboard to update it with the latest developments from the case. He was soon frustrated. This was because, even when Richard put aside the 'who', 'why' and even the 'how' of the murder, there were still so many unknowns. For example, did the piece of paper they'd found in Freddie Beaumont's pocket with '11am' written on it mean that Freddie's presence in the shower room was pre-arranged, or did it mean something else? And talking of pieces of paper, what was written on the burnt piece of paper that they'd found in Tom's office? Richard had locked the bound packages of charred paper in the bottom drawer of his office desk while the photo paper developed, but he knew he wouldn't be able to open the packages to see if the experiment had worked for another week at least. And there was no guarantee that the photo paper would have picked up what had previously been on the piece of paper, even then.

Oh, Richard thought to himself, and while he was considering all of the unknowns of the case, he couldn't possibly forget the mystery that sat at its very heart: just how had the killer managed to escape from a locked room after killing Freddie Beaumont?

A few minutes before it was time to close the station up for the day, a dusty Fidel trudged back into the office with Dwayne at his side. But whereas Fidel looked ready to drop, Dwayne was relaxed, and his uniform was crisp and freshly pressed.

'Fidel!' Richard said, desperate for some good news. 'Tell me that this time you've found our mystery three-wheeled van.'

Fidel looked at his boss and shook his head, the shame of his failure eating away at him.

'I'm sorry, sir. I haven't. And I've spoken to every owner of a three-wheeled van on the island as far as I can tell. And driven past every house within a two-mile radius of the Beaumont Plantation to see if anyone has a Piaggio 50 three-wheeler van parked outside their house. And I found one.'

'You did?' Camille asked.

'But I don't think it's the van we're looking for.'

'Didn't its front wheel have the distinctive cut in it?'

'It didn't have any wheels. And it was up on blocks. It didn't even have an engine inside it.'

As the young Police Officer slumped down at his desk, Richard began to realise that if Fidel had been unable to find their three-wheeled van, then maybe it really was undiscoverable. After all, there was no doubting Fidel's diligence and commitment to the job. And it would be easy to hide such a small vehicle in a barn under some tarpaulin almost anywhere on the island.

'How about you, Dwayne?' Richard said. 'Did you find anyone down at the old port who knows what Lucy Beaumont was doing there this morning?'

'Sorry, Chief. No dice. And I asked everywhere. All the nearby streets. The bars. Everywhere.'

'You did?'

'Sure did.'

Richard looked at how fresh and clean Dwayne looked.

'In the dust and sunshine? You really pounded the streets all afternoon?'

'Tell me about it!' Dwayne agreed, and turned his attention back to his computer monitor.

'Dwayne?' Richard said.

'Yes, Chief?'

'I don't believe you've spent all afternoon going door-to-door. Not from the state of your uniform.'

'Oh,' Dwayne said, finally understanding. 'You're wondering how I managed to stay so clean? Well that's easy enough to explain. You see, it was so hot and sweaty down by the old fish market that I had to go home and have a shower and a change of clothes afterwards.'

'You did?'

'Which was lucky, I can tell you.'

'It was?'

'Sure. Because you know how the best ideas hit you when you're having a shower?'

Richard didn't particularly, if only because, when he was standing in his shower in the shack, he was usually terrified that he was about to be attacked by flying-crawling-biting-stinging things.

'You see, it occurred to me, Lucy could have gone anywhere after she parked at the fish market. I mean, you looked for her on the streets and couldn't find her. And I asked my contacts and no-one had seen her, either. So I thought to myself, what we needed to do was narrow down the search area. And to do that, maybe we should go through Lucy's computer and phone records to see if we can find any text messages – or contacts – or emails – that Lucy has sent or received with anyone who's based down by the old fish market in Gosier. Maybe that'll help us work out where she was going this morning.'

'You thought that, did you?' Richard asked.

'Sure did, boss,' Dwayne said, beaming.

'In the shower?'

'In the shower.'

'I see,' Richard said, and as much as it chagrined him, he could see the logic of what was Dwayne was suggesting. After all, there was no doubting that Lucy had refused to tell them where she was going that morning – and had looked shifty as hell as well. She'd been up to *something*. Maybe the evidence of that 'something' would be in her records somewhere.

'Fidel?' Richard said. 'I'm going to release you from trying to find the van.'

'You are, sir?' Fidel said with all the disbelieving hope of someone who'd been in solitary confinement for months and had just been told that the door was open and he was free to leave.

'I am,' Richard said. 'Help Dwayne go through all of Lucy's contacts, phone records and financial statements, and see how many times she's had any kind of interaction with people and companies in Gosier, would you? It could be phone calls, diary appointments or purchases in shops. Just find every link she has, and then we can work through them.'

'Yes, sir!' Fidel said, and then headed over to Dwayne's desk before his boss changed his mind.

Selwyn ambled into the office.

'Good afternoon, sir,' Richard said, and it was only as he spoke that he realised he'd done next to nothing about the Commissioner's rum seller ever since Dwayne had chased and lost him.

'So,' Selwyn said. 'How's the case going?'

'The case?'

'That's what I said. "The case".'

Having been caught out before, Richard wasn't going to be caught out again.

'And by "the case", do you mean our ongoing murder case of a member of the Beaumont family, or do you mean the case of the man who's suspected of selling bootleg rum?'

'Our bootleg rum seller, of course.'

'Of course, sir. Just checking.'

'So how's it going?'

'Well, since you're asking, Officer Myers went down to the Toubana hotel and saw that the suspect was indeed selling rum from the roadside. Just as you said. However, when Officer Myers approached to make his arrest, our suspect made a run for it. And despite Officer Myers' valiant attempts, he lost the suspect in the jungle behind the Toubana hotel.'

'So the sly dog saw you approaching, did he?' Selwyn said to Dwayne.

Dwayne stood up from behind his desk to answer.

'He did, sir. I was wearing my uniform. And when he saw that I was a member of the Saint-Marie Police, he took off like a rocket. And I gave chase, but he had a head start on me.'

'Hmm,' Selwyn said, as he considered what Dwayne had just said. After chewing it all over for a little while longer, he turned back to Richard. 'Then it seems there's only one course of action that remains open to us.'

'It does?'

'We need someone to approach our suspect who's not in uniform. And, seeing as our suspect's *modus operandi* is to prey on innocent tourists, I think we need to serve him up an innocent tourist.'

'I don't understand, sir,' Richard said.

'I think you should go undercover, Inspector.'

'I'm sorry?'

'I think you should go undercover to catch our bootleg rum seller. In fact,' Selwyn said, warming to his theme, 'I think you should go undercover as a British tourist who's here on holiday, and then I bet you'll be able to get close enough to our suspect to arrest him.'

'But sir, this just isn't possible.'

'Why not?'

'Well, for starters, I've got a murder case to run.'

'Of course. I quite understand. So I suggest you go undercover this evening – when you've finished up here for today. For overtime, of course.'

'You want me going undercover *today*?'

'This evening,' Selwyn said with relish.

Richard threw a desperate glance at his team for help, but he could see that Fidel was already back at his desk, making a phone call – damn Fidel and his unswerving work ethic, Richard thought to himself – and while Dwayne and Camille were free to help him, it was clear from the grins on their faces that they had no intention of doing so. Damn them as well, Richard thought to himself as he headed over to the whiteboard to buy himself time.

'Well, sir,' he eventually said. 'I'd love to help you. I really would. But unfortunately I can't.'

'Why not?' Selwyn said with an edge to his voice.

'Well, sir… you see… we've just made a crucial break-through in our case.'

'You have?'

'Yes we have,' Richard said, going over to Dwayne's desk. 'Because Officer Myers here has just found a crucial link between one of our suspects – Lucy Beaumont – and a contact of hers that she visited clandestinely in Gosier this morning.'

Dwayne smiled broadly at the rare compliment, and only subsequently realised that the compliment wasn't entirely true.

'I have?' he asked his boss.

'Of course you have,' Richard said. 'And following up on your lead will take me all evening.'

'It will?'

'Yes, Dwayne,' Richard said, desperately trying to communicate with his eyes that he needed to be saved. 'It will.'

While Dwayne tried to work out why his boss was looking at him like a tropical frog with constipation, Fidel said, 'Okay, thank you very much for your help,' into his phone and then slammed it down into its cradle.

'Okay, sir, I think I've found it already,' he said, and it was clear from his tone of voice that he hadn't been following the conversation in the office while he'd been on the phone.

'You see?' Richard said, now going over to Fidel's side. 'This is a fast-moving case, sir. It really needs my full attention.'

'It is fast-moving,' Fidel agreed, still with no idea of just how high the stakes were for his boss. 'Because I typed Gosier into the search field of Lucy's emails on her phone, and there was only one hit. But it was an email that Lucy sent in January of this year to a woman called Zoe Winstanley who works for a firm of solicitors who are based in Gosier.'

'And what was the email about?'

'It was to ask for a meeting.'

'In January of this year?'

'That's right. And when I looked the company's address up, I discovered that not only are their offices in Gosier, they're actually only two streets away from the fish market. So I rang the number at the bottom of Zoe's email – that's who I was speaking to just now – and she's just confirmed that she saw Lucy Beaumont again this morning. But more than that, Zoe said that she'd been thinking of ringing us anyway. Because she thinks she's got information that's pertinent to the murder of Freddie Beaumont. In fact, she said that she thinks she maybe knows why Freddie was murdered.'

'She does? But what reason did she give?'

'I'm sorry, sir, she said she couldn't possibly tell me over the phone.'

'But she thinks she knows why Freddie was killed?'

'That's what she said.'

'And she's the person who Lucy secretly visited this morning?'

'She is. She said she wants to talk to you as soon as she could.'

'Then wait there a second, Fidel,' Richard said, turning back to the Commissioner and privately marvelling at how life had, for once, dealt him an Ace at the precise moment that he needed it. 'You see, sir, as I was saying, I'd love to go undercover for you tonight. I can't think of anything I'd rather be doing. But, unfortunately, I really ought to interview this Zoe woman as a matter of urgency.'

Selwyn looked disappointed.

'Yes. I can see that's a priority.'

'And I promise to get to the rum seller case just as soon as I can after that.'

'Oh don't worry about that, sir,' Fidel said to Richard. 'Zoe said that she's out of the office now. She won't be able to see you until tomorrow morning.'

'*What*?'

'So that's when I arranged your meeting with her. For first thing tomorrow morning. Which will allow you to go undercover after all.'

Richard's mouth opened, but he discovered that he'd

lost the power of speech. He could understand it when
Camille betrayed him – she was French, and a woman to
boot – but how could a junior officer like Fidel double-
cross him like this?

Much too late, Fidel realised that maybe his boss hadn't
been telling the truth when he'd told the Commissioner
that he'd rather spend the evening working undercover.

'Oh,' Fidel said. 'I think I see what I've done now.'

Richard leant in close to Fidel's ear and whispered with
a voice like dust, 'You have no idea.'

'Well that's sorted,' Selwyn said with finality. 'Seeing
as you have to wait until the morning before you can get
back to the Beaumont case, that leaves you with the perfect
opportunity to go undercover as a tourist this evening. I
suggest you start with the beaches near Honoré, Inspector.
I want our rum seller caught.'

'But sir,' Richard said, trying to buy himself time, 'I've
got nothing to wear.'

'What's that?'

Out of the corner of his eye Richard saw Dwayne leave
his desk and go into the back office, but he didn't have
time to worry about what Dwayne was up to.

'Well,' Richard said, knowing that this was his last line
of defence, 'if you want me to look like a British tourist,
I don't suppose many of them dress in suits.'

As Richard said this, he indicated his polished brogues,
dark suit, white shirt and tie. The Commissioner frowned.

'You've maybe got a point there.'

'In fact, I don't own any clothes that are even remotely touristy. And I can hardly go onto a beach wearing a suit and tie, can I?'

'Yes. I see what you mean.'

'No worries,' Dwayne said with a smile as he stepped back through the bead curtain holding a pile of colourful clothes in his arms. 'You can choose your outfit from this lot.'

Richard realised that Dwayne was holding all of the shirts and shorts that he'd tried to get him to wear the week before.

'Perfect!' the Commissioner said, heading over to Dwayne and picking up a brown Hawaiian shirt that was covered in shiny yellow pineapples.

'How about this one?' the Commissioner asked.

'Sir?' Camille said to Richard, finally joining the conversation. 'Can I make a suggestion?'

'Please do,' Richard said, desperate for any kind of help his partner could offer him.

'Well, sir, it's just an observation, really.'

'Go on, then. Whatever you've got, Camille, I want to hear it.'

'Well it's just that I think the shirt the Commissioner's holding would look *perfect* on you.'

Richard looked at Camille and realised that he now knew what true betrayal was.

CHAPTER NINE

Richard didn't want to get changed into his undercover outfit anywhere near his team, so he took his new clothes back to his shack and decided to have a shower first. But it was only when he finally got into his shower that Richard discovered the water had been cut off. So, wrapping his towel around his waist, he went to his desktop computer to find out from the utility company's website if there was a problem with the water supply, only to discover that the electricity to the shack wasn't working, either. So he picked up his phone to complain to the electricity company that he couldn't use his computer to look up why the water wasn't working, only to discover that the phone line was down as well.

Richard sat down on his lumpy bed. His phone line was dead, the electrics were out, the water was cut off, and he knew there was no point trying to use his mobile phone to sort out any of these problems. There wasn't any kind of mobile phone coverage on the beach anywhere near his shack.

And as he sat on the bed with only a thin towel wrapped around his waist, a quiet despair gripped Richard's heart. He was living in a wooden shack in the Caribbean where the culture was French, the food was French, and where even the doors that led out of his main room were bloody French. And, to make matters worse – if that were even possible – he knew that he was now going to have to go out in public dressed like an idiot.

Richard looked at the chair where he'd dumped the least offensive 'tourist' clothes that he'd been able to find from Dwayne's selection, and he decided with a sigh that perhaps the only way he was going to put this whole sordid affair behind him was if he just got on with it. So, refusing to engage his brain too much, he got dressed in the shorts and Hawaiian shirt and then went into his little bathroom to check out his reflection in the mirror.

The pasty-faced middle-aged man who was looking back at him was wearing a maroon Hawaiian shirt that was covered in yellow and red flowers, and a pair of loose denim shorts that had been cut off just above his knees. He'd been assured by his team that this was a 'good look', and yet, now that he was looking at himself in the mirror, Richard knew that this was very much the opposite of the truth.

Why did he look so wrong in these clothes?

It was his knees, Richard realised. His knees looked incongruous somehow. Not that they were ugly as such, but it was obvious even to him that his legs didn't look right sticking out of a pair of shorts. His legs were too 'English'. That was the problem, Richard decided. He had 'English' legs. So, although the rest of his body could go undercover, his legs quite clearly couldn't. And nor could his white and sweaty face, now he was looking at it in the mirror. His face didn't seem to fit his outfit any more than his legs did.

As he looked at his full-length reflection, Richard found himself reminded of those shops in London that were always advertising 'Closing Down Sale, Everything Must Go' – and yet never seemed to close down, because there they'd be, weeks later, still advertising the 'Closing Down Sale, Everything Must Go'. Richard's shoulders slumped. Was that basically what his life was? A closing down sale for a failing shop that never quite managed to close down?

Richard turned from the mirror and trudged back into the main room of his shack. After all, it didn't matter how stupid he looked. The Commissioner expected him to go undercover, so he had to go through with it.

Now all he had to do was find a pair of shoes he could wear. The only problem was, he didn't own a single pair of shoes that even began to suit the rest of his outfit. Never mind, he thought to himself. He would just do the best he could. He wouldn't be deterred.

It was barely five minutes later that Richard Poole found himself picking his way across the golden sands of Grand Anse beach wearing a floral Hawaiian shirt, cut-off denim shorts, black socks and a pair of polished black brogues. Luckily for him there were very few people about. But, unluckily for him, nor was there a young dreadlocked man trying to sell bottles of bootleg rum. Richard would have to go and look for their suspect on the other nearby beaches. And, as he thought this, Richard had a creeping realisation. He was standing on a beach wearing 'touristy' clothes (the polished brogues notwithstanding).

He tried to imagine himself wearing clothes like this on a more regular basis.

He couldn't.

However, he did notice that the shorts and thin cotton shirt allowed the warm air to circulate better around his body, and he realised that, for the first time since he'd arrived in the Caribbean, he wasn't actively sweating.

Were light cotton clothes like this the answer, and the devil take his knees? It seemed impossible to imagine, so Richard stopped trying to imagine it. Instead, he turned to leave the beach, only to see Dwayne and Camille heading directly over the sand towards him.

'Loving the outfit!' Camille called out, and as much as her face was split with a wide grin, Richard could see that it was as nothing compared to the delight he could see on Dwayne's face.

Richard turned bright red with embarrassment.

'What are you two doing here?' he asked, as Dwayne and Camille approached.

'Offering mission-critical support, sir,' Camille said.

'Oh you are, are you?' Richard said, trying to use bravado to hide the fact that he was shrivelling up with shame on the inside.

'Of course. What if you need back-up?'

'Well, as you can see, our bootleg rum seller isn't here.'

'He isn't?' Dwayne said, as though this was the biggest disappointment he'd ever faced in his life, and then he balled up his fist and smashed it in apparent frustration into the palm of his other hand. 'He's outsmarted us again!'

'So there was no point you coming down here at all.'

Dwayne pretended that this was now the second biggest disappointment he'd ever faced in his life.

'Although, sir,' Camille chipped in. 'Now we're here, can I say something?'

'No you can't.'

'It's just—'

'I said no, you can't say anything.'

'I just wanted to say I think you're looking good.'

It took Richard a few moments to realise what Camille had just said to him.

'What's that?'

'I just thought you'd want to know. I think that outfit suits you.'

'Camille's right,' Dwayne said. 'You're looking good there, Chief.'

Richard tried to see sarcasm in the eyes of his subordinates, but all he actually saw were looks of kindness. Richard concluded that they were therefore dissembling.

'Well, if you've finished laughing at me – and seeing as we all agree our bootleg rum seller isn't here – then I think I'll be on my way. I've got at least another five beaches I need to visit tonight.'

'I'm being serious, sir,' Camille said, as Richard started to head off. 'You look great in that outfit. Apart from the shoes. You need to sort out your footwear, sir.'

Richard didn't break step as he left the beach, but as he finally made it up to where he'd parked the Police jeep, he found himself wondering if he did indeed 'look good' in the stupid outfit after all? It wasn't possible – how could it be possible? – but even Dwayne had said he'd looked okay in the shirt and shorts combination, so maybe he did in fact look okay? After all, Richard had gathered plenty of empirical evidence since he'd arrived on the island that these were precisely the sorts of casual clothes that other people seemed to wear.

Could he even begin to think the unthinkable? Could he maybe consider getting himself some new clothes? Some new *casual* clothes?

★★★

The next morning, Richard was back in his suit, shirt and tie, and waiting with Camille in the main reception of Zoe Winstanley's firm of solicitors.

'You hot there, sir?' Camille asked.

'No,' he said.

The pair fell into an uneasy silence.

A bead of sweat rolled down Richard's forehead and stopped on the end of his nose. Richard dashed it away with the palm of his hand.

'So,' Camille said, 'you didn't find the Commissioner's rum seller last night?'

'I've already told you I didn't.'

'Does this mean you'll be going undercover again tonight? Because if so, Dwayne and I are *very* happy to offer back-up again.'

Before Richard could come back with a suitably withering reply, a secretary appeared and ushered the two Police officers into Zoe's office.

'Good morning,' Zoe Winstanley said crisply from behind her desk, and Richard took a moment to look about himself as he settled into one of the two chairs that were already set out for him and Camille. The office was somewhat tatty and was covered in piles of files in a seemingly haphazard fashion, but Ms Winstanley had a purposeful manner about her that Richard found instantly engaging. He knew he wasn't going to be wasting his time here.

'My apologies I couldn't see you last night,' Zoe offered.

'No worries,' Camille replied with a smile. 'It allowed us to work on another case.'

'Which we don't need to mention right now,' Richard said. 'But I understand that Lucy Beaumont came and saw you yesterday morning? Is that right?'

'It is.'

'And, because of that, you think you know why Freddie Beaumont was killed?'

'I think so.'

'Then can you tell us all you know?'

'Of course. I'd be happy to. But first, I'll need to fill you in on a bit of history between our firm and the Beaumont family.'

Zoe explained that her company was one of the oldest legal firms on the island, and they traditionally handled the legal affairs of the island's many importers and exporters. That's why the office was based down by the old port in Gosier, where trade had historically been centred. What was more, the Beaumont family had been one of their most important clients since the early nineteenth century, so the affairs of both her solicitors' firm and the Beaumont Plantation were tightly intertwined. Even so, Zoe said she'd been glad when a Police Officer had called her the night before because she'd had an encounter with Lucy that day that had troubled her, and she already knew she wanted to talk to the Police about it.

'So what happened yesterday?' Richard asked.

'Well,' Zoe said, gathering her thoughts, 'did you know that the Beaumont family instructed me to try and sell the plantation earlier this year?'

'They did?' Richard said, surprised.

'That's right. Or rather, Lucy did. She got in touch with me in January and told me that the family wanted to sell the plantation. Could I see if I could find a buyer for it.'

'And did you?'

'I most certainly did. And quite quickly, actually. It was a company we sometimes do business with, and they offered the Beaumont family five million dollars for the plantation.'

'How much?'

'I know. It's a lot of money.'

'But the family told us the plantation was worthless.' Zoe was surprised. 'They did, did they?'

'And we've seen the accounts. It's been losing money for years.'

'It has, I'd agree with you there. And, as long as it remains as is, I'm sure it would continue to lose money. But the buyers are a holiday property company who want to buy the land to build a bunch of holiday villas up that side of the mountain. After all, there's already a good service road, and the holiday company can really trade on the Beaumont brand to make it feel like a heritage holiday destination. That's why the land is so valuable.'

'Five million dollars,' Camille said in wonder, more to Richard than to Zoe. 'So why have they kept that hidden from us?'

'They really didn't tell you they were trying to sell the plantation?' Zoe asked.

'They didn't,' Richard said. 'In fact, very much the opposite. They kept saying how little money it was worth. Even Lucy – when she told us she wanted to sell – gave no indication that it would be worth millions of dollars to her.'

h,' Richard said, still not really understanding.
t. How very sad.'

gree,' Zoe said. 'But it meant that, once I'd calmed
nd the rest of the family down, I was able to explain
 didn't much matter that Tom didn't want to sell,
e they'd still not be able to sell the land unless they
eddie to sign the document of dissolution as well.
 I said. Everyone had to sign.

at's more, I explained that I'd then have to split
 million dollars equally among the whole family.
er, if I didn't split the money equally – or tried
 anyone out, whether it was Freddie or anyone
en the rest of the family would find themselves
 the next few years trying to defend that decision
 expensive court case they'd almost certainly lose.'
money had to be split equally?' Richard asked.
 the five family members named in the trust.'
ding Freddie?'

ding Freddie. You see, I also had to take into con-
 our firm's relationship with William Beaumont.
 although I wasn't around when he turned the
 into a trust, we acted on his behalf in drawing
 up. So, as far as I'm concerned, if every member
ily now wishes to dissolve the trust, and I get
 money equally among William's heirs, then I
ve the trust with a reasonably clear conscience.
William wouldn't have been able to predict that
ss would stop being profitable at some stage in

'But why wouldn't they tell you the truth?'

'I look forward to finding out.'

'Yes. Because it's a lot of money, isn't it? Although
they maybe didn't tell you because the negotiations have
somewhat ground to a halt. You see, there are a few legal
difficulties with selling the land.'

'There are?'

'Even with all that money on the table. Because the
land isn't owned by a single person. As you may or may
not know, Hugh's father, William, turned the estate into
a trust before he died.'

'Yes, the family told us. To make sure that his first-born
Freddie didn't inherit.'

'That's right. It's a trust with Hugh in charge. But that
means that every trustee and named beneficiary of the
trust has to sign a document that dissolves the trust before
I can even begin to sell the land. And that decision has
to be unanimous.'

'I see,' Richard said, trying to process what he'd just
heard. 'So are you saying that not everyone wanted to
sell the land?'

'Let me answer your question by saying that the situation changed considerably yesterday. But originally, there
was indeed one person in the family who was refusing
to sell.'

'And who was that?'

'Tom Beaumont.'

'Of course,' Richard said, remembering how Tom had

been in his father's office working through the company books. 'He thinks he can make the plantation profitable again, doesn't he?'

'He does. He believes he can turn the business around and earn more money for the family in the long term by keeping it rather than selling it. And he makes quite a persuasive case, if you ask me. As an impartial third party, I can see the logic of what he's suggesting. After all, there are now so many mass production coffee plantations, there's room in the market for a niche supplier of the highest quality. But they'd need to invest heavily in new machinery. Not that it's ultimately my decision, of course.'

'So you've not been able to get everyone to sign the document to dissolve the trust because Tom wouldn't sign?' Camille asked.

'That's right. I had the whole family in here earlier this year telling Tom to sign, but Tom refused to.'

'And when you say the whole family, who do you mean?'

'Well, Lucy, Tom and Matthew, of course. And Hugh and Sylvie as well.'

'Is Sylvie named in the trust, then?'

'No. But she's still a member of the family.'

'I see. And they were all putting pressure on Tom to sell?'

'They were.'

'And how did Tom react, would you say?'

'Not all that well if I'm honest,' Zoe said. 'He lost his

temper, and started calling Hugh an
names and accusing them of taking
plantation when it should have been
Things got ugly real fast until I exp
actually a fifth person who'd also h
ment before I could dissolve the tru
to be sold.'

'There is?'

'There *was*. Because, if you reca
named in the trust had to sign any
before I could dissolve the trust.'

'Oh I see,' Richard said, final
that includes Freddie Beaumont,

Richard was pleased to see a lo
on Zoe's face.

'Quite,' she said. 'He had n
or the money. The control we
sole executor of the trust. But I
Nominally. I guess he was nam
so that there'd always be a leg
return to the family if Hugh d
been rehabilitated.'

'How very sad,' Camille sa

'Why's that sad?' Richard

'Well, think about it. Willi
of his will. That's how muc
him. And yet William left t
onciliation. And it never ca

'O
'Righ
'I a
Tom a
that it
becaus
got Fr
It's like
'Wh
the five
Or rath
to leave
else – t
spendin
in a very
'The
'With
'Inclu
'Inclu
sideration
Because,
plantatio
the paper
of the far
to split th
can dissol
After all,
the busine

the future. And it was fair to argue that were he still alive he'd want the family to cut their losses now. But, as I say, it has to be unanimous.'

'I see,' Richard said, 'meaning you needed Freddie's signature. So did you get it?'

'That's the thing,' Zoe said. 'When I explained to the family that William had five direct relatives – Lucy, Tom, Matthew, Hugh *and* Freddie – and all five people would have to get an equal share of the five million dollars – Lucy said that she'd changed her mind. In fact, she went so far as to say there was no way she'd sign a document that would give her biological father the best part of a million dollars. So she'd now side with Tom and refuse to sell.'

'How did the others take that?'

'They didn't have much chance to take it one way or another. Lucy announced that she'd never sell as long as Freddie got even a dollar, and then she got up and walked out without another word. The rest of the family didn't know what to do. So they all got up and left themselves. And that was the last I thought I'd hear about it.'

'I see,' Richard said. 'So, to sum up, Lucy asked you to look into selling the plantation at the beginning of the year. But when you found someone who'd buy their land for five million dollars, the plan first faltered because Tom refused to sell. And then it faltered again when Lucy learnt that Freddie would make a million dollars from the sale, so she refused to sell from that moment onwards.'

'That's right,' Zoe said. 'And then we come to the Monday before last.'

'Why? What happened then?'

Zoe took a moment before answering. It was clear that she wanted to pick her words very carefully.

'Well, it was on the Monday before last that I received a rather surprising visitor.'

'You did?'

'It was Freddie Beaumont.'

'*What*?' Richard and Camille both said at the same time – and Richard tried to work out the timings in his head. If Freddie visited Zoe the Monday before last, then that meant that he saw Zoe three days before he was murdered.

'He didn't make an appointment,' Zoe said. 'He just walked in here with his brother Hugh.'

'Hang on, you're saying Hugh was with him?'

'He was.'

Camille turned to her boss, amazed.

'Your hunch was right.'

Richard frowned. Was Camille right?

'So why did Hugh and Freddie come and see you the Monday before last?' Camille asked.

'Well, as Freddie put it to me at the time, Hugh had phoned him in the UK and explained that if he came to Saint-Marie, he could sign a document that would make him a million dollars.'

'So did Freddie sign it?'

'He did. Here, let me show you.' Zoe handed over a thick document that had been on her desk all through the interview, and Richard could see that it was the paperwork to dissolve "The Beaumont Trust". On the last page, there were five typed names: Freddie Beaumont, Hugh Beaumont, Lucy Beaumont, Thomas Beaumont and Matthew Beaumont.

There was a scribble of blue ink above the printed-out name of Freddie Beaumont. And, looking elsewhere on the page, Richard could see that Matthew and Hugh had also signed their signatures above their names. So that was three of the five signatures.

Tom and Lucy were the only two members of the family who hadn't signed.

Richard looked up from the document.

'Can you tell me,' he asked, 'how was Freddie when you saw him?'

'Good question,' Zoe said. 'I think he was drunk. Or jet-lagged. But he seemed somewhat strange, I can tell you. Disconnected from reality. And he didn't look as though he'd washed in days. Not that any of this matters of course. His signature was still legal. Which finally brings me to yesterday. Because, yesterday, I received a visit from Lucy Beaumont. And she explained to me that Freddie had been murdered.'

'You didn't know already?'

'I didn't. And I was shocked, I can tell you. I'd only seen him the week before. But Lucy wanted to double check that she now inherited the whole estate on her own. So I got out her grandfather William's will. Let me show you.'

Zoe picked up a second document from her desk that Richard could see was titled 'Last Will and Testament'. Turning a couple of pages to find the relevant passage, Zoe then said, 'Here we are. Because it says quite clearly here that the estate only remains in trust for as long as Freddie Beaumont is alive. The moment he dies, then Freddie's oldest surviving child inherits, as long as he or she is "over eighteen years old, is legally sane, has no unspent prison time, and hasn't been declared bankrupt in the last five years." As Lucy clearly meets all of these criteria, I was able to tell her that it didn't matter that Freddie had signed the document of dissolution, his death had automatically triggered the dissolution of the trust and she'd indeed just inherited the whole estate.'

'How did she react when you told her this?'

'She wasn't very happy.'

'She wasn't?'

'No. Although she was pleased to discover that she'd just inherited the estate. The problem was that she didn't know that Freddie had signed the document of dissolution the week before. And, I must say, I was somewhat confused myself. You see, I'd rather presumed that the whole family had known that Freddie was on the island and had signed the document.

'But as soon as Lucy found out that it had been Hugh who'd been in here with Freddie, things got really strange.

First of all she went silent. I've no idea why. But we sat in silence for so long that I started talking. You know, trying to explain how I couldn't have stopped Freddie from signing, and it didn't matter anyway. Because Freddie had died, so Lucy still inherited everything. There was no real harm done.

'In the end, she just stood up, told me to proceed with selling the plantation as soon as possible, and then turned and walked out of here. But there was a look in her eyes that was so cold and calculating that it frightened me. That's why I was thinking of ringing you anyway. It was like she was planning to do something… drastic. Although I've no idea what that "something" was of course. She was gone before I could ask her. But either way, I was troubled to learn that Freddie had died so soon after signing the document.'

'You think it's suspicious?'

'I wouldn't like to say. But in our business it's considered a surprising coincidence if someone dies within a few months of signing an important legal document. Freddie only survived three days after signing his.'

'I agree,' Richard said, his mind already trying to organise the facts that he'd just learned. In particular, he felt a dark sense of fury that even though Hugh had finally admitted to the Police that he recognised Freddie the moment he saw his dead body on the floor of the shower room, he'd still not told them that he'd actually been with Freddie three days before he was murdered.

Richard thanked Zoe for her help and he and Camille left the solicitor's office. It was obvious they needed to talk to the Beaumont family again as a matter of urgency. So, as Camille drove them both to the plantation, Richard phoned Hugh and told him to assemble the whole family at the house.

'Thank you all for meeting us,' Richard said as he entered the sitting room where the family were waiting – but Richard noticed that while Tom, Matthew, Hugh and Sylvie were all present, Lucy was missing.

'Where's Lucy?' he asked irritably.

'I don't know,' Sylvie said, looking up from her phone. 'I rang her on her mobile, but she didn't answer. So I left a message that she was to meet you here. I'm just texting her now.'

'Maybe we should wait for her?' Hugh said, and Richard could see that he was nervous. Good, Richard thought to himself. He should be.

'No need,' Richard said, deciding that he didn't have the patience to wait any longer before Hugh started telling him the truth. 'I'm sure she'll be with us soon enough. In the meantime, my partner and I still have a few questions. You see, we've just come from Zoe Winstanley's office. And she told us a very different story about your plantation than the one you've told us. You see, according to her, the estate isn't worthless. It's worth five million dollars. To the right buyer. As you all knew, but didn't tell us.'

Richard saw looks of surprise ripple through the room,

but it was Hugh that Richard was most interested in. He looked guilty as sin, and Richard could well imagine why. After all, Hugh must have guessed that if the Police had just spoken to Zoe, then presumably they now knew that Hugh had been with Freddie when he signed the document of dissolution, three days before he was murdered.

Sylvie could see how Richard had turned his attention to her husband, and she drew herself up in her seat.

'Yes, well, I don't see why we had to tell you,' she said as regally as she could.

'You don't?'

'Because we looked into selling up earlier in the year, but we didn't all agree that it was a good idea to sell, so the plan was shelved.'

'That's right,' Richard said. 'Tom was originally the only one of you who didn't want to sell.'

'So?' Tom said.

'So, Zoe told us that when Tom refused to sign the document of dissolution, things got heated. In fact, she went so far as to say that Tom had accused Hugh and Sylvie of gross financial mismanagement of the plantation. Is that true, Tom?'

Tom didn't answer, but Richard could see that he wanted to.

'Look, people say things in the heat of the moment,' Matthew said, trying to act as peacemaker. 'And it doesn't much matter who said what or when, because Tom wasn't the only person who was opposed to the sale. Later on,

Lucy also decided that she didn't want to sell. When she found out that Freddie would have to sign as well. So that made things more equitable. Tom and Lucy didn't want to sell. Father and I did.'

'So you always wanted to sell?' Camille asked Matthew.

Matthew was surprised by the question, and then he looked a little shifty.

'I did. But only if we all agreed. It had to be unanimous.'

'And what were your reasons?'

'For wanting to sell?'

'Yes.'

'Well… I know it's a bit craven, but my interests have always been somewhat short term. I'd just like my share of five million dollars. Considering my prospects at the moment. After all, a bird in the hand and all that.'

As Matthew was speaking, Richard could see him looking at his family. It was as if he was trying to communicate something without the Police noticing, Richard realised. But what was that message?

'So you see,' Sylvie said, trying to draw the whole sordid conversation to a close, 'it's quite understandable why we didn't tell you about any of this. As Matthew's saying, only he and Hugh wanted to sell. So it was never going to happen.'

'I see. So you'd all stopped trying to get the required number of signatures on the document of dissolution, is that what you're telling me?'

'How do you mean?'

'It's a simple enough question,' Richard said, seeing that Sylvie's confidence was already beginning to waver – and when he looked back at Matthew, he could see that he still seemed to be trying to pass a message on to the others with imploring eyes.

'So tell me,' Richard continued. 'Have any of you managed to add a signature to the document recently?'

'Why can't we just tell them the truth for once?' Matthew said to the room angrily. 'Why do we have to lie about everything?'

Matthew stared at his family, and Richard could see how indignant he was. Even more interestingly, Richard could see that none of the rest of the family were daring to meet his gaze.

'I'm sorry,' Matthew said a lot more calmly to Richard, 'but we were talking about what we should tell you before you arrived, and I don't agree with the others. I believe we should tell you the truth.'

'We wish someone would,' Camille said.

'Don't worry, it's not that hard to explain. But you're right. We'd decided that the document of dissolution was a dead end. Or rather, that's what we thought until yesterday.'

'Why? What happened yesterday?'

'Well, Lucy went off somewhere. We didn't know where. But when she got back, she was acting really weird, and wouldn't tell us why. She just went to her room upstairs. But when she came down to dinner, she let rip. She told us how she'd been to the solicitors that morning and learned that Father had brought Freddie over to Saint-Marie to sign the document of dissolution behind her back – and she could never forgive him.

'And the thing is, we're all used to Lucy's rages, but this was something else. She was spitting mad. Frothing almost. And then she dropped the bombshell. She said that because Father had betrayed her like this, she was going to betray him. Now that Freddie was dead and she'd inherited the plantation, she was going to sell it for five million dollars and divide the money equally between her, Tom and me. She said she'd make sure Mother and Father never saw a cent. They had to be punished. Those were her words. They had to be punished. Not that she'd have seen it through, of course,' Matthew added, trying to stick up for his older sister. 'But it's what she said, so we should be telling you.'

'And that's everything?' Richard asked.

'That's everything.'

'Lucy said that she was going to sell the plantation and make sure that Hugh didn't make any money from the sale?'

'That's what she said, but that was just her speaking in the heat of the moment. She didn't mean it.'

'Are you sure?'

'Of course. I mean, don't get me wrong, Lucy's always been volatile. But she's a bit like Mount Esmée. She blows her top from time to time, but she calms down again afterwards. She'd have changed her mind in time. I'm sure of it. She'd have forgiven Father. After all, it would have been so incredibly wrong to cut him out from the proceeds of any sale.'

'It would, wouldn't it?' Richard agreed, before turning to face Hugh. 'So this is where you start talking, Hugh. Is Matthew telling the truth?'

Hugh looked at Richard a long moment before daring to reply.

'He is,' he eventually whispered.

'So you're now admitting that you've seen Freddie since he came to the island?'

'I am.'

'In fact, you not only saw him, it was you who took Freddie to your solicitor's office to sign the document of dissolution?'

'It was.'

'But why didn't you say?' Camille asked. 'I don't understand. Why didn't you just tell us the truth?'

'All I've tried to do my whole life is protect my family. And that's what I was doing when I didn't tell you that I'd gone to see the solicitor with Freddie. Protecting my family.'

'But how was that protecting them?'

'Because I knew that if Lucy found out, she'd go crazy.'

'As yesterday evening proved,' Sylvie said, wanting to

make her position clear to the Police. 'I've never seen her so out of control.'

'And don't get me wrong,' Hugh said, 'I don't want to sell the plantation any more than Tom does, but I don't think we've got any choice. We either sell now and take the money or we risk running the business even further into the ground. And I'd do anything to get this place sold. I want to get on with the rest of my life. I just want to get on,' Hugh said with a sudden catch to his voice, and Richard saw how very desperate Hugh was. This wasn't the patrician 'man in charge' that Richard had first met in the shower room. This was a man who was fraught, highly strung, and *very* close to the edge.

'But I don't understand,' Camille said. 'You'd have had to tell Lucy that you got Freddie to sign the document eventually, wouldn't you?'

'I know, but only when it was all done and dusted. When Freddie had left the island. And I was going to pick my moment. I was going to wait until I felt that Lucy was in a receptive mood, and then I was going to try to get her to agree in principle that she was happy for Freddie to get his share of the cash before I dared tell her that I'd already got his signature on the document.'

'But why did you even need Freddie's signature?' Richard asked.

'Because we all needed to sign before we could dissolve the trust.'

'I know, but surely there was a part of you that thought

there was a fair chance that Freddie would be dead soon anyway. At which point, the trust would be dissolved and you wouldn't need his signature.'

'Ha!' Sylvie said dismissively. 'But that presupposes that we believed that he really did have cancer.'

'What's that?' Richard asked sharply.

'What's what?' Sylvie said, unsure why Richard was so interested.

'How do you know that Freddie had cancer?'

'Well, Hugh told me that Freddie had written to Matthew saying that he had cancer.'

'Oh, Hugh told you about Freddie's letter, did he?'

'Hugh tells me everything.'

'Which is more than he does to us. Isn't that right, Hugh? Because you very specifically told us that you didn't tell Sylvie about Freddie's letter to Matthew.'

'Yes, well it hardly matters, does it?' Sylvie said. 'Because it was obvious that Freddie was lying in the letter. He *always* lied. Therefore, if he said that he had cancer, then you could guarantee that that was the one thing he didn't have. And so it was very much our view that we would still have to get the document of dissolution signed if we were ever going to sell the plantation.'

'So was it your idea to secretly contact Freddie?' Richard asked, finally guessing that maybe Sylvie wasn't just the power behind the throne, she *was* the throne.

'Of course. Hugh can't decide anything. It takes a woman to be decisive.'

'So what was your plan?'

'Well, as far as I could see, as long as Freddie came to the island and signed the document without Lucy finding out, then I was sure she'd eventually thank us for our intervention. It's like Hugh just said. But we hadn't counted on how much of a bitch she is.'

Seeing the outrage on the rest of the family's face, Sylvie laughed.

'Oh right, so Lucy gets to call me all those names yesterday afternoon, but I call her a bitch once and that's considered unacceptable? After all the years I've wasted raising her when her own drunkard father wouldn't.'

Hugh looked ashen.

'Sylvie, you don't mean that.'

'Oh I bloody do,' Sylvie said, now on a roll. 'Because I know the kids look all nice and grown up now, but Lucy and Tom were wild when we first got them. They swore, they stole, they smashed things. They were a nightmare. For years. And although Tom soon buckled down, Lucy never did. She was selfish. She was angry. Matthew was right. She's like Mount Esmée. She can blow her top at any time. And she never makes an effort in the home. She doesn't clear from the table after meals, she doesn't say thank you, she doesn't tidy her room, or do anything. And in all the years Hugh and I have put ourselves second, not once has she ever said thank you. That's what I can't forgive. I mean, Tom and Matthew show their gratitude all the time, but not Lucy. Never

Lucy. She's too precious. Too damaged. So yes, I'm happy to admit I don't like her. I've *never* liked her. And I definitely don't like her on the day after she told me that she'd make sure I didn't get my share of cash from the sale of this plantation.'

In the silence that followed, Richard tried to work out what the family were thinking. It was easy to see that Matthew and Hugh were horrified by Sylvie's outburst, but Richard thought he saw a look of satisfaction in Tom. It was as if he'd just realised that all of his suspicions about Sylvie had just been proven true.

Before Richard could ask any further questions, there was a banging noise from upstairs, and everyone looked up at the ceiling. The noise was then followed by a loud clatter, and then the sound of something smashing.

'What's that?' Hugh said.

There were footsteps from outside the room and the door flung open to reveal a panicked Rosie.

'Did you hear that?' she asked.

As she said this, there was a very definite thud, again from the room directly above their heads.

Hugh said one word – 'Lucy' – and everyone dashed out of the room and into the hallway at speed. But as the Police, the Beaumonts and Rosie reached the bottom of the staircase, they were met with a chilling sight.

Lucy was standing at the top of the polished staircase, bent double in pain as she clawed at her stomach, and Richard could see that there was blood at the corners of her mouth as she desperately tried to gather her breath to speak.

She raised a trembling arm and pointed an accusatory finger at the people gathered at the bottom of the stairs – at Richard, Camille, Hugh, Sylvie, Rosie, Matthew and Tom – although it wasn't quite possible to work out exactly who she was pointing at.

'You killed me…' she wheezed.

Just as she was about to speak again, she let out a sudden gasp of pain and tumbled down the staircase in a shocking tumble of limbs before coming to rest near the bottom step.

'Everyone stand back,' Richard announced as Camille went to Lucy's body and checked the pulse in her neck.

Camille looked back at her boss.

'There's no pulse, sir,' she said. 'She's dead.'

'No!' Rosie called out and tried to run for Lucy, but Richard held her back.

'There's nothing you can do for her. And I have to ask you to step back. All of you. This is now a crime scene. Everyone, please leave the hallway at once.'

As Richard spoke, he held his arms wide and walked the family back a few paces from the foot of the stairs. Camille had pulled out her mobile phone and was already calling for an ambulance.

Richard continued edging the family members back, and while he noticed that Hugh, Tom, Matthew and Rosie were reeling from what had they'd just seen, Sylvie was already weeping fat tears. Richard couldn't tell whether this was because she'd just lost her adopted daughter or if it was because she'd been so contemptuous of her only moments before she died. All speculation would have to wait for the moment. First they had to work the scene.

Richard told the family to wait in the sitting room for him and went back to the staircase.

'Okay, sir,' Camille said, as Richard approached. 'I've just called Dwayne and Fidel. They're on their way. And the ambulance should be here before them.'

'Good work. But what the hell happened?'

'At this stage, sir, there are no obvious wounds to her body as far as I can tell, and yet she was bleeding from her mouth, and clutching at her stomach, wasn't she? And look at her lips, sir.'

Camille indicated Lucy's lips, and Richard could see a tinge of greyish blue to them.

'Poison?'

'It's a possibility.'

Neither Police Officer mentioned that Lucy had accused one of her family of killing her just before she died.

Leaving Camille to continue processing the body, Richard went upstairs. There was nothing of note to see on the staircase or main landing, but he could see that the door to Lucy's room was open. Entering, he saw that a free-standing mirror had been knocked over and lay smashed to the floor. There was also a china cup on the floor by the shattered glass, and a black liquid had spilled from it onto the old rug. Looking at the cup more closely, Richard could see a residue of what looked like coffee grounds at the bottom. Richard bent down and smelled the strong aroma of coffee. Of course. It was a coffee plantation. Lucy had been drinking coffee. And the bitter taste of coffee would have been perfect for masking the taste of poison.

It very much looked as though Lucy had been drinking from this cup when she started to convulse from a poison that was mixed in with the coffee. She then knocked over the mirror, dropped the cup, staggered from the room and then died where she stood at the top of the staircase.

Richard looked over at the coffee-making apparatus at the end of Lucy's bed and saw that there was a swill of black liquid at the bottom of the cafetiere. Richard knew they'd need to test the whole set-up to find out if any of it contained poison.

But as much as Richard was trying to focus on the cause of Lucy's death, he couldn't stop replaying in his mind the moment that she'd stood at the top of the stairs and then, with her last dying breath, pointed down at them all and said, 'You killed me'.

But who exactly had she been pointing at?

★★★

After the ambulance arrived – with Dwayne and Fidel roaring up on the Police bike and sidecar a few minutes later – Richard and Camille went back to the sitting room to talk to the family, and walked in on an atmosphere that was fraught with tension.

'What happened?' Sylvie asked, rising from her chair.

'I'm sorry,' Camille said.

'She's really….?' Rosie said, unable to finish her question.

'It looks like she died from poisoning,' Richard said.

'She took an overdose?' Hugh asked.

'That seems very unlikely,' Richard said. 'I've looked through Lucy's room. There's no suicide note. No obvious source of the poison. And I'm sorry to be indelicate, but we also all saw her point at one of you just before she died and say that you'd killed her. That's the other clue.'

Looking around the room, Richard could see only shock on the family's faces.

'So I'm sorry to ask, but it feels important. With Lucy dead, who's just inherited the plantation?'

The family were surprised by the question, but Hugh worked it out first.

'Tom does,' he said.

'What?' Tom said, not understanding.

'According to the terms of William's will, the estate was to be held in trust until Freddie died. Then, with his death, his oldest surviving child would inherit it all. Which was Lucy. But if she's not…?' Hugh trailed off, unable to complete his sentence.

Richard could see that the other members of the family

were still too stunned by the death of Lucy to fully under-stand what had just happened – and then Richard saw Sylvie slowly put a hand to her mouth in shock. She'd finally worked it out.

Tom had just inherited everything.

And Tom was the only member of the family who had *never* wanted to sell the plantation.

CHAPTER TEN

By the following morning, a few things had become clear.

Firstly, the only fingerprints that Dwayne and Fidel were able to lift from the cup and coffee apparatus they'd recovered from Lucy's room belonged to Lucy herself. So, assuming that it had indeed been a substance in her coffee that had killed her, then the killer must have been wearing gloves when he or she had laced Lucy's coffee-making equipment with poison.

Then, by the afternoon, any doubt about whether Lucy had been poisoned was removed. The autopsy on her body confirmed that she had died from a fatal overdose of a substance called sodium fluoroacetate. The report explained that sodium fluoroacetate was normally used for pest control, and went by the trade name of '1080'. When Richard looked up '1080' online, he discovered that the pesticide was strictly controlled, if only because it was a seriously lethal poison that was odourless, tasteless, and highly water-soluble. As far as Richard could tell, it was pretty much the perfect poison with which to commit murder.

The labs also found traces of sodium fluoroacetate in the coffee that Lucy had been drinking, and in the cafetiere that the Police had collected from the end of Lucy's bed.

Someone had put 1080 pesticide into Lucy's coffee-making apparatus. She'd drunk the poisoned coffee and died.

As for establishing where the 1080 poison had come from, Dwayne said that there were only two chemists on the whole of Saint-Marie who were registered to sell agricultural poisons, and he knew that they both kept a 'poison register' that listed the names of anyone who even enquired about the purchase of poisons.

Richard despatched Dwayne to the two chemists' shops to check their Poisons Register. Had anyone from the Beaumont family bought any 1080 pesticide recently?

Richard went to inspect the information that was written up on the whiteboard. As he tried to work out which of the names on the board had first killed Freddie, and had now killed Lucy, Camille came over holding an ice-cold bottle of water she'd got from the office fridge.

'You may want this, sir,' she said.

'Thank you,' Richard said, and then rubbed the ice-cold plastic bottle around the back of his neck.

'Ah,' he said, 'a brief respite from the furnace.'

'You really need to stop wearing a suit, sir,' Camille said.

'You really need to stop telling me to stop wearing a suit.'

'But Dwayne and I weren't joking when we said you looked good on the beach the other day. I mean, you'd maybe want to get a different pair of shoes, but I thought you looked very handsome in a casual shirt and shorts.'

Richard looked at his partner. Had Camille just said he'd looked 'handsome'? Before things got any more confusing, Richard knew he had to get away from the conversation as fast as he could.

'Fidel!' he barked, heading over to his subordinate's desk. 'What are you doing?'

'What am I doing?'

'Yes. What are you doing? It shouldn't be a difficult question to answer.'

'Well, sir,' Fidel said, indicating his computer monitor. 'I'm trying to see if there are any other outlets on the island where it's possible to buy 1080. Or if sodium fluoroacetate can be bought under different trade names.'

Richard saw Camille return to her desk shaking her head to herself, but he wanted to concentrate on the case.

'So is it for sale under different names?'

'No, sir,' Fidel said.

'Then what about the black market? Do you think our killer might have got hold of their 1080 illegally?'

'It's a possibility. You can generally get hold of anything on the island if you try hard enough.'

Richard wasn't surprised to hear this. It was like the illegal three-wheeled vans all over again. Did *nobody* abide by the law on Saint-Marie?

'Then I know, sir,' Camille said from her desk, as though a thought had just occurred to her. 'How about you look at the burnt bits of paper?'

'What's that, Camille?'

'If you're looking to move the case on, we should see what was written on those burnt pieces of paper we found in Tom Beaumont's bin.'

'But the FBI manual says we have to leave the photographic paper undisturbed for two weeks.'

'Of course it does. And we have to do everything by the rule book, don't we?'

Richard had a feeling that his partner was still talking about his refusal to wear anything other than his woollen suit.

Richard fixed Camille with a stare that would have made a Gorgon blush.

'We do, Camille,' he said. 'Or I tell you, madness will ensue.'

'Oh, okay,' Camille said, apparently unbothered, and then she got on with her work.

Richard couldn't work out what Camille was up to. Why was she behaving so oddly?

'Camille's maybe got a point, sir,' Fidel said. 'Maybe we don't have the luxury of waiting two weeks.'

'Look,' Richard said, struggling to keep his temper in

check. 'If the FBI say we have to leave the photographic paper in the dark for two weeks, then that's how long we have to leave it. Okay? Now, I suggest we try and focus on what we *do* know. For example, the fact that we're now dealing with two murders. Firstly, the estranged father Freddie Beaumont. An alcoholic and abusive man. Secondly, his first born, Lucy. A troubled young woman who hated her biological father. Theories?'

'Well,' Fidel said, 'this second murder has to be connected to the first.'

'I'd agree,' Richard said, happy to get the conversation back on track. 'But why did she have to die?'

'What if it's connected to her announcement that she was going to cut Hugh and Sylvie out of the profits from the sale of the plantation?'

'It seems the most natural answer, doesn't it?'

Fidel picked up on Richard's sceptical tone.

'But you don't think so, sir?'

'Well, just because that seems the most obvious conclusion, it doesn't mean it's the correct one. After all, say you wanted to poison me with 1080 pesticide.'

Fidel and Camille's faces both lit up with smiles.

'Do you mind?' Richard said, tightening the tie at his neck. 'It's just a theoretical question.'

'Don't worry, sir,' Camille said, her grin no less dimmed. 'This is just a theoretical smile.'

'But what's the fastest you reckon it would take to put in place a plan to poison me?'

'Well, sir,' Camille said, happy to speak for herself and Fidel. 'First I'd have to get hold of the poison.'

'I don't think so,' Richard corrected. 'First you'd have to decide that poison would be the best way of despatching me.'

'Oh I already know that,' Camille said. 'Poison's always the best way. If you can get hold of it. That's the problem.'

'I see,' Richard said a little uneasily. This wasn't by any means the first time that he'd discovered that one of his team had a rich fantasy life as a murderer. 'So, you'd have to decide to use poison, and then you'd have to work out what poison would best suit the murder. Whether it should be quick-acting, slow-acting, or whatever. And then you'd have to get hold of that particular poison – which we know isn't easy in general, and is particularly difficult when it comes to 1080. And even if you had some to hand, you'd have to work out how to get into Lucy's bedroom and then get the poison into her coffee paraphernalia.'

'Oh, I see what you mean,' Fidel said. 'It takes time.'

'It takes time. All of which leads me to guess that Lucy's murder was premeditated *before* her announcement that Hugh and Sylvie weren't going to get any money from the sale of the plantation. I don't think there would have otherwise been time to set it up.'

'So she was always going to die that morning?'

'It's certainly a possibility we can't rule out.'

'Or maybe,' Fidel offered, 'Lucy's killer had everything prepared in advance, but only as an insurance policy. So it *was* premeditated, but it was only to be enacted in a worst case scenario. Which maybe came about when she announced that Hugh and Sylvie wouldn't get any money.'

'Yes. That's also a possibility, I suppose,' Richard conceded, frustrated that there were still so many ways of interpreting how the killer had managed to strike again. Mind you, it wasn't a surprise. After all, that's why poison was such an effective murder weapon. It could be put into place any length of time before it was needed, and the killer could be sure to be far distant when it was ingested.

'In which case,' he said, moving the conversation on. 'Let's consider our suspects again. So what about Hugh Beaumont? Could he be our killer?'

'He could easily have killed Freddie,' Camille said. 'Especially considering how much he's lied to us about his contact with him.'

'I agree,' Richard said. 'But I have to confess, I don't currently see why he'd then kill Lucy. After all, Lucy's death is the worst possible outcome for Hugh. Because Tom now inherits, and he won't sell the plantation. So there's no longer a million dollar cash windfall for Hugh.'

'And it's just the same for Sylvie,' Camille said.

'Exactly,' Richard agreed. 'So she's just as unlikely to be our killer. Although there was clearly no love lost between Sylvie and Lucy. Of all of them, she's the most capable of killing her adopted daughter, but I just don't see how she benefits from her death. Not with Tom inheriting.'

'And Chief,' Fidel added, 'the same goes for Matthew, doesn't it?'

'It does. He didn't make any secret of wanting to sell the plantation to us, did he? Because this is what the case is about, isn't it? The inheritance of a plantation worth five million dollars. And yet, I can't see who benefits from Lucy's death apart from Tom.'

'So maybe Tom's our killer?' Camille asked.

While Richard considered whether this could be true, Fidel said, 'Can I make a crazy suggestion, sir?'

'No,' Richard said.

Fidel looked crestfallen.

'Oh alright, then,' Richard said wearily. 'Go on. What's your crazy suggestion?'

'Well, it's just that there's one person we've not considered yet.'

'And who would that be?'

'Nanny Rosie.'

Richard was perplexed. 'She was on a boat to Montserrat when Freddie was killed.'

'But was she, sir?'

'Yes,' Richard replied. 'Her boat left at 11am that morning, ten minutes before Freddie was shot dead in the shower room.'

'I know, sir,' Fidel said, 'but we still don't know for sure that Rosie was on the 11am sailing to Montserrat. Not exactly. We know she bought a ticket that morning. Our witness sold her a ticket at 9.30am. But Customs here in Honoré don't check passports when people leave the island, do they? They only check the passports of people who are arriving.'

'Correct,' Richard said, already beginning to see where Fidel was maybe going with this.

'So the next time her alibi actually checks out is at 12.30pm when the Customs shed at Montserrat have a record of her going through passport control there.'

'Along with all the other passengers from the 11am sailing from Saint-Marie,' Camille said, also realising the truth of what Fidel was saying.

'But that's the point I'm making. I mean, don't get me wrong sir, I don't think this is very likely, but just because she went through Customs at the same time as the rest of the passengers, it doesn't mean that she was on the same boat as them. There's room in the harbour at Montserrat for more than one boat to arrive at the same time.'

Against his better nature, Richard was intrigued.

'Go on,' he said.

'So I was just thinking that it's maybe possible – in theory at least – that she bought her ticket at 9.30am, as we know. Then she went back up to the plantation. Somehow. Don't ask me how. But she then killed Freddie at 11.10am, got away real fast, and went straight down to the harbour at Honoré. Then, all she'd have to do is hire a much faster boat, and I reckon she could easily catch up with the ferry and arrive on Montserrat at 12.30pm at the exact same time that ferry docked.'

'Yes, Fidel,' Richard said, considering what he'd just heard. 'I can see the logic of what you're saying. But why would Rosie want to kill Freddie?'

'No idea, sir,' Fidel said, nonetheless beaming at the fact that one of his theories was being taken seriously by his boss.

'And why would she then kill Lucy?'

'Still no idea, sir,' Fidel said, still smiling.

'I'll tell you what,' Richard said. 'Why don't you go down to Honoré harbour? Speak to the boat charter companies, and just double check to see if Rosie Lefèvre chartered a boat on the morning of the murder to go to Montserrat.'

'Yes, sir,' Fidel said, still unable to wipe the smile from his face. He put on his Police cap and strode out of the station.

Once he'd left, Richard turned back to his partner.

'So, in summary, it looks like Tom is our most likely suspect,' he said.

'I'd agree.'

'After all, he's now inherited the plantation. But do we really believe that he'd kill both his estranged father and his older sister to get his hands on the family business?'

'People have killed for less,' Camille said.

'I suppose so,' Richard agreed. 'You know what I keep thinking? We're missing something.'

'You think so?'

'I do. The case just isn't adding up for me. I think

there's something fundamental we're not getting. Some fact we've got the wrong way round. Or aren't looking at the right way. And then if we could just invert it – or flip it over so we could see the other side – then we'd finally understand why Freddie had to die, and why Lucy then had to die a week later.'

There was a clatter of footsteps on wood, and they all looked over to see Fidel re-enter the Police station at speed.

'Okay, you won't believe this,' Fidel said, 'but I think I may have just broken the case wide open.'

'You have?' Richard said in amazement. 'You've already found someone who hired Rosie a speedboat?'

'No sir, not that case.'

'What on earth are you talking about?'

'Well, sir, I was on my way to the harbour on foot, but you know how it's market day today?'

'Of course.'

Richard always knew when it was market day, because he had to fight through the various tourist nick-nack stalls, rum, DVD and clothes sellers, just to get to work – and with everyone irritatingly wishing him a 'good morning, Inspector!' when all he wanted to do was get to work unharassed.

'Well, I was just heading down through the market when I saw a young man selling bottles of rum out of a rucksack at his feet.'

Richard and Camille were stunned.

'Our rum seller is currently in the market just outside our Police station?'

'It's what it looks like to me.'

The three Police officers went over to the window that overlooked the veranda and the car park beyond. It was just as Fidel said. The market was in full swing, but at the far end of it, they could see a young man sitting by a load of old bottles of clear liquid with a hand-made sign that said 'Local Rum, $5 a bottle'. The man was wearing a filthy old vest and tatty shorts, but what drew Richard's eye was the mass of blonde-ish dreadlocks piled up in a bun on top of the man's head.

There was no doubt about it. This was their fabled bootleg rum seller.

'Well, this shouldn't take too long,' Richard said, and strode out onto the veranda and down the steps to the yard to effect his arrest.

'Wait, sir!' Camille called, knowing that the young man would guess that Richard was a Police Officer the moment he saw him approaching. Camille wasn't wrong.

The rum seller looked over as Richard strode down the steps, saw Camille and Fidel emerge from the Police station just behind, and he then scrabbled a few of the bottles into his canvas bag before legging it.

'Stop that man! Police!' Richard shouted, but that only made everyone in the market look over at Richard.

'No, don't look at me! Catch that man!' Richard shouted at the various market sellers, gesticulating wildly at the rum seller's fast-departing back as he dashed down the hill and out into the main road. But the Police were after him. Or at least, Fidel and Camille were after him, because Richard soon found that he'd lost sight of the rum seller through the market.

Camille and Fidel chased the man across the main road and down onto the strip of beach that ran all the way around the bay of Honoré. Arriving at the sea was something of a dead end for the man, so he turned left and ran along the white sand just as Camille and Fidel stormed onto the beach themselves.

'Keep on his tail!' Camille shouted to Fidel, and swerved back up the beach – dodging under a washing line of colourful clothes that was strung between two houses – and emerging at full pelt onto the main road. She knew that unless the man was going to attempt to swim to safety, he'd eventually run out of beach and would have to head back up onto the road – where she'd make sure that she'd be waiting for him.

With her feet pounding the hot tarmac, Camille saw the man dash across the road only twenty yards ahead of her, and then he raced into the small car park that serviced the harbour. Camille crossed the road to cut the man off and saw Fidel emerge – fists and knees pumping – from the side of the houses by the beach.

They had their bootleg rum seller in a pincer.

The man ran up to his vehicle, slung his rucksack into the back of it and then scrabbled a set of keys from his pockets, but before he could get his keys into the lock, Camille caught up with him and smashed the keys out of his hand – the keys flying through the air and skittering to a stop on the hot asphalt – and then she yanked the man's other hand behind his back and slammed his body over the bonnet of his vehicle.

'You're under arrest,' she said as she pulled out her handcuffs and started to cuff the man who was panting hard from the exertion of the chase.

But even as Camille let the adrenaline of the chase wash out of her body, she couldn't stop grinning at what she was seeing. Fidel arrived only seconds later, his face shining with sweat, and he stopped a few feet short of where Camille was standing.

And then he grinned just as widely as Camille.

'I don't believe it,' he said.

'I know,' Camille said. She grabbed the man roughly by the scruff of his shirt collar. 'You're coming with us.'

The man didn't put up any kind of resistance as Camille started to walk him back to the Police station, but – as she'd known would happen – Fidel wasn't looking at their captured rum seller. Instead, he only had eyes for the vehicle that the man had been trying to get into.

It was a Piaggio 50 three-wheeled van.

Fidel went up to the vehicle, got down onto his hands and knees and looked at the front wheel. It only took him a moment to find what he was looking for.

There was a distinctive cut across the tread of the front wheel.

'Camille,' he called out as he rose to his feet. 'This is the three-wheeled van I've been looking for all this time.'

'Then congratulations, Fidel. You've finally found it.'

Camille and Fidel shared a moment of triumph, and then they had the same thought at about the same time and turned and looked at their suspect.

Just who the hell was he?

And what on earth had his vehicle been doing up at the Beaumont Plantation on the morning that Freddie had been murdered?

★★★

When Camille and Fidel marched their handcuffed suspect into the Police station, they found Richard already waiting behind his desk, a fresh pen and pad of paper in front of him.

'I knew you'd catch him,' Richard said, trying to cover for how inept he'd been as the chase started.

'Thanks, Chief,' Fidel said. 'But it's even better than that.'

As Camille pulled up a chair for the suspect to sit in, Fidel explained that the man had tried to get away in a three-wheeled van that had a distinctive cut in the front wheel.

'You're kidding me?'

'I'm not, sir,' Fidel said, thrilled that he had finally delivered the three-wheeled van to his boss.

'Fidel, I never doubted you,' Richard said, before turning his attention to the man who was sitting in front of him.

'Good morning,' he said in his most teacherly voice. 'My name is Detective Inspector Richard Poole. What's yours?'

The dreadlocked man didn't say anything.

'Very well. Camille, take our friend here to the cells. We can leave him overnight and interview him tomorrow.'

As Camille reached for the man's arm, he pulled away.

'Alright,' he said, in what Richard guessed was a London accent, 'I'll answer your questions.'

'Good. Thank you. So let's start with, what's your name?'

'Andy Lucas.'

'You're from the UK?' Richard said.

'Essex,' the man said.

'Where in Essex exactly?'

'Does it matter? I'm a citizen of the world.'

'I'm sure you are, and I'm thrilled for you, I really am, but where are you from originally?'

'Maldon.'

The mention of Maldon sparked half a memory for Richard.

'You are?' he said. Maldon was a coastal town in Essex, but Richard couldn't work out why it had just chimed with him. He was sure he'd heard it in connection with the case, but who'd said it? 'Then can you tell me, how long have you had that three-wheeler van for?'

'You want to know about my van?'

'If you could just answer the question.'

'Alright. I've had it a year or so.'

'And do you have the requisite papers and licence for it?'

'What?'

'It's not a hard question. Do you have the correct insurance and vehicle registration documents for your van?'

Andy looked for help from Camille.

'What's he talking about?'

'I'm talking about whether your van is legally roadworthy,' Richard said.

'Well,' Andy said, still unsure as to why it was so important, 'if you're going to put it like that, then maybe not.'

Richard harrumphed to himself. He then made a sharp note on a fresh piece of paper, and Andy got the impression that maybe, in the Police's eyes, his lack of proper paperwork was somehow a worse crime than anything else he'd been up to.

'But seriously. What's my van got to do with any of this?'

'Now can you tell me about the rum you've been selling on the island?'

'What do you want to know?'

'I'd like to know where you get it from to start off with, because it's not legal.'

'You don't know that.'

'You left some bottles behind when one of my Officers chased you the other day. It's very clearly bootleg. So where do you get it from?'

'Alright,' Andy said reluctantly. 'A guy.'

'You get your rum from "a guy"?'

'That's what I said.'

'And does this "guy" have a name?'

'He lives on Guadeloupe.'

'That's not much help.'

'It's a guy I met on Guadeloupe, okay? He sold me a few crates of rum a couple of years back, but I couldn't sell them anywhere near where he was. He'd already got that market sewn up. So I sailed the rum to Saint-Marie and sold them here.'

'You have a boat?'

Andy shrugged, indicating that maybe he did.

'Where is it?'

'In Honoré harbour.'

Richard got the name of the boat and the keys from Andy, and told Fidel to go down to the harbour to search it.

Once Fidel had left, Richard turned back to Andy.

'So, you're saying that this "guy in Guadeloupe" sold you the bootleg rum "a few years ago"?'

'That's right.'

'And it's taken you this long to sell it?'

'No. I came to Saint-Marie and spent a few months

selling it in the bars around the island. And I liked it here.
I mean, who wouldn't? And you don't need much money
to get by if you're living on your boat and are prepared to
do odd jobs here and there. Anyway, when I ran out of
rum to sell, I went back to my contact on Guadeloupe,
bought some more, came back here and sold it around
the bars of the island again. But, if I'm honest, the rum's
not the best quality stuff, so I've been running out of bars
who are prepared to buy it from me.'

'Which explains your recent push into direct selling
to tourists?'

'Maybe. But I've done nothing wrong.'

'Have you paid duty on the rum you've been bringing
into the country?'

'It's not much rum. If you want to fine me for non-
payment of duty on a few crates, go for it.'

'But the rum's not legal in the first place.'

'It isn't?' Andy asked, pretending to be surprised by
the news. 'I didn't know that. Are you telling me my
contact on Guadeloupe has been selling me hooky rum?
No wonder people get ill when they drink it. But then,
you only have to look at me to know I'm not a great
businessman.'

'Yes, I was coming to that,' Richard said. 'What exactly
are you doing on the island?'

'How do you mean?'

'Well, Saint-Marie is a long way from Maldon.'
Richard once again felt a resonance when he said the

word 'Maldon', but what was it? Where had he heard the name before?

'Alright,' Andy said with a sigh. 'If you must know, I got into a bit of trouble with a gang I used to run with back in the day. When I still lived in Essex. I had to get out of Dodge City, and fast. So I got on a ferry down to Spain. This was a good decade or so ago. And in Spain, I started working on boats. They've always been an interest of mine. And I got to be crew on a boat that came out to the Caribbean. When I got here, I realised this is where I should have been my whole life. I mean, the people, the pace of life, the sunshine – I fell in love with the place.'

'But why Saint-Marie?'

'How do you mean?'

'Of all the islands in the Caribbean?'

There was the briefest flash of indecision in Andy's eyes, and Richard suddenly remembered why the town of Maldon had resonated with him.

'So tell me about you and Sylvie Beaumont.'

'What's that?'

'You and Sylvie Beaumont.'

'I don't understand.'

'What is there to understand? I mean, you're from Maldon. And I remember now that she's also from Maldon originally. So what's the connection? And before you consider denying your relationship with her, we know that you and your van were up at the Beaumont Plantation just before Freddie Beaumont was murdered.'

'What's that?'

'You heard me.'

'Who's Freddie Beaumont? And what do you mean, "murder"?'

Richard's mobile started to ring, and he could see on the Caller Display that it was Fidel who was phoning. Perfect timing, Richard thought to himself. He could take the call and let Andy sweat.

Richard answered his phone, listened for a few moments – all the time keeping his eyes on Andy – and then, with a curt 'thank you', hung up.

'Now that's very interesting,' Richard said. 'Because my officer tells me that he's just boarded your boat at the harbour. And first of all he says it's far more powerful than he'd have expected you to have.'

'I travel around the Caribbean,' Andy said, trying to sound as though this was the most natural thing in the world.

'But he also says that it's full of contraband. There are crates of bootleg rum. Packages of cigarettes. But he's also found a dozen twenty kilogram bags that are labelled as being high grade Bonifieur coffee beans from the Beaumont estate.'

'So?'

'So where did you get two hundred and forty kilograms of finest Bonifieur coffee beans from?'

'You can't prove it's contraband.'

'But I can prove that you were up at the Beaumont

Plantation just before Freddie Beaumont was murdered. So unless you want us to connect you to his murder, then I suggest you start telling us the truth, and fast.'

Andy looked from Richard to Camille, and thought that he could see genuine sympathy in her eyes. He was wrong. And he was still misjudging Camille when he relaxed as she smiled.

'I'm sure you've got an innocent explanation for all of this,' she said.

'I have,' Andy said to her. 'I'm totally innocent.'

'Then what's your connection with Sylvie?' Richard asked.

Andy held up his palms as if he was admitting that it was a 'fair cop' and that he'd come quietly.

'Alright, then. I've got nothing to hide. She's my cousin. About a million times removed. She's one of my uncles' in-laws' kids or something.'

'You're related to Sylvie Beaumont?'

'Barely. And I wasn't joking when I said I fell in love with the Caribbean when I first came out here. But after a while, I remembered that I had a relation out here. Sylvie. And that she was rich. That's what the family thought. She'd hooked herself a rich guy on an island called Saint-Marie. So I did the natural thing. I came here looking for her. But she wasn't anything like I expected. And nor were her family.'

'How do you mean?'

'Well she hated them.'

'She does?'

'That's how it looked to me. Her husband in particular. She said he had no backbone. That he'd tricked her into marrying him and now she was stuck with a man who couldn't support her, and his brats. That's what she always called her kids. "The brats". When I asked her for some cash to help me out, she just laughed in my face. She said she didn't have any money of her own.'

'Is that what she said?'

'That's what she said. And I'd already told her I kind of kept body and soul together by doing this and that. So she said she had an idea. If I could get up to her family's plantation, there was a place we could meet and she'd be able to give me twenty bags of coffee, each one weighing ten kilograms. She worked it all out, and she told me that each bag had a wholesale price of $400. If there were twenty of them then that meant they had a combined value of…'

'Eight thousand dollars.'

'Right. Eight thousand dollars. But I'd obviously have to sell them for less. She suggested selling them for about $350 per bag and then we'd split the money sixty-forty in her favour.'

'Netting you a cool $2,800. And her, $4,200.'

'You can work all that out that quickly?'

'It's just maths. But are you telling me she took sixty per cent to your forty?'

'Sure. Mind, I was actually able to sell a few of the

bags for a bit more than she thought I would. So I did okay. But the point is, the whole thing went like a dream.'

'Even though it was illegal?'

'Hey. As far as I was concerned, it was her coffee, so there was nothing illegal going on. I was just her sales rep. That's all.'

'A sales rep who just had to be kept secret from the rest of the family?'

'Who she told about our business relationship had nothing to do with me.'

'But I take it you always had to meet behind the farm buildings. Where no-one could see you?'

'Maybe,' Andy said with a crooked smile.

Richard considered what Andy was saying and realised that his story rang true. After all, Richard remembered how their background checks had thrown up the fact that Sylvie ran multiple credit cards – that they were mostly maxed out – and that, every now and again, there'd be a large cash injection of a few thousand dollars to help pay them off. It hadn't made much sense at the time, but Richard guessed that he'd just uncovered the explanation. She was selling bags of coffee on the black market and using the cash to pay down her credit card bills.

But did any of this tie in with the murder? That was the important question.

Richard mentioned the date that Freddie had been killed and, after a bit of prompting, Andy admitted that

that had almost certainly been the day he was last up at the plantation.

'And what time were you there?' Richard asked.

'I had to get there at nine.'

'In the morning?'

'That's right. We had to be finished before anyone else went down to the plantation buildings. So I drove up there in my little three-wheeler for 9am. Sylvie had already got the bags of coffee into the outhouse where we always met. I loaded them up. The whole thing took about ten minutes. And then I drove back down the mountain and loaded the coffee onto my boat.'

'And did you see Sylvie that morning?'

'No.'

'You didn't?'

'Except for in exceptional circumstances, we try not to meet. I'm telling you, she had the whole thing organised like a dream. There's this empty plastic water butt in the outhouse. That's where she leaves the bags of coffee for me to pick up. It's also where I leave her share of the cash when I'm done with selling it. Not that it happens that often. This is only the fifth time I've done it.'

'Then tell me, when you were up at the plantation this last time, did you see anyone else?'

'No.'

'Are you sure?'

'Yeah. I mean, I'm on the lookout for people, so I'd have seen if anyone had been around.'

'You didn't, for example, see an old man in his late fifties lurking around? A Caucasian male with shaggy white hair and a beard?'

Andy shook his head, and Richard was just wondering how much the testimony of a known criminal could be trusted when Dwayne burst into the office holding an old ledger.

'Okay, Chief, you have *got* to see this!' he said, but then he stopped dead in his tracks when he saw Andy.

'Oh. It's you.'

However, Dwayne's desire to share his news was greater than his embarrassment at coming face to face with a criminal who'd outrun him wearing flip flops, and he beckoned for Richard to join him at his desk.

Asking Camille to stay with Andy, Richard went and joined Dwayne.

'Okay,' Dwayne said, holding up a hard backed notebook. 'This is the Registered Poisons Log for the pharmacist on the other side of the island. And look,' Dwayne said, turning the pages of handwritten entries until he found what he was looking for. 'Here it is,' he said. 'A 500 milligram packet of "sodium fluoroacetate, trade name 1080" was sold for cash five weeks ago.'

'But who bought it?' Richard asked.

Dwayne pointed at the name, address and signature of the purchaser.

'You're kidding me?' Richard said, seeing what was written there.

According to the ledger, the person who'd bought the 1080 poison was Tom Beaumont.

'I know, Chief,' Dwayne said. 'But, unless this name is a forgery, it's who bought the poison that day. And, if you're asking me, that kind of suggests to me that it was Tom who killed his sister. But, either way, I reckon he's got some serious questions to answer.'

'You know what?' Richard said. 'For once, Dwayne, I'm in one hundred per cent agreement with you.'

CHAPTER ELEVEN

Leaving Dwayne to take Andy Lucas' formal statement, Richard and Camille drove up to the Beaumont Plantation to interview Tom again. But he wasn't at the main house. They found him in the old shower room where Freddie had been murdered.

'Oh,' Tom said as the Police entered. 'What are you doing here?'

'Actually,' Richard said, 'I could ask you the same question.'

'How do you mean?'

'I'm just interested to know what you're doing at the murder scene of Freddie Beaumont.'

Tom was put out by the question.

'This is my home,' he said. 'I can go where I like. And if you must know, this room used to be used for drying the coffee cherries. After they'd been soaked and before they were husked. Sylvie converted it into a shower room years ago, but it's never really worked as a shower room.

The ventilation is terrible. Which is hardly surprising. It was always designed to retain heat. But if we're to go back to traditional production methods, I want to see if it's still fit for purpose.'

'And is it?'

'I reckon so. We'll have to strip out the shower, of course.'

'So you're really committed to keeping the plantation running?'

Tom understood the implied subtext.

'There have been Beaumonts here for hundreds of years. I'm not going to be the one who ends that tradition.'

'Even though you could just sell it right now and pocket five million dollars for yourself.'

'When are you going to get it? This plantation is worth so much more than five million dollars. Its coffee plants come from the same cuttings that were used to establish the Blue Mountain Plantation in Jamaica. That's how prestigious our coffee is. But you can have the best plants in the world. As we do. And one of the best situated plantations in the world. As we do. And some of the most fertile soil in the world. As we do. But if you don't have the right machinery, or the right training for the workers, or the right drying sheds or packaging plant, then it doesn't matter how fine your raw ingredients are. What you're going to produce will be junk.'

Richard couldn't help but notice that Tom had almost entirely dropped his island 'surfer dude' pose. There was steel in his voice. And Richard found himself remembering a comment that Nanny Rosie had made about Tom the very first time they'd spoken to her. She'd said that Tom was a very determined young boy who always had to get his own way.

'And that's what you think is currently produced here? Junk?'

Tom didn't say anything. But Richard noticed that he didn't deny the statement, either.

'When we last interviewed you with the family, you didn't answer my question when I asked you if you thought Hugh was mismanaging the plantation.'

Tom still didn't reply, but Richard had had enough of Beaumont family members not telling him the truth.

'There's no point denying it. After all, your solicitor told us that that's what you said in front of her. And we've been through the company accounts ourselves. So I can tell you that I think I agree with you. At the very least, seeing as the business is losing money, I don't see how Hugh and Sylvie have been able to justify the hundreds of thousands of pounds they spent sending Matthew to Eton.'

Richard saw Tom's brow furrow. Good, he thought to himself. The last time he'd spoken to Tom about his brother's school fees, Tom had tried to brush them off as irrelevant.

'In fact,' Richard continued, 'it's just throwing good money after bad, isn't it? I mean, there's you – with your free education from Saint-Marie – getting a degree from

Miami University, but after all that money was spent on Matthew, he doesn't even get any decent A-levels.'

'They're idiots,' Matthew said quietly.

'Your parents?'

'I mean, I kind of forgive Father. You heard him in the sitting room. He's not really cut out to run this place. But Mother? The way she lords it over the rest of us?'

'While also paying herself forty thousand dollars a year.'

'Precisely. All Mother wants is money. Money and status. That's why she spends all her time sitting on committees and doing her charity work. She's not trying to do good, she just wants everyone to see how important she is.'

'When in reality she's a one-time travel rep from Essex?'

It was clear from Tom's half-smile that he agreed with Richard's summary.

'In which case, it's all worked out rather well for you,' Richard said. 'Because, instead of Hugh and Sylvie continuing to run the business into the ground – or, worse still, Lucy selling it – it's you who's just inherited it. The whole shebang.'

'I didn't want to inherit *anything*.'

'But nonetheless, you did when your sister died.'

'You really think I'd kill my own sister?'

'I don't know. Why you don't tell me?'

'There's no way I could kill Lucy,' Tom said in a burst of anger. 'Ever. She's my sister. I loved her.'

'Even though she seemed to like Matthew more than you?'

'*What*?' Tom was appalled by the suggestion.

'Only, I couldn't help noticing that whenever the family were gathered, Lucy always sat with Matthew, and you always sat on your own.'

'That's not true,' Tom said, but Richard could see that he was rattled.

'No, it is true. You always sat on your own in the window seat.'

When Tom didn't say anything, Richard decided to throw him an olive branch.

'But maybe it's a "middle child" thing? The oldest sibling bonds with the youngest, and vice versa. So Lucy and Matthew become inseparable. It's understandable. And you, the middle child, get left out. Excluded.'

'Okay,' Tom said. 'Maybe you're right. Lucy *maybe* got on better with Matthew than she did with me. But it's kind of bound to happen. Lucy got to look after Matthew from the moment he was born. I mean, I was four years old when we left the UK, and Mother was right about one thing. I was pretty uncivilised back then. It wasn't my fault. But I was wild. Angry. Everything had to go my way. Whereas Matthew was a brand new baby, and Lucy was twelve years old – the perfect age to fall in love with a new-born. She doted on him. Nothing was too good for Matthew.'

'Which must have been hard on you. An older sister who was more interested in your sibling, and an adopted mother who I understand from Rosie was never all that maternal.'

'Ha!' Tom said. 'That's the understatement of the year. I struggle to remember any memories of my mother playing with me when I was small. Or reading a book to me at night. Or doing *anything* with me. She's totally absent from my early memories of being on Saint-Marie.'

'So why did she adopt the three of you?'

'Isn't it obvious? She guessed that if she did what Grandfather wanted – and kept us on Saint-Marie – he'd leave his whole estate to her and Hugh when he died. Well, he didn't, did he? Because he still left it to Freddie, the crazy old bastard. And then Lucy got it when he died.'

'And now you have it.'

Richard realised something.

'And once again I notice that you've sidestepped my question.'

'What question?'

'About your father. You've said that he's not really cut out to run the plantation, but you've not told me whether you think that he's actively to blame for mismanaging the place?'

Tom ran his hands through his hair – just the way Hugh did, Richard noted. And as he did so, Richard was briefly struck by how much Tom looked like Hugh – even though Hugh was only his uncle rather than his father.

'Alright,' Tom said, once he'd gathered his thoughts. 'If you want chapter and verse, I've been going through our historical accounts. You know, from before 2001 when Grandfather died. And the place was run completely differently then. Surplus money was ploughed back into the business, there was a regular plan for maintaining and replacing machinery, and during boom years money was set aside to cover for when times were tougher. But since William died, there's been no capital investment, and the farm machinery has got old and inefficient. And father doesn't even come close to pushing our workers hard enough. They're allowed to come in late – or not turn up at all – and their productivity is just shot to hell. We've got to fire a rocket up their arses. Get everyone upping their efficiency.'

'Or sack them?' Camille asked.

'If need be. We're a business, not a charity. And while the place is falling down around our ears, Father just lets Mother keep splashing the cash. So whenever there's been a surplus, they've spent the profits, and when there's a loss they still pay themselves the same salary – even if they can't afford it. As far as I can see, their only financial planning is to wait until we run out of money and then sell another family heirloom to fund the shortfall.'

'Like the house in Fulham?'

'Exactly!' Tom said, suddenly animated. 'That's what I keep telling the others. We used to own the freehold to a property in Fulham. And sure, we coined it in when we sold it, but that money's now been spent. And if we'd just kept it, imagine the rental income we could be getting from it now? Or we could have used the capital we had in the house to get a mortgage to help us out here. But once it's sold, that's it. You don't sell the family silver.'

'I see,' Richard said, fascinated to see just how passionately Tom believed in his mission to save the plantation. 'So tell me, what do you plan to do with Hugh and Sylvie now?'

'How do you mean?'

'Well, do they stay on once you've inherited the plantation?

'You mean, having a job here? No way.'

'Wow,' Camille said. 'That's pretty brutal.'

'It's the facts.'

'So what will you do with them?' Richard asked again.

'I don't know. Can't say I've thought much about it. But I suppose there'll be some job I can give to Father. Like PR or something. Or brand ambassador. But as long as he has time to do his painting, I know he'll be happy enough. I mean, you saw him – he wants to step aside. He never wanted to run the plantation in the first place. But Mother? If you really want to know, I think it's about time she learned that life's not a free lunch.'

'You'd stop giving her a salary?'

'You have to do work to get a salary.'

Richard looked at Tom's resolve and decided that he'd been circling his prey for long enough. It was time to move in for the kill.

'Did you know that your sister died from an overdose?'

'Yes. You said.'

'But it wasn't just any substance that she overdosed on. It was sodium fluoroacetate.'

Tom's eyes widened.

'What?'

'Which I don't need to tell you is a pesticide that goes by the trade name of 1080.'

'No way. That's not possible.'

'And, as I'm sure you've already worked out, we've also found evidence that you bought a packet of 1080 last month. In fact, it's quite a damning piece of evidence, because it's your signature, name and address all written out in your handwriting in the poison register of the pharmacy where you bought it.'

Tom was reeling. Unable to speak.

'Okay,' Richard said, like a disappointed parent. 'Then let's start at the beginning. Do you admit that you bought 1080 pesticide five weeks ago?'

Not trusting his voice, Tom slowly nodded his head.

'Could you speak out loud, please?' Richard asked. 'Did you buy 1080 poison five weeks ago?'

'Yes,' Tom said desperately. 'I bought a packet of 1080 a few weeks ago, but it wasn't my idea.'

'It wasn't?'

'It wasn't.'

'Then whose idea was it?'

Tom crossed the floor and sat down on one of the slatted benches to the side of the shower room. Camille gave Richard a look to stay quiet.

'Who told you to buy the poison?' she asked.

'It was Lucy,' he said.

'What?'

'It was Lucy who told me to buy the 1080 poison.'

Richard and Camille exchanged a glance. This wasn't what they'd expected to hear.

'When was this?' Richard asked, going over to join Tom and Camille.

'Last month. Just like you said. She told me she'd seen a mongoose with rabies in the jungle. It used to be a big problem when we were growing up. Rabies in the local rodent population. And she said she couldn't remember what the poison was that we used to get rid of the problem. I told her it was 1080. So she asked me to get some the next time I was in town. Which is what I did. I got her some.'

Tom realised something.

'So that's why she wanted it,' he said. 'She used it to end her own life.'

'Is that what you think?' Camille asked.

'It's the only thing that makes sense. She asked me to get the poison. I gave it to her. And then she used it on herself.'

'Then can you tell me why you didn't go to the pharmacy in Honoré?' Richard asked.

'What?'

'There are two pharmacies licensed to sell agricultural poisons on Saint-Marie, but you didn't go to the one in Honoré. Even though it's your nearest by some distance.

Instead, you went to the pharmacy five miles further away. On the other side of the island. Why was that?'

'I didn't want anyone in Honoré knowing I was getting it. Our reputation's bad enough without people thinking we've had an outbreak of rabies. So I went to the pharmacy further away.'

'How very convenient.'

'I'm telling you the truth.'

'Then where is it now?'

'What do you mean?'

'Where's the 1080 poison you bought for Lucy?'

'I don't know. I gave her the packet and haven't seen it since.'

'Really? Then why didn't we find the box in her room?'

'I don't understand. How do you mean?'

'Only, if this was a suicide – like you're saying – she wouldn't have needed to hide the box once she'd taken the poison, would she? After all, she'd have known that her autopsy would reveal that it was 1080 that had killed her. So how come she apparently took this overdose and then hid the box somewhere so that we'd not be able to find it afterwards?'

'Have you looked in her safe?'

'Yes. It wasn't in there. Any more than there was a suicide note anywhere in her room. And let's not forget her last words. Just before she died, she tried to tell us that she'd been murdered by one of her family. And she was very much pointing in your general direction.'

Tom rose from his seat, anger boiling up in him.

'No! She took her own life, that's the only thing that makes sense! She killed Freddie. I mean, she's spent long enough openly saying that she'd kill him if she met him. And she's unstable enough to have done it, I tell you. But she wasn't a bad person – not really – so I reckon she felt remorse afterwards, and that's why she took her own life. Or are you really saying that I'm actually so stupid that I'd use poison that I'd bought from a central register – that I'd *signed for myself* – to kill my own sister with?'

'You have to admit – ' Camille said, but Tom interrupted her before she could get any further.

'Just because I didn't go to Eton, doesn't make me an idiot.'

'Mr Beaumont!' Camille said, but it was too late.

Tom had stormed out of the room, leaving a somewhat flabbergasted pair of Police officers behind.

After a moment, Richard straightened the knot of his tie.

'Well I think we touched a nerve there,' he said.

Camille was thoughtful.

'He's got a point, though. Hasn't he?' she said. 'What sort of killer would sign for the poison he then used to commit murder with?'

'A very stupid one,' Richard said, and turned to look at the room. But he tended to agree with Tom. The killer wouldn't commit murder with a poison that he'd so obviously bought. Unless it was all an elaborate double bluff, of course. But that didn't seem too likely, did it? So, if Tom was telling the truth, why on earth had Lucy wanted him to buy the 1080 pesticide in the first place? Or to put it another way: what had Lucy done with the poison once Tom had given it to her? How on earth had it ended up being the substance that ultimately killed her?

With his mind now whirling with all of the unanswered questions of the case, Richard walked out of the building without another word, and Camille was left behind to marvel at how very ill-mannered her boss was. In fact, Camille had occasion to note her boss's lack of basic manners for the rest of the afternoon, because, once they were both back at the Police station, Richard continued to work silently at his desk. Or he'd get up and look at the whiteboard. But always on his own, and always in silence.

As for the rest of his team, they didn't want to admit as much, but they didn't quite know what direction to take the case. After all, Fidel had finally found the three-wheeled vehicle that had been at the plantation on the morning of the murder. So that was explained now. And Richard hadn't specifically tasked Dwayne with anything since he'd finished processing the physical evidence from Lucy's murder.

As for Camille, she decided that, in the absence of any further instructions, she'd dip back into the mystery of exactly where Lady Helen had got to after she'd walked out on her family – even though she'd failed to find any official customs records of Lady Helen leaving the UK in June or July of 1999.

Camille found herself wondering if maybe the problem was that they were presuming that Helen had been up to some subterfuge at the time. It was an understandable presumption, of course. After all, according to Rosie, Helen had walked out of the house wearing only her red and white dress and white shoes, with no handbag or other bags to hand, and clutching only a twenty-pound note. However, Camille found herself thinking, what if they'd been overthinking the situation and Lady Helen really had been 'going home' that day? Home was surely her parents' house that was just outside Dorchester in Dorset. So – continuing the process of trying to keep things as simple as possible – Camille tried to imagine what could have happened to Helen on the way 'home' that might have stopped her from arriving.

What if she'd had an accident? An accident in which she'd lost her memory maybe? Or worse, had died?

Although it was something of a long shot, Camille got up a rail map of Britain on her computer and looked at how Helen might have used her twenty pounds to return to Dorchester on public transport. The nearest train station to Lady Helen's house was Maze Hill, and Camille could see that it was a relatively easy journey to get a train from Maze Hill up to Waterloo station. And from there, Lady Helen could have got a direct train from Waterloo that arrived in Dorchester two-and-a-half hours later. Then, once she'd arrived at Dorchester South, she'd have only been a few miles from her parents' house. So maybe that's what she'd tried to do that day?

Feeling a bit of a fool, but – again – without anything much else clamouring to get done, Camille started to contact all of the hospitals and police stations that were on the train route that Helen might have taken from Maze Hill back to Dorchester. Were there any women being admitted to hospital – or dying, even – whose identities were never established during June and July of 1999?

As for Richard, he remained a restless and snappy presence all afternoon. When it came to 6pm and time to finish up for the day, he bid everyone a terse goodnight and left without further comment. Camille continued to be unimpressed with her boss's manners.

But what Camille didn't appreciate was that Richard had spent the afternoon wrestling with an existential crisis. When he was investigating a murder case, he normally had a sense of forward momentum. Even if he didn't know who the killer was, the leads always suggested where he should be focusing his attention. And, as the Beaumont case had unfolded, he'd felt that that was exactly the process that he was involved in. And then Lucy had been murdered, and that was what had been upsetting Richard so much. It wasn't so much that he now didn't know which way was up or down in the case any more, although that was certainly true. Nor was it the fact that his instincts couldn't even begin to give him a sense of why Lucy had to die after Freddie had been murdered. No, what was gnawing at Richard was the sense that if he'd acted faster, or been smarter, Lucy might still be alive.

As an evening of self-reproach turned into a fitful night's sleep of self-reproach, Richard increasingly found himself focusing on the fact that he had in his hands what could possibly turn out to be the key clue: the burnt piece of paper that he'd found in Tom's bin on the day that Freddie was murdered. Putting aside the fact that the FBI manual said that Richard should leave the photographic paper undisturbed for at least a fortnight, he couldn't help wondering what might have happened if he'd chanced his arm – like Camille had suggested to him – and discovered what had been written on the paper much sooner?

Would Lucy still be alive now?

By 5am, Richard gave up on ever getting to sleep and instead decided to go to the Police station. Desperate times called for desperate measures, and he unlocked his desk drawer that contained the packages of burnt evidence. Each sandwich of glass was wrapped inside a thick black plastic bag that was held tightly in place with rubber bands.

But did Richard have the courage to open the bags before the FBI manual advised? That was the question.

Richard remembered how he'd had a hunch that Hugh was still lying to them – and he'd later been proven correct. Maybe the time for following precise rules was over? Maybe he was a maverick rule-breaker now? It didn't feel possible, but Richard felt he had run out of other options.

So, looking about himself to make sure that no-one could see him, Richard took his suit jacket off, folded it up, and put it carefully to one side. He then loosened the tie at his neck and undid the top button on his shirt. But that felt wrong, so he did his top button up again and re-asserted his tie knot. There – that was better, he thought to himself. He might be about to bend a few rules, but this wasn't Las Vegas.

Richard picked up the plastic bag he'd already stuffed full of his photographic kit and started constructing a quick studio at his desk. As it was the dead of night, he didn't have to worry too much about light pollution, but he swapped his desk lamp's light for a red lightbulb so he could have some light of the correct wavelength to see by. He then put out two plastic trays, each about A3 in size and a couple of inches deep. He filled one of them with developing liquid, and the other with fixing solution. And then – again, without stopping to think in case he lost confidence – he reached into the drawer of his desk and lifted out the four black plastic-wrapped packages of evidence.

He snapped the rubber bands from the first package, and then he cut open the black plastic bag to reveal the two glass plates that were held together by the next set of rubber bands. Holding the glass plates together with one hand, he picked up his scissors and snipped through the rubber bands. He then eased the top piece of glass off to reveal the 'top' piece of A4 photographic paper.

Richard knew that what he was about to do would irreparably destroy the burnt pieces of paper that were squashed to the other side of the photo paper. This was the moment of no return. If the photographic paper hadn't had time to develop, there'd be no second chances.

Richard peeled the photographic paper up, and the charred paper that had attached to the other side of it fragmented and fell away in a mess – some of the black bits continuing to stick to the photographic paper underneath, some of them coming away still attached to the underside of the piece of photographic paper Richard was now holding in his hands. Next he picked up a blusher brush he kept in his desk drawer for such occasions, swept all the charred bits from the photographic paper so it was clean, and then slipped the now-clean photographic paper into the developing liquid. He then started his stopwatch.

This was the moment of truth – an image of whatever had been written on the burnt paper should appear magically before his eyes.

Nothing happened.

The seconds ticked past on his stopwatch. Twenty seconds gone. And still no image appeared. Thirty seconds. Forty seconds. Fifty seconds.

Nothing.

Although, was there perhaps the faintest of grey blushes appearing on the photo paper where the charred piece of paper had been? It was hard to tell. The stopwatch reached sixty seconds and Richard pulled the photographic paper out of the developing solution and dunked it into the fixing solution.

There was a barely-visible area of light grey on the photo paper, but no handwriting could be seen to the naked eye. The whole experiment was a busted flush, Richard thought to himself. But he'd started on a course of action now, and he knew he couldn't turn back. He would develop every single piece of photo paper. Hopefully, one of them would have picked the indentations of the handwriting that had been on the paper before it was burnt.

An hour later, Camille, Fidel and Dwayne entered the station, having just had their breakfast at Catherine's bar, but they stopped in mid-conversation as they saw their boss standing by the bead curtain at the back of the office. He was holding a magnifying glass to eight glossy pieces of photographic paper that he'd attached to the curtain with clothes pegs.

'Sir?' Camille asked.

Richard didn't even turn around.

'And good morning to you too, sir,' Camille said as she went to her desk.

Richard still didn't acknowledge his team's arrival. Instead, he kept looking over the sheets of photo paper with his magnifying glass.

'Chief, what's up?' Dwayne said, and crossed the Police station to join his boss by the bead curtain.

'I opened the packages,' Richard said.

'*What*?' Dwayne asked.

From the depths of his disappointment, Richard explained how he'd spent the night developing the pieces of photo paper that he'd attached to the burnt evidence they'd found in Tom's bin.

'But sir,' Fidel said, 'you said they wouldn't be ready yet.'

'I know,' Richard said crankily, 'but I changed my mind, didn't I?'

'You broke the rules?' Camille asked, just as amazed as the others.

'And as always happens when you break the rules, it hasn't worked,' Richard said, and stepped to one side so his team could see that although there was a light area of grey in the centre of each developed piece of photographic paper, it wasn't really possible to see if there were any areas of white writing within the grey areas. The image was just too indistinct.

'I can't see any images of the handwriting,' Dwayne said.

'I know,' Richard said. 'I've ruined everything.'

'You know what, sir,' Fidel said. 'We might be able to enhance this. All we need do is change the white and black balance.'

'We do?' Richard asked, not really understanding what Fidel was talking about.

With his boss's permission, Fidel took one of the pieces of photographic paper over to his desk and used the office scanner to digitise the image. He then loaded the image into a photo editing programme.

'Now, sir, all we need to do is tell the software to find everything that's light grey in the image and turn it to jet black.'

Using the mouse, Fidel moved a pipette cursor on the screen until it was hovering over the area of light grey. He then clicked to load that colour into the palette of the software. He then moved a slider so that the grey colour turned black, and now that the greys of the image had become black, it was possible to see that there was the faintest – and thinnest – scrawl of white on the page.

It was handwriting. Old-fashioned handwriting.

'You did it, sir,' Fidel said to his boss, and Richard realised that he was dumbstruck. Not just because it looked as though his experiment had worked after all, but because he'd managed to get it to work even though he'd not followed the rules to the letter. In his mind, a strange and impossible-to-believe thought was beginning to form. Was this what spontaneity felt like? What being a rule-breaker felt like? After all, he'd rolled the dice – he'd gambled – and it had paid off. It was an intoxicating feeling.

It didn't take long for Fidel to scan and change the colour balance of all of the photos. Four of them had no writing on them at all, as could be expected – they'd been attached to the side of the burnt piece of paper that had no writing on – but four of them were covered in

scrawls of old-fashioned handwriting. Fidel matched up
the images on the screen so that he was able to create a
virtual image of the original piece of paper. It wasn't an
easy task, because the writing was so illegible – and there
were plenty of lines and imperfections in the image from
where the paper had once been folded over. There were
also a few gaps in the list where the burnt edges of the
paper didn't quite match up. But Fidel got the images
aligned so that it was possible to see what had been written
on the paper before it had been burnt.

It was a list of names. Richard quickly checked them
over.

Lily Aquarele
Sylvaine D'Or
Christophe de Souza
Julian Renouf
Morgane Pichou
Pierre Colville
Gabriel Lefèbvre
Vivien Bowyer
Pamela Logut
Kirsty Harrison
Lucy Hanham
Stéphane Carrié

It seemed fair to assume that the piece of paper was the
very same list of slave names from 1777 that Tom had

asked Lucy to store in her safe three days before Freddie had died. But why on earth had someone removed it from the safe and then set it on fire in Tom's bin?

Richard heard an email notification chime from Camille's computer. As she went over to see what had just arrived, Richard got Fidel to print out the image of the list and he then took it over to the whiteboard and pinned it to the top of it. Richard guessed that it had to be connected with the murder somehow, but it seemed so improbable. How could a list of names from two hundred years ago be related to a modern-day murder? It just didn't make sense.

'Oh okay, sir, you need to see this,' Camille said without looking up from her computer monitor.

'Why? What have you got?'

'I think I've finally found out what happened to Lady Helen.'

'You have?' Richard said, amazed, and he, Fidel and Dwayne converged on Camille's desk at speed.

'Because I contacted the hospitals and police stations that were on the train route Lady Helen would have used if she really was going home on the day she walked out on her family.'

'You did?' Richard asked, impressed – and he had one of his very brief flowerings of respect for his number two. This is why Camille was so good at her job, he found himself thinking – despite her very many and very obvious flaws. When she got her teeth into something, she didn't let go.

'So what did you find?'

'Well, the first stop on the train line from Waterloo to Dorchester South is a place called Winchester, and Winchester Police Station was one of the places I sent my enquiry to. Anyway, they've just got back to say to me that on the 13th of June, 1999, a woman threw herself in front of a train at Winchester Station. She was killed instantly. And when they looked through her pockets, they didn't find a single identifying document on her. She didn't have a handbag. Or a wallet.'

'Just like Nanny Rosie told us,' Richard said.

'That's right. But this woman didn't even have a train ticket. All the Police were able to find was £1.20 in the pocket of her dress.'

'But is that woman Lady Helen?'

'That's the thing, sir. They've sent through the photos from the crime scene.'

Camille scrolled down the pdf of the report, and there were a number of crime scene photos of the crumpled body of a woman at the side of the train track.

The dead woman was wearing a red dress with white polka dots. Just like Rosie said Helen had been wearing when she walked out on her family. And there was a white shoe on the gravel to the side of her body. Just as Rosie said Helen had been wearing that day.

The next photo removed all doubt. It showed a picture of a woman's head, and although her skull had been crushed at the back – with black blood matting her blonde hair – most of her face was relatively undamaged.

The woman was Lady Helen Beaumont.

'It's her,' Fidel said.

'So what does the report say?' Richard asked eagerly.

Camille scrolled back up through the document.

'Okay,' she said, 'it says here that after they failed to identify the dead body at the scene, the Winchester Police issued photographs of the deceased around the county, and appealed for witnesses who could identify the body. But no-one came forward. And there was no CCTV footage of her death. So the Coroner ruled it death by misadventure, but the presumption was that it was a suicide. After six months, the Police closed the file.'

'So they never identified her?' Dwayne asked.

'That's what it says here,' Camille said.

As his team started discussing Lady Helen's death, Richard felt something tickle at his memory, but he couldn't quite place it. What was it? He could tell that whatever it was, it was the faintest of connections, and he decided to try and forget all about it. Sometimes you could frighten ideas away if you thought about them too closely. Instead he tuned back into the conversation his team were having.

'She did this on purpose,' Camille was saying.

'What's that?' Richard asked.

'The Police didn't find her train ticket on her. Which suggests to me that she didn't want to be identified after she'd killed herself.'

'But why did she kill herself?' Fidel asked.

'That's the million dollar question,' Richard agreed.

'Although we don't know the stresses she'd been under,' Camille said. 'Or just how bad it really was living with Freddie. Because if he'd been hitting her – like Hugh, Rosie and Lucy all said he did…? The moment Nanny Rosie walked in – and she knew her children would be safe from that moment onwards – I could imagine a woman who was already unstable just giving up. Just walking out of the door – too ashamed to carry on with her life.'

'So you think she already knew she was going to kill herself when she left?' Fidel asked.

'I'm not sure. The fact that she died on the journey back to her parents suggests that she at least set out that day with the intention of going home. So maybe something happened on the journey that made her change her mind. Or maybe she just changed her mind anyway. But, either way, she threw her train ticket away and made sure no CCTV cameras could see her before she committed suicide.'

'Although, what if she was killed?' Fidel said, getting everyone's attention.

'Go on,' Richard said.

'Not that there's any proof, but the absence of a train ticket isn't really proof that her death was definitely suicide, either. Maybe she lost the ticket on the way. Maybe her killer took it from her before pushing her in front of a train. But if she was murdered then that would also explain why her death didn't happen near any CCTV cameras.'

'But who'd want to kill her?' Dwayne asked. 'Who benefits from her death?'

'And how did her murderer – if it was murder – know that she'd be on that station at that time?' Fidel asked.

Richard found himself remembering how he'd briefly wondered if Lady Helen had had an accomplice of some sort when she walked out on her family.

'And why wasn't there any luggage with her when her body was found?' Dwayne asked.

'Wait!' Richard said, holding up his hand for everyone to stop talking. He was sure of it now. There'd been a critically important piece of information that he'd heard in the last few minutes. Something that contradicted what he thought he already knew – or threw a new light on a previously-gathered piece of evidence. But what was it?

Turning his back on his team, Richard went to the whiteboard and looked at it for inspiration. His eye took in the names of the suspects, the key pieces of information, the list of slave names he'd only just pinned to the board, and then, before he'd even consciously had the thought, an ice cold shiver ran through his body. It was like a sudden shock of precognition, because he knew – just *knew* – what he'd just heard that was out of place.

'Good grief,' he said quietly to himself.

But it couldn't be true, could it?

Richard turned to face his team.

Fidel started to ask a question, but both Dwayne and

Camille shushed him into silence before he'd even opened his lips.

Richard barely noticed. Instead, he dashed over to his desk and grabbed up the bulging case file for Freddie's murder. Allowing statements and reports to tumble onto the desk, he eventually pulled out a document, slapped it onto his desk and bent down to inspect it carefully. After a moment, he looked up at his team.

He'd got it. Or had he?

Richard crossed to Camille's desk and quickly scrolled through the crime scene report for Lady Helen's death – and saw, once again, that she had indeed been wearing a red dress with white polka dots when she died.

'But it's not possible,' he mumbled to himself, before biting his lip. What did this mean?

Richard's mind raced back over the case from the moment that Lucy had entered the Police station saying that there was a man at the plantation stalking her. Richard considered what they'd learned about Freddie and his life with Helen before she left him. He then considered Lucy's relationship with Freddie, and everyone else's relationship with her. Who wanted to sell the Plantation, and who didn't. And then – almost unbidden – Richard had a stunning realisation as he remembered a throwaway remark that the solicitor Zoe had said when they interviewed her. Dear god, he thought to himself, was this it? The reason why Freddie had to die? And Lucy afterwards?

But even if it was, how did the killer murder Freddie

inside a locked room and then manage to be outside it when it was opened up?

And that's when Richard got it. The whole plan. It was so obvious when you thought about it, he realised. *That's* how the killer did it.

'Got you,' he said in quiet wonder.

'Sir?' Camille asked tentatively. 'You're not saying you know who our killer is, are you?'

Richard's attention returned to the room, and he looked at his partner as though he were surprised to see her standing in front of him.

'You know what?' he said. 'I think I am.'

'You know why Freddie had to die?' Dwayne asked.

'I do.'

'And was it the same person who then went on to kill Lucy, sir?' Fidel asked.

'It was, Fidel. The same person killed both Freddie and Lucy.'

Camille, Dwayne and Fidel exchanged stunned looks, and then Camille turned back to face her boss.

'Then do you also know how the killer got out of the locked room after they'd killed Freddie?'

Richard looked at Camille with a twinkle in his eye.

'Of course I do. Don't you?'

CHAPTER TWELVE

As the Beaumont family entered the shower room, they found Richard already waiting for them, looking out of the window. As they settled themselves on the slatted benches in the changing area, Richard kept looking out at the tarmacked road and thick jungle outside. What he found so interesting was the way that the jungle just stopped at the very edge of civilisation. But it was always there. On the edge of things. Wild and threatening. Waiting. All it took was one step. One step, and you moved from the ordered world of roads and buildings and were plunged into the untamed wilds. Because that's what had happened on the day that Freddie was murdered. The killer had, in one step, moved from civilisation and entered the lawless anarchy of the jungle.

Richard looked at the watch on his wrist. He'd sent Dwayne and Fidel to search Beaumont Manor ten minutes ago, and he hoped that they'd be back soon enough.

There was a clatter of footsteps, and Richard turned

to see Camille walking a handcuffed Andy Lucas across the room. Andy didn't look anyone in the eye as Camille made him stand on his own to the side of the family, although Richard could see that Sylvie was looking at Andy with shock. Yes, Richard thought to himself. Sylvie *should* be shocked.

But now they were all gathered. Hugh Beaumont. Sylvie Beaumont. Their two adopted children, Tom and Matthew. The family's one-time nanny Rosie. And the semi-criminal Andy Lucas.

'Thank you for all meeting me here,' Richard said.

'What choice did we have?' Tom said.

'Indeed,' Richard said with what he knew wasn't even the beginnings of a smile.

'But what do you want with us?' Sylvie said.

'I want to tell you who killed Freddie and Lucy Beaumont,' Richard said, and was gratified to see the effect that his words had on the suspects. 'But first, let me tell you how we all ended up here.

'The Beaumonts are a proud and noble family who can trace their lineage back many centuries. And the Saint-Marie Beaumonts have been one of the island's most important and wealthy families for well over two hundred years. Or, that's the impression you'd all like to give, because the reality is somewhat different. Your plantation has been steadily losing money for decades, you've been selling off family assets for just as long, and most of you have felt hard done by one way or another ever since Grandfather William died. But then, that's no surprise, is it? Grandfather William sewed the seeds for this particular tragedy when he left a will that turned the estate into a trust because he wanted to cut out his wastrel first born son, Freddie Beaumont. In truth, it's hard to know what else he could have done to stop Freddie from inheriting. Although, of course, he could have left the estate outright to you, Hugh. After all, he knew that you'd adopted Lucy, so the line of inheritance would have eventually reverted back to the family's firstborn. Which is the real reason you adopted Freddie's children, isn't it?'

'What?' Hugh said, appalled by the suggestion. 'No. We adopted our three children because it was the right thing to do. And it was the best decision we ever made. They've brought nothing but joy to us.'

Richard glanced at Sylvie, but she was looking away, and Richard didn't push the point. Sylvie had made her feelings about her children clear the last time they'd all been gathered. As Andy Lucas had told them, she thought they were 'brats'.

'Okay, so let's park your exact motives for adopting your brother's children for a moment. It's still true to say that you felt snubbed when William's will didn't leave his estate to you, didn't you?'

Now it was Hugh's turn to look away from Richard's gaze.

'And it's easy to see why. You'd had to sacrifice your dreams of being an artist to run a plantation you'd always

presumed would have been Freddie's responsibility. And –
worst of all – even after your father died and you learned
that you hadn't even inherited this place, you still had to
stay on as the plantation's proxy owner. Because you either
ran the plantation as a trust, or you walked away – in
which case the solicitors would have got someone else in
to take over, and you'd have lost all control. And with
that, your salary. And Sylvie's. You were handcuffed to
this place. Whether you liked it or not.

'But then Lucy came up with a plan earlier this year,
because she shared your dislike of the plantation. Although,
for her, it wasn't so much that the plantation was no longer
profitable, it was more that she felt your family's history
on this island needed to be erased. I mention this because
it gets to the heart of why Freddie had to die, and why
Lucy then had to die afterwards. Your history.

'Anyway, I bet no-one was more surprised than Lucy
when she discovered from Zoe, your solicitor, that
although the plantation wasn't making any money, the
land you owned was worth a small fortune. Five million
dollars in fact. Five million dollars to share between the
four of you. Or so you thought, because – to start off
with – Tom refused to sell. And then you all learnt that
Freddie would have to sign the document of dissolution as
well. And not only did he have to sign, but he would also
have to get his share of the five million dollars. And that's
what put paid to the whole plan, because Lucy point blank
refused to sell if her biological father benefited in any way.

Which is interesting, isn't it? Because that's a truly twisted level of hatred when you think about it. That you'd pass up getting a million dollars yourself just to stop some third party from also getting a million dollars. Which rather begs the question: what was it that drove Lucy's hatred of her father? Why was it that she could never forgive him?

'But once Lucy said she refused to sell, the situation became an impasse with no way out. Because that meant that there were now two family members who were opposed to selling. Tom. And Lucy. And this must have been so frustrating for the rest of you,' Richard said, turning to face Hugh, Sylvie and Matthew. 'Because the three of you wanted to be shot of the plantation, but there was no way of convincing both Lucy and Tom to change their minds. They were too set in their ways. So that was that. You were thwarted.

'And then, quite unwittingly, Matthew set off a train of events that would lead to his biological father and his sister's murder. He wrote to Freddie, as he always did on the occasion of his birthday. And this one entirely inno-cent letter was enough to set the first domino toppling. Freddie wrote back and told Matthew that he was dying.

'As Matthew had never understood why his family had refused to reconcile with Freddie, he did the honourable thing. He went to Hugh – as the head of the family – and showed him the letter, and asked him to reach out to Freddie before he died. But Hugh refused to, and sent Matthew away, telling him to break all contact with his biological father. So Matthew stopped all communication with Freddie. No more letters. No phone calls – as we were able to prove when we looked into his and Freddie's records. Matthew really did just walk away, as Hugh had asked him to.

'Which is more than we can say about Hugh. Because he was in a quandary. Did his brother have cancer, or didn't he? Was he going to live for many years, or would he be dead soon? So Hugh did the most natural thing. He shared his concerns with his wife. As she inadvertently ended up admitting to us. And, as she also made clear to us, she had no such doubts. To her mind, Freddie was a liar. Therefore, if he said he had cancer, it wasn't true. As far as she was concerned, all the letter really proved was that Freddie was alive and well and still hustling. As it happens, Freddie did indeed have cancer, but there was no way for Sylvie or Hugh to know about this at this time. Instead, I think Sylvie decided that if Freddie was out to get himself some money, then – for once – his interests aligned with hers. Because it's clear to me that it's been Sylvie who's been driving her husband's actions all of this time.

'So I think it was Sylvie who got Hugh to ring Freddie up and tell him that if he wanted cash, then there was a million dollars waiting for him. All he had to was come to Saint-Marie and sign a document. And Freddie agreed. Of course he did. And all along, Sylvie hoped that if she stayed in the background, no-one would work out how involved she was. Well, her plan backfired – and backfired spectacularly – when Lucy found out what Hugh had done. Because this was when, like Mount Esmée, Lucy erupted.'

'If you think I could kill my own daughter...?' Hugh said incredulously. 'There are simply no circumstances under which I could ever do harm to any of my children. Whether it benefited me or not. They're mine. I love them. They're the only good I've achieved with my life.'

Seeing the desperation in Hugh's eyes, Richard decided that it was time to put the man out of his misery.

'I know. And that's the real reason why you kept lying to us, isn't it? You said at the time that you were trying to protect your family, but I think you've only actually ever been trying to protect yourself. Because you knew that if this became an investigation into your brother's death, we'd uncover how badly you've been mismanaging the plantation, and how you've allowed your own wife to bleed this place dry. And you were also petrified that we – and therefore your children – would find out that you'd gone behind their backs to get Freddie out here. The shame you felt – at your failures as a businessman, and as a father – is what has driven you to continuously lie to us and try to cover up your role in what happened here. But you're no killer. I know that now.'

'You do?' Hugh asked.

'I do.'

Hugh turned from Richard and looked pleadingly at Matthew and Tom.

'I'm sorry,' he said. 'I'm so sorry.'

Looking at Hugh, Richard had a sudden insight that he could see through the decades and observe the young schoolboy inside the older man. And the young boy that Richard could see was nervous, insecure, and desperate for approval. How very sad, Richard thought to himself. Hugh's self-confidence was really not much more than a glossy haircut and a posh accent. There was nothing else there.

'Which brings me to you, Sylvie,' Richard said, turning to Hugh's wife. 'Because if your husband is mostly innocent, the same can't be said for you.'

'What?' Sylvie said. 'I don't know what you mean.'

'Tell me, do you know the man standing just here?' Richard said, indicating Andy Lucas as he stood off to one side.

Sylvie looked over at Andy and shook her head.

'No. Sorry. I don't.'

'Oh dear,' Richard said. 'Andy?'

Andy didn't seem to be looking at anyone in particular as he spoke in a monotone.

'I'm Sylvie's cousin. From Maldon. And we're business partners. Of sorts. She steals coffee from here. I sell it.'

'*What*?' Tom said, rising to his feet in anger.

Sylvie's smile had frozen, and it was clear that she didn't know what to say.

'That's right,' Richard said for the benefit of the rest of the family. 'Sylvie has been stealing your coffee, getting Andy to sell it, and then splitting the profits with him.'

'Is this true?' Matthew asked, just as appalled as the rest of the family.

'Of course not,' she said, but the look of guilt on her face betrayed her. 'And anyway,' she said, knowing she'd need to mount a stouter defence, 'it's not stealing. I own it.'

'You don't,' Tom said.

'Of course I do. This is my plantation as much as it's yours.'

'It's the *family* plantation,' Tom said, his voice tight.

'Oh, put a sock in it.'

'What?' Tom said.

'You're just a snob. Like all the others. A bloody snob. I was never good enough for you. Was I? Because of my background. Because your family always thought I was just a gold digger. Well, you had the last laugh there, didn't you? There wasn't any gold. But you still thought that's why I married your father, so I decided, well, if you thought I was only here for the money, then I might as well try and make some money.'

'So you admit it?' Hugh asked in stunned amazement.

'Wasn't forty thousand dollars a year enough for you?' Tom asked.

'Get over yourself. It was only a few bags here and there.'

'A few bags when we weren't making a profit.'

'And it wasn't just a few bags,' Richard said. 'It was worth quite a few thousand dollars each time.'

'It was the least I was owed!' Sylvie spat.

The family looked at her in shock.

'Oh come on, stop looking like a slapped arse the lot of you. I was duped when I married Hugh. I thought I was marrying someone special. But he's not. And all along, he's said he'd have been a famous painter if he'd not had to run this place, but I can tell you now, Hugh, that your paintings are crap. You've no idea how much pressure I had to put on Pascal to show them in his gallery last year.'

'What?' Hugh said.

'It was only because of me that you got your bloody exhibition. Because I'm telling you now, Pascal didn't think your paintings were any good, either. No-one does.'

'But the paintings sold. I sold plenty of them.'

'Which just proves how gullible people are. Pascal was laughing at you the whole time. We all were.'

Richard looked at the family, and could see outrage in the faces of Hugh, Matthew and Tom as they realised just how monstrous Sylvie was. But Richard could also see a look of quiet satisfaction in Rosie's eyes. She wasn't in any way surprised to see Sylvie reveal herself like this.

Richard could also see that Sylvie was looking with contempt at the rest of her family.

'So you can all continue being obsessed with your past, obsessed with your history, but you don't need to worry about me ever. I'm on the next flight out of here. God knows to where, but as long as it's as far away from you lot as I can get, I'll be happy.'

'I wouldn't be so sure you'll be on the next flight out of here,' Richard said.

'What?' Sylvie said.

'Because we know that you've been breaking the law. There's the small matter of whether the family wish to press charges.'

'I've not broken any law. I owned the coffee I sold. Good as.'

'But what if that's not the only law you've broken?' Richard asked, taking a step towards Sylvie. 'What if you're also a murderer? Because, God knows, you've already made it clear to us how much you hated Lucy. And when she told you that you wouldn't get any money from the sale of the plantation, I could well imagine you being driven into a rage that would end in you killing her, the adopted daughter who'd never once thanked you for raising her.'

'What is this?'

'It's called a motive.'

While Richard let this hang in the air, he glanced at the door to the room. Where the hell were Dwayne and Fidel? If his theory was right – and he knew his theory had to be right – they really should have returned by now. He'd just have to plough on until they arrived.

'But would you have killed Lucy having first killed Freddie? That's a far more ticklish question. Because, with both Freddie and Lucy dead, it's Tom who inherits – and he's the only member of the family who's never wanted to sell. Which is the worst possible outcome for you. And as much as I can see you killing Lucy, I think your hatred of her isn't anywhere as large as your love of money. As we can tell from the salary you pay yourself. And the fact that you'll even indulge in petty theft to boost your cash reserves. No, as long as Tom inherited, I can't ever see you killing Lucy under any circumstances. You lose everything with Tom in charge.'

'So you admit I'm innocent?' Sylvie said, drawing herself up and trying to recapture her status.

'No. You're not innocent. But you didn't commit murder, I'll agree to that.'

Richard looked at Sylvie and saw a woman who was trying to project haughty defiance, but all he saw was anger. There was such a fury inside her, Richard thought to himself. And an arrogance, too. It was clear to him that Sylvie felt that she deserved more from life. And now that it hadn't gone to plan, she was going to blame everyone in the world for her misfortune apart from the one person who could do anything about it: herself.

'Which brings me to you, Matthew,' Richard said, turning to face the youngest member of the family. 'And I have to admit to a prejudice here. You see, when I meet a young Etonian, I'm not necessarily predisposed to like him. It shouldn't have affected how I judged you. I'm sorry to say that it did. At least at first.

'But let's look at the facts. Seeing as you were only a baby when you left the UK, I can't see how you could have had any significant grudge against your biological father. In fact, to all intents and purposes, you never even met him. What's more, you're the only member of the family who's got a track record of treating Freddie with any kind of kindness. You wrote to him once a year on your birthday. And the fact that Freddie's last letter to you told you that he had cancer makes it all the more improbable that you could be his killer. After all, why would anyone risk a murder conviction when their potential victim would be dead soon anyway?

'And as for murdering Lucy, that's even more unlikely. As Tom later admitted to us, she's the member of the family that Matthew was closest to. His big sister. The person who'd all but raised him when he was growing up. So when we look at the facts rationally, it's impossible to imagine Matthew committing either murder. Even if he went to a posh private school,' Richard said with a rueful smile, tacitly admitting to the family that his prejudices against Matthew had briefly got in the way of the facts of the case.

Richard heard footsteps on the cobblestones outside, and Dwayne and Fidel bustled into the room. Dwayne was wearing evidence gloves and holding a cardboard box.

'You were right, Chief!' he called out as he joined his boss. 'We found it at the back of Tom's wardrobe.'

'Has it got everything inside?'

'It has,' Fidel said, marvelling. 'Although I still don't know how you knew it would be there. Or what would be in it.'

Richard was thrilled to have his theory proven correct, and he turned with a deadly smile to face Tom Beaumont.

'And now we come to you, Tom. And I think my officers have just found some very incriminating evidence in the wardrobe of your bedroom.'

As Richard said this, Fidel lifted a little metal tin out of the cardboard evidence box and held it up for everyone to see. It was an old metal cash box.

Tom was panicking.

'What's that?' he asked.

'An old cash box we just found hidden in your bedroom at the back of your wardrobe,' Dwayne said.

'You did?'

'Because you have to admit,' Richard said, turning to include the whole family as he spoke, 'Tom's name has kept cropping up in the case right from the start. Think about it. The gun that was used to kill Freddie might have belonged to Lucy, but she told us that the only other member of her family who knew about the gun's existence was Tom here. What's more, it was Tom who found the list of slaves' names in his office, and it was Tom who then asked Lucy to store that list in her safe three days before Freddie was killed. And we know that the list of slaves' names is somehow connected to Freddie's death, because we found it burned in the bin in Tom's office just after the murder had been carried out. And while all of these little facts are perhaps circumstantial, what *isn't* circumstantial in any way is the fact that it was Tom who bought the poison that was then used to kill his sister Lucy.'

'No,' Tom said in alarm, 'that's just bad luck on my part. It was Lucy who asked me to get the 1080 poison.'

'Which, rather conveniently for you, she's no longer here to confirm or deny.'

'But it's what happened. She asked me to buy the poison. So she must have killed Freddie and then killed herself.'

'But how did she kill Freddie, Tom? She was with me and my Detective Sergeant at the precise moment that Freddie was murdered. In fact, she's the only person on the whole island who couldn't have been his killer.'

Tom looked panicked. 'I don't know. What if Freddie was already dead beforehand?'

'You mean, did Lucy kill Freddie *before* she'd even come to the Police station that morning? And then, once we'd gone to the plantation with her, she somehow created the sound of gunshots at 11.10am so we'd think that that was when he was killed?'

'Yes! What if that's what happened?'

'Unfortunately for you, that's simply impossible. Not seeing how the water from the shower hadn't even begun to seep under Freddie's body by the time we got to the scene. He could only have been dead for a matter of moments – and Lucy was in our sight the whole time. She wasn't the shooter. So, Dwayne, can you tell me what you found in the box in Tom's bedroom?'

Dwayne lifted the lid on the little metal box and pulled out a box of bullets.

'9mm bullets for a Glock 19 handgun,' Dwayne said.

All the blood drained from Tom's face. It looked as though he was going to faint.

Next, Dwayne took out a make-up brush, a small glass jar full of graphite powder, and a light blue cloth.

'We've also got everything you'd need to reveal the fingerprints on the keypad of a safe. Including a blue cloth that I bet will be made of fibres that will match the blue fibre we found snagged on the hinge on Lucy's safe.'

Next, Dwayne lifted out a small cardboard box that was painted bright yellow. There was a black skull and crossbones on the front of the box above big red numbers that said '1080'.

'And finally,' Richard said, 'we have the box of 1080 poison that was used to kill Lucy. A box of poison that Tom told me he didn't know the location of, even though it turns out that it was hidden in the back of his wardrobe in an old metal tin.

'So, seeing as we've just found physical evidence hidden in his bedroom that suggests that Tom's our killer, let's see if we can't also work out why he'd want to kill both Freddie and Lucy. But then, that's hardly a challenge. Because he's not this laid back cool dude islander that he'd like everyone to think. He's actually a lot more like his grandfather William than he'd ever let on. He has a ruthless streak. And he knew perfectly well that if he wanted to take control of the plantation and stop it from being sold, then two people first had to die: Freddie and Lucy. And there isn't a jury in the land who won't notice that they're precisely the two people who are now dead.'

'But none of this is true,' Tom said in desperation. 'I didn't kill anyone.'

'Even though you were the only member of the family who knew about Lucy's gun? And the only person here with a motive to want both Freddie and Lucy dead? You don't even have an alibi for the time of Freddie's murder, do you?'

'I was out in the fields.'

'Which was always rather convenient, I thought. That you were miles away and on your own when Freddie was killed.'

'But I always check over the fields at about 11 o'clock every day.'

'And that's a critical piece of information, so thank you for bringing it up. As you told us at the time, you *always* go into the fields to check on the coffee plants at about 11 o'clock every morning.'

'Why's that important?' Sylvie asked, her interest suddenly piqued.

'Before I explain,' Richard said, 'I should also add that Tom had a point when he told us that the killer wouldn't have been so stupid as to sign his name for the poison that was then used to kill his sister as well. Any more than he'd leave such incriminating evidence in an unlocked box at the back of his wardrobe.'

'Hang on,' Hugh said. 'What are you saying?'

'Isn't it obvious? Right from the start it was always the real killer's plan to set Tom up for the two murders. Isn't that right, Rosie?'

Richard turned and looked at Rosie as she sat on the bench, her hands folded neatly in her lap.

'What's that?' she said, confused.

'Tom's being framed by the murderer, isn't he?'

Rosie opened her mouth to say something, but no sound was forthcoming. She'd finally caught up with what Richard was saying.

'Very well,' Richard said. 'If you want to play the innocent. Because we've always presumed you couldn't have killed Freddie. Or rather, the fact that you were on a boat to Montserrat that left Saint-Marie ten minutes before Freddie was killed certainly suggested that you were in the clear. But can I ask, seeing as you bought your ferry ticket at 9.30 that morning, why did you not get on the 10am sailing?'

'What's that?'

'Well, we know you were down at the harbour buying your ticket at 9.30am. So I eventually found myself wondering, why didn't you just get on the next boat to Montserrat? Which was at 10am that morning. Why did you wait an extra hour until the 11am sailing?'

'Well, I don't really know.'

'You don't?'

'It was so long ago. Hold on,' she said, suddenly

remembering. 'I wanted to get a present for my god-daughter, that's it! I went along the shops of Honoré looking for something. I'm sure that's why I ended up getting the 11am sailing.'

'And did you get a present?'

'For my goddaughter? As it happens, no. There was nothing appropriate.'

'So you looked for an hour, but found nothing?'

'Yes. That's right.'

'How interesting. But, as Police Officer Fidel Best here realised, what if you used that missing hour to go back to the plantation? Because you could easily have hidden in the shower room and been the person who killed Freddie at 11.10am.'

'But I was on the boat to Montserrat at 11am that morning.'

'And yet, the only proof we have of this is the fact that you arrived on Montserrat at 12.30pm with the other passengers from the 11am sailing.'

'That's what I'm saying. I was on that boat. I went through customs with the other passengers. That's all the proof I need. Isn't it?'

'Then let me offer up another scenario. And in this version of events, I think it's perfectly possible for you to have committed murder at 11.10am in the shower room of the plantation. And then, all you'd need is some kind of transport to get you down to the harbour and onto a fast boat and you could have caught up with the ferry to Montserrat. Meaning you arrived on a different boat at Montserrat, but at the same time as the ferry. And if we're looking for other means of transport, I can't help noticing that Andy Lucas was up at the plantation in a three-wheeler van that morning.'

Andy was thrown.

'What's that?' he asked.

'You were up at the plantation that morning.'

'But that's because I was picking up a delivery of coffee.'

'So you say. But *someone* killed Freddie – and seeing as it didn't make sense to me that it was one of the Beaumont family – this is what I found myself thinking: what if your presence at the plantation that morning wasn't just because you were picking up illegal coffee? What if that was just your cover story? Because all along I've been presuming that your vehicle must have left before the murder – because it briefly rained at 11am that morning. And the tyre prints we were able to pick up in the mud had clearly been left *before* it started raining. But what it took me too long to realise is that the tarmacked road that led down the mountain was only twenty or so yards away. So there was nothing stopping you from driving up to the outbuilding across the dry mud to pick up your coffee, and then returning to the tarmacked road to wait for Rosie there. Either because that was always the plan for where you were going to meet her, or because you could see that it was going to rain, and you didn't want to leave any prints in the wet mud that would later prove to us that you'd only left the plantation after it had rained. Because that would suggest that you'd maybe had something to do with the murder.'

'You've got no evidence for this,' Andy said.

'But that's not the end of the story,' Richard said, ploughing on. 'Because, when my officer boarded your boat, he reported to me that it was far more powerful than he'd expected. And I'm sure that if you'd driven down the mountain after the murder with Rosie in your three-wheeler van, you could easily have got her onto your boat and arrived in Montserrat at 12.30, thus giving her an apparently unbreakable alibi.'

'But I don't even know this woman,' Andy said, angrily.

'And we're supposed to believe you, are we?' Richard asked. 'A known criminal?'

'But he's telling the truth,' Rosie said, just as panicked as Andy. 'I've never seen this man before in my life.'

Richard held Rosie's gaze for a long moment.

'Very well,' he said. 'Then tell me about the list of slaves' names you found in Tom's study.'

'What?'

'Because I remember that when Tom told us he'd found a handwritten list of slaves' names in an old book, he hadn't been on his own. There'd been two other people with him at the time. And those two people were Matthew and you. Isn't that right, Matthew?'

Matthew looked at Richard awkwardly. He didn't want

to implicate Rosie, but it was obvious that he couldn't lie, either.

'You're right,' Matthew eventually said. 'The three of us found the list of names together.'

'Thank you,' Richard said, turning to face Rosie. 'So you admit it? You saw the list of slave names that day?'

'I suppose so,' Rosie said, now desperately confused by Richard's questioning.

'And after the murder, we found that same list of names burned in Tom's bin. A list of twelve names. And while eleven of them weren't that interesting, there was one name that I couldn't help but notice.'

As he said this, Richard reached into his pocket and pulled out the printout of the re-joined burnt pieces of paper. He held it up for everyone to see.

'You worked out what was written on the paper?' Tom asked, amazed.

'It was a name in the middle of the list,' Richard said. 'A man's name. "Gabriel Lefèbvre",' Richard said. 'And I can't help noticing that, as surnames go, it's extremely similar to yours, Rosie. Because your surname is Lefèvre. In fact, when you consider how names can change over two hundred years, it's *extremely* similar. And because I knew this list of names had to be important – or it wouldn't have been burnt – I then remembered the story we'd learned about "Mad Jack" Beaumont, and how he'd killed a whole dormitory of slaves, even though there was one witness. And when this witness tried to testify against

"Mad Jack", "Mad Jack" rigged the evidence and the jury so that this one witness was convicted of the crime and therefore hanged.

'But what I finally remembered was the fact the innocent man who "Mad Jack" had hanged was called Gabriel. It's not too much of a stretch to imagine that the Gabriel who Mad Jack had hanged was the self same Gabriel Lefèbvre who'd come over on the first boat with Thomas Beaumont. And it's also not that much of a stretch to imagine that this Gabriel Lefèbvre was also one of your ancestors. So, if a mad and crazy drunk had killed one of your forebears, what if it was you who'd now killed Mad Jack's mad and drunk descendant, Freddie?'

'But why would I do that?' Rosie asked, still reeling from Richard's accusations.

'Indeed,' Richard said. 'And why would you then kill Lucy? It doesn't make much sense, does it? But it just goes to show how fiendishly clever the real killer has been – that I even began to wonder if a woman very much in the Autumn of her years might have been our double killer.'

'Hang on,' Hugh said. 'Are you saying that Rosie is innocent?'

'Of murder? One hundred per cent. She had nothing to do with either death. But she's by no means blameless. Like Hugh, she's been lying to us from the start. But unlike Hugh, she's also been lying to the whole family for the whole time she's been working for them.'

'What's that?' Rosie said, confused.

'Rosie,' Richard said, turning to face the old woman, 'I think that Freddie and Lucy's killer will strike again. Unless you tell us the truth right now.'

'But I've only ever told the truth,' Rosie said.

'Then prove it. Tell us the identity of the killer.'

'What?'

'You know who the killer is.'

'But I don't know. I don't.'

'Oh you do. You've known from the start. When you really think about it.'

Richard held Rosie's gaze for a long moment, and then she looked away.

Richard pounced. 'I'm right, aren't I?' he said.

It was barely noticeable, but after a long moment, Rosie nodded her head.

'But I don't understand,' Sylvie said. 'Who killed Freddie and Lucy?'

'It's obvious, Sylvie,' Richard said. 'There's only one person here who could possibly be our double killer.'

'And who's that?'

'The person who cut up the bird.'

'What bird?' Hugh asked.

'I'm sure you know the story, but the first time we met Rosie, she told us how, many years ago, she'd been walking in the garden when she discovered a bird that had been ritually disembowelled. It's such a sick thing to have done, it's always felt to me as though whoever had experimented on the bird in the past was almost certainly our killer in the present. Even if they were only five years old at the time. Isn't that right, Matthew?'

'What's that?' Matthew asked.

'It was you who ritually disembowelled that bird all those years ago. And it was you who killed Freddie Beaumont. And then killed your sister Lucy.'

Matthew still didn't seem to understand this statement, and he remained just as confused as Dwayne stepped towards him and started to handcuff him.

'What's this?' Matthew said. 'What are you doing?'

'Arresting you for murder,' Dwayne said as he yanked Matthew's arms hard behind his back. 'For *two* murders.'

Hugh, Sylvie and Tom were too stunned to speak, but as Matthew started finally to profess his innocence, Richard turned to face Rosie and saw tears in her eyes.

'And you've suspected that Matthew was the killer for some time. Haven't you?'

Rosie didn't say anything.

'But it's not possible,' Hugh said, finally finding his voice. 'Matthew was Lucy's favourite. He could never kill her. And why would he kill Freddie? It's like you said. He never even met him.'

'That's right,' Richard said. 'And those are the reasons why – when I managed to put my prejudices to one side – I found myself naturally wanting to discount Matthew as our killer. After all, there really does seem to be no rational reason for him to have killed a man he'd never met – and who was dying anyway – and then a sister who he loved. But these murders weren't entirely rational. In fact, although they were meticulously planned, the motive behind their deaths wasn't even close to rational.'

Richard looked at the room. This is what he lived for. Delivering justice.

'Let me tell you what happened.'

CHAPTER THIRTEEN

'The past casts a long shadow,' Richard said. 'And, as I said before, these two murders are all about the past. Not that Matthew started out planning to kill anyone. In fact, as far as he was concerned, he was just trying to make contact with his biological father after he'd learned that he was dying of cancer. But Hugh told Matthew that Freddie was lying. That it was all a ruse, and that he should cease all contact with Freddie. So that's exactly what Matthew did. He did as he was told. But we also know how honourable Matthew is. And I don't think this decision would have sat well with him. After all, it wasn't the honourable thing to do to abandon Freddie in his last hours.

'But unbeknownst to Matthew, Hugh decided to take matters into his own hands. Now, I don't think we'll ever know the precise order of events. Did Matthew overhear Hugh telling Sylvie that he'd paid for Freddie to come out to the Caribbean? Or did he find out by some other means? It doesn't much matter, because what we *do* know is that when Lucy started saying that she'd seen an old guy spying on her, Matthew guessed who it might be. Or maybe he also saw the old man hanging around the plantation, spoke to him, and found out that he was Freddie, his biological father. Again, it doesn't much matter what the precise order of events was, because it's obvious from what followed that Matthew worked out that it was Freddie who was the plantation's Peeping Tom. But to be clear: Matthew still had no thoughts of murder. Not yet. He just wanted to do the honourable thing.

'And once again, we have to speculate, because Lucy is no longer here to tell us exactly what happened, but it would only be natural that Matthew would go to his closest ally in the family. His big sister, Lucy. And whether or not he'd told her everything before, he did now. He explained how he'd been writing to Freddie for years, how Freddie was now dying of cancer, and how it wasn't right that Freddie should now be reduced to skulking around in the undergrowth trying to steal glimpses of his family.

'But Lucy's reaction shocked Matthew, because she still refused to have anything to do with Freddie. In fact, I think her reaction to the news was extremely violent – in the same way that we were told that Lucy was like Mount Esmée. Quiet for long stretches of time, and then she blows her top. But Matthew's sense of duty towards Freddie was a match for Lucy's loathing, and I bet he argued back. Forcefully. They *had* to see Freddie. And I imagine that it was Matthew's insistence that they should behave with honour that tipped Lucy into making a terrible mistake. She told Matthew the truth. I'll explain what she said in a moment, but for the time being, all that matters is that, by doing so, she sealed her fate. And she sealed Freddie's.'

'I imagine Matthew took time to digest what he'd just learned. But very soon afterwards, he went back to Lucy and told her that he now agreed with her. Freddie deserved to die. And of course Lucy agreed like a shot. She'd always wanted Freddie dead – as she was so happy to tell us. But what poor Lucy didn't know was that Matthew wasn't going to stop with Freddie's murder. He was going to kill Freddie, and then he was going to kill her.'

Richard looked at the witnesses and was gratified to see that they were hanging on his every word. Everyone, that was, apart from Matthew. His head was bowed. In shame – or denial – it was hard to tell.

'But how to kill Freddie, that was the question. Well, living on an old plantation like this, it didn't take Matthew and Lucy too long to remember the odourless, colourless and soluble pesticide, 1080, that was once used for controlling pests. That would be a perfect murder weapon. But how could they get hold of it? They both knew that it was strictly controlled. So Matthew told Lucy that they should get Tom to buy the poison for them. You see, not only did Matthew want to kill both Freddie and Lucy from the off, but it was also always his plan to pin both murders on his brother Tom.'

'But why?' Hugh asked.

'Don't worry. He had his reasons,' Richard said darkly. 'But going back to the chronology of the two murders, Matthew had now tricked Lucy into asking Tom to get hold of a box of 1080 poison. And that's when he enacted stage two of his plan. Again, we'll never know the precise order of events, but I think that, once they'd got the poison, Matthew pretended to realise that it wouldn't work. He no doubt told his sister that, once the Police did an autopsy on Freddie's dead body – as they were bound to do – they'd discover that he was killed with 1080 poison. They'd then check the poison registers, and they'd discover that Tom had bought some 1080 poison recently. And when interviewed, Tom would just tell the Police that it had been Lucy's idea to get the 1080 poison. She'd be implicated in his murder.

'So Matthew told her they needed to come up with an alternative plan. A *better* plan. And it was at this point that Matthew suggested they use Lucy's Glock 19 pistol to shoot Freddie dead. Now, I'm sure Lucy had told Matthew all about her gun long before they bought the 1080 poison. And I'm sure that Matthew had discounted it as a possible murder weapon at the time. After all, it belonged to Lucy. If they used it, they'd risk implicating her even more than the poison would.

'But this is when Matthew made his big play. He

suggested that maybe they could use Lucy's gun after all, as it wouldn't much matter whose gun was used if they made Freddie's death look like suicide. After all, if an old tramp is found shot dead inside a locked outhouse with a pistol in his hand, how could it be anything other than suicide? And if Lucy was still worried about being implicated, they could make sure that she was with the Police when Matthew killed Freddie. She'd then have an unbreakable alibi to prove that she didn't pull the trigger. She'd be in the clear.

'And Lucy finally agreed. They put the 1080 poison aside. Matthew would use her gun to kill Freddie. And it's here that I have to apologise to you all. Because I've been guilty of committing the crime of *post hoc ergo propter hoc.*'

'You have?' Dwayne asked, as if his boss had just confessed to having a highly contagious disease.

'Or to put it in English?' Camille asked, not entirely politely.

'It's a Latin phrase, Camille. And it means "after this therefore because of that".'

'Well I'm glad we've cleared that up,' Camille said.

'In other words,' Richard said, deigning to explain, 'it's a logical fallacy where you say that since event Y followed event X, then event Y must have been caused by event X. And that's the mistake I made when we found that Lucy's safe had been broken into and that her gun and box of bullets were now missing. I presumed that it had been her gun and bullets that had been stolen from the safe.'

'Because of Post Hic… whatever-it-was-you-said,' Dwayne said.

'Exactly,' Richard said, delighted that Dwayne had caught up with him. 'And it's such a clever trick, really. We see that the safe has been broken into. The gun and box of bullets are missing. Therefore, it must have been the gun and box of bullets that were stolen. But the reality is that they were never stolen from the safe.'

'Then how did Matthew get the gun from the safe?' Hugh asked.

'Lucy just took the gun and bullets out herself, and then handed them to Matthew. *That's* how her gun got out of the safe.'

'But I don't understand. If that's what happened, why did anyone have to break into the safe?'

'Because it wasn't good enough for Matthew that Lucy just give him her gun. That only suited the plan that he'd agreed with Lucy. He also had his secret plan to frame Tom for the murder. But how could Matthew make it look as though Tom had broken into the safe to get the gun? Well, it was quite simple, really.

'First, he wiped the keypad on Lucy's safe – removing all fingerprints. He then offered to help Tom go through the old papers in his office. And, as Matthew rather foolishly confirmed to us only a few moments ago, it wasn't just Rosie who was present when the old document was found. Matthew was there as well. And I don't think it much mattered what the document was. All that mattered was that Matthew could convince Tom that it was important enough to put in Lucy's safe. And then, once Lucy had put the document in her safe, Matthew went up to Lucy's bedroom and used graphite powder to reveal the code on the safe's keypad.

'He then broke into the safe and left a thread of blue cotton on a hinge that he knew he could later use to frame Tom to make it look as though this was when and how the gun had been stolen. But Matthew also realised – once he'd got the safe open – that there was one more thing he could do. He could remove the old piece of paper that Lucy had only just put in there. And, having done so, he then took it downstairs and set fire to it in Tom's bin. Because he knew that if the Police later found a burnt piece of paper in Tom's office, we'd have it analysed and would discover that it had originally been an old document. And, from there it would have been a short step to discover that Lucy had recently put the document in her safe – at Tom's bidding.

'As for what the piece of paper was now doing burnt in Tom's office, Matthew knew it would have been quite reasonable for us to then make the false assumption – seeing as it was Tom who'd got Lucy to store the piece of paper in her safe, and now here it was in his bin – that it must also have been Tom who'd opened the safe to remove Lucy's gun and bullets at the same time that he'd taken the piece of paper. And now Tom had burnt the incriminating piece of paper in a botched attempt to destroy the evidence that apparently linked him to Lucy's safe.'

'Hold on,' Sylvie said, 'are you saying that Matthew set all this up *before* he'd even committed murder?'

'That's exactly what I'm saying,' Richard said. 'His whole plan was thought through in advance. You see, Matthew may not be all that good at acing exams – or standing out from the crowd when he's at an overachieving private school – but that doesn't mean he hasn't got plenty of cunning. And a desperate point to prove.

'Because I think that Matthew's felt inadequate his whole life – when compared to his father's illustrious ancestors, whose great deeds go back to the time of William the Conqueror. That's why he's been writing a history of the family. I think he's fatally fascinated by his family – and not in a way that's even remotely healthy. Especially seeing as he's the third-born of his three siblings. He could never inherit anything. The rules of primogeniture make sure of that.

'And if the history of the Beaumont family is enough to give Matthew an inferiority complex, let's consider his mother Lady Helen's family, who count Earls and Countesses in their number stretching back in greatness just as far as the Beaumonts. And still, Matthew knew he'd not inherited anything from her, either. Certainly not brains. Certainly not money. Not even a title.

'So this wasn't just a murder for Matthew. This was also his vindication. The proof he'd craved his whole life that he had it in him to be a "great man".

'Or that was the plan at least, because now we come

to the day of his first murder. The day he shot Freddie dead. Or the day before, to be more precise. Because the note we found in Freddie's pocket – with "11am" written on it – made it clear to us that Freddie's presence in the drying room on that fateful Thursday morning had been pre-arranged. Now, I don't know what lie was used to make Freddie agree to the meeting, but I imagine Lucy or Matthew promised Freddie the big family reconciliation that I think he secretly craved. After all, why else was he spying on his family, if not because he wanted to see them but was too scared to approach? And why else had he kept the letters that his son Matthew had written to him for all of these years if not because – at some level – he'd always been desperate for some kind of a reconciliation? So yes, I think it would have been tragically easy for Lucy or Matthew to trap him with a promised meeting of the whole family.

'And Matthew chose 11am because, as Tom told us the very first time we interviewed him, he always goes into the fields at about 11am every day to check on the coffee plants. So by killing Freddie just after 11am, Matthew knew that Tom would almost certainly have no alibi for the time of the murder. That's why Matthew got Lucy to walk into our Police station at exactly half past ten that morning saying that there was a stalker at the plantation. Of course we said we'd investigate. Then it was just a matter of Lucy making sure that we were nowhere near the old drying shed at 11am when Matthew went in, met with Freddie, and shot him dead.

'But how did he then get out of the room afterwards?' Hugh asked.

'You mean, considering how it was locked from the inside?'

'Of course. It's not possible.'

'But it becomes far easier to understand when you realise who else was involved in Freddie's murder. Lucy herself. In fact, it becomes extremely easy to explain. Matthew shot Freddie dead in the shower room. He then turned the shower on, locked the main door, and then he left through the window here.'

As Richard said this, he moved over to indicate the old metal window on the far side of the room.

'It would then have been a simple matter to land on the tarmac just beyond the flower bed, and then reach back and push the window shut.'

'But I thought that window was locked on the inside?' Hugh asked.

'It was,' Richard agreed. 'The latch was jammed into the window frame, and the butterfly lock on the window's metal lever was firmly screwed down. But remember, Matthew turned on the shower before he left the scene. I couldn't work out why at the time. I assumed that maybe the killer had been trying to wash some kind of evidence away, but now I understand, because – as Tom told me yesterday – this room has never worked very well as a shower room. The ventilation's terrible. But that's hardly surprising, the clue has always been in the name: this is the old Drying Shed. It's supposed to have poor ventilation. But that's why Matthew set the shower to its hottest setting and turned it on after shooting Freddie dead. He knew that the shower would start to fill the room with steam.

'This meant that when we smashed the door open, the room was thick with steam. I mean, don't get me wrong, it wasn't so heavy that DS Bordey and I failed to see that there was a dead body lying in the middle of the floor. And, as Police officers, we of course both rushed to the body to see if we could offer any assistance. As Matthew and Lucy knew we would. And it was then, as we were briefly distracted by the dead body – while the steam was still filling the room – that Lucy came to the window here and quickly closed the latch and screwed the lock down.

'It was so simple, really. Matthew would commit the murder but leave one thread sticking out – the fact that while he'd been able to close the window, he couldn't lock it from outside the room. Then, once he'd got clear of the scene, Lucy would tuck that one thread back in for him. And Lucy must have been so pleased with herself when she managed to lock the window without us seeing. Because, as far as she was concerned, that was going to be the end of the story. It would now look as though an unidentified tramp had been alone inside a locked room when he committed suicide.

'But what Lucy didn't know was that Matthew wasn't just content with killing his biological father. He also wanted to kill her. So, although he'd got her to help him by promising that he could make the scene look like a suicide, he left behind two very simple clues that he knew would make the Police conclude that Freddie's death had to be murder.'

'He did?' Hugh asked. 'What clues?'

'Well, the first was the fact that Freddie was shot twice. Because, when we found the second bullet, we quite naturally began to wonder how Freddie could have shot himself dead with a gun that he was holding with a hand that had already taken a bullet to the wrist. In fact, it made us realise that Freddie's death couldn't have been suicide. It was almost certainly murder.

'However, this second gunshot wasn't a mistake. It had always been Matthew's plan to shoot Freddie twice so that we'd think that this was a murder that had gone wrong. I presume that the first shot was the killing shot to Freddie's heart. But then, once Freddie was lying dead on the floor, Matthew then took the gun and very carefully fired a second bullet into Freddie's right wrist to make it look as though there'd been a tussle of some kind that had resulted in a wild shot being fired. Matthew then placed the gun in the dead man's right hand as if the killer had then been forced to go through with his plan even though it was now botched. And we fell for the bait. Just as he knew we would.

'As for the second clue, Matthew made sure that one of the bullets he used to kill Freddie had Lucy's fingerprint on it. Because, as soon as we found Lucy's fingerprint on the bullet casing, he knew we'd ask her how it might have got there, and she'd be forced into revealing that she owned a handgun. A handgun that she kept in her safe. And when we opened the safe, we'd discover that her gun and box of bullets were no longer there, and that the keypad had been wiped clean of fingerprints with a blue cloth.

'And if we really didn't pick up on either of these clues, Matthew also left the box of 1080 poison – and Lucy's remaining box of bullets, and the blue cloth he'd used to wipe the safe clean – and the graphite powder he'd used to reveal Lucy's fingerprints – in a tin box hidden at the back of Tom's wardrobe. As an insurance policy in case the Police were too stupid and ever needed a nudge towards believing that Tom was the killer. Well, Matthew was fortunate and unfortunate here. Yes, we were clever enough to follow the trail to Tom for ourselves. But we were also clever enough to realise that the trail of clues we were following was false.'

Richard was looking directly at Matthew, but he was still looking down at the floor, refusing to meet anyone's gaze. Very well, Richard thought to himself. It was time to test Matthew's self-control.

'And now we come to the murder of Lucy. Because everything had been going so well for Matthew. The Police had uncovered Freddie's real identity without help. We'd even found the clues at the scene that proved that Freddie's death was in fact murder – and taken the bait that a lot of the evidence seemed to be pointing to Tom. But Lucy still had to die, didn't she, Matthew?

'After all, you knew better than most how emotionally unstable she was, and while she'd maybe have been able to keep her composure if Freddie's death had been ruled a straight suicide, you knew that we'd soon be treating it as a murder. And yet, I think you were still surprised by how quickly she began to fall apart under the pressure of the Police investigation.

'And when you discovered – at the same time as us, as it happens – that Lucy had even started eavesdropping on you, I think it made you realise that maybe Lucy was even beginning to think that you couldn't be trusted. When she came back from the solicitors and had her complete meltdown that evening, I think you decided you could delay no longer. The sister you'd loved your whole life had to die. By the following morning, you'd poisoned Lucy's cafetiere with 1080 – I imagine by inserting the 1080 in between the metal meshes of the plunger so it was released and dissolved into the coffee when she pushed it down.'

'But that's what I refuse to believe,' Hugh said. 'How could he kill her? He loved her. More than any of us.'

'And that's why I said earlier that there didn't seem to be any *rational* reasons for Matthew to be the killer. But his motive to kill Freddie and Lucy isn't entirely rational. And remember: Matthew is sick in his soul. He always has been. Think about it. He was five years old when he cut that dead bird open. Can you imagine that?

A five-year-old boy stumbles across a dead bird on the lawn, and isn't repulsed. In fact, he's fascinated by what he's seeing. And not just fascinated, he wants to see more. So he goes and gets his sister's knife and cuts the dead bird open.

'And there's something else that that incident teaches us about Matthew. Because maybe he saw his brother Tom approaching, dropped the knife and ran away. Or maybe he'd already got bored and had left the scene. But, either way, it was Tom who stumbled across the bird and picked up the bloody penknife. And it was then Tom who got the blame when Nanny Rosie found him standing over the dead bird holding a knife only a few moments later.

'Matthew learned a very important lesson that day. Because he saw how much trouble Tom got into with Nanny Rosie. Simply for being in the wrong place at the wrong time. Even though Matthew knew that Tom was blameless. And here we are, all these years later, and Matthew has done it again. But this time it wasn't Lucy's knife he used. It was her gun. Even if the person who he framed for the crime was the same. His brother, Tom.'

Richard got out his hankie and wiped the slick of sweat from his face and neck. It really was very hot inside the old drying room. Or rather, it really was hot inside his thick woollen suit whilst standing inside the old drying room. It was like being inside an oven that was inside another oven.

'From that day to this, I think Matthew has learned

to hide his fascination with death. Now, imagine what happens when a child who's already learned to hide his obsession with the macabre is sent to the other side of the world to a boarding school where he knows no-one. I think the shock of suddenly being abandoned like that – even if Matthew had thought it was a good idea at the time – is something that he never quite overcame. Having to cope on his own. Having to shut down his feelings because he had no-one to share them with. And, like anyone who tries to repress their feelings, I think those dark feelings grew inside him like a cancer.

'And to make matters worse, as Matthew told us himself, at Eton he was now surrounded by Maharajahs and millionaires. Baronets and billionaires. And I think that Matthew felt as though he should fit in, but he didn't. After all, he might have been the son of a Lady, but she'd run away years ago, and he had no title himself. And while his family had once been rich, they were now poor. In Eton terms at least. Even more tellingly, his real parents had abandoned him as a baby and he was now being raised by his uncle and aunt. And, not to put too fine a point on it, I can't imagine he ever told his Etonian friends that his adoptive mother was a one-time holiday rep from Maldon.

'I think Matthew's five years at Eton took him from being a disturbed child and turned him into a *very* disturbed adult. That's why he wrote to Freddie every year. I think he was desperately trying to understand who he was by making contact with the man who'd made him. But

Freddie – his own biological father, remember – continued to reject him. Year after year.'

As Richard said this, he went over to the ledge to the window and picked up a pile of paper he'd placed there earlier. Each A4 piece of paper was a scanned copy of one of Matthew's letters.

'But we should be grateful for the fact that Matthew sent his letters every year on his birthday. Because now we're closing in on the dark heart of this case. The secret that Lucy told Matthew, which meant that she and Freddie had to die. But I wouldn't have got there if it hadn't been for the diligence of Detective Sergeant Camille Bordey.'

Richard went back to the window and picked up another printout.

'Because Camille decided that she was going to track down Matthew's mother, Lady Helen Beaumont, née Moncrieff. After all, it seemed so suspicious that she'd vanished so thoroughly off the earth. Especially now that her children had grown up. So where exactly did she get to when she left you that day? And why hasn't she resurfaced since then? Well, I'm sorry to say that she hasn't turned up since then because she died on the same day she walked out on you all.'

The family took a few moments to digest this. Richard could see that in some ways they weren't surprised, but there was still a deep grief to Tom as he turned to the Police and asked what had happened.

'She committed suicide,' Camille said as kindly as she

could. 'On the train journey back to her parents. She stopped at a station and stepped in front of a train. It would have been instant.'

'Do you know why?' Hugh asked.

'It's hard to know for sure after all this time. But I think she maybe realised that she was doing the wrong thing. Her parents had cut her off years before. They'd made it clear that they never wanted to see her again. So she was already dead to them. I think this meant she realised she couldn't go forward. And she already knew she could never go back. She was trapped. With no money. No family. And I think that that's when she decided to do what she did.'

'And although we'll never know all the details, we do know for sure that that's the day she died because we have the Police report of her death,' Richard said, holding up a copy of the report from the Winchester Police. 'And here at the very top it says that your mother died on the thirteenth of June, 1999. The date didn't register as being important to me at first. But then I realised what was wrong with it.'

Richard held up the photocopies of Matthew's letters to Freddie.

'Because here we have the letters Matthew wrote to Freddie. And rather fortunately for us – if not for Matthew – they're written on the same day each year. Matthew's birthday. Which is on the fifteenth of June. And, as Hugh told us, Matthew was born in 1999, so that means that Matthew was born on the fifteenth of June, 1999. Which is impossible when you think about it. So Matthew, can you please tell me how your mother managed to give birth to you two days after she'd already died?'

Matthew's mouth twitched, his eyes shining with a terrifying intensity. Richard turned to face Rosie.

'And this is the secret that Rosie has kept for all these years. Isn't that right, Rosie? Because, when you arrived in London, it wasn't Lady Helen who you discovered was pregnant, was it? It was her twelve-year old daughter, Lucy.'

Very slowly, Rosie nodded.

'That's right,' Richard said. 'Lucy's not just Matthew's sister. She's also his mother. And it was kept a secret from Matthew his whole life.'

Again, Rosie nodded.

'But the story doesn't end there, does it? Because you also know who the father of her baby was, don't you?'

Rosie didn't move. She didn't dare move.

'Don't you, Rosie?'

Rosie mumbled something that was hard to hear.

'Who was it, Rosie? Who was the person who'd made the twelve-year old Lucy Beaumont pregnant?'

'Freddie,' Rosie said in a hoarse whisper. 'It was her own father. Freddie Beaumont.'

There was a gasp from Sylvie, and everyone turned to look at Matthew. Fury was burning in his eyes.

'Go on, Rosie,' Camille said.

Rosie tried to focus on her story.

'It took me years to find out the truth. Although I think I'd maybe come to suspect – seeing how Lucy never forgave Freddie. How she continued to hate him. And then, she told me one day. How Freddie had raped her. His own daughter. And she'd never told anyone. No-one apart from me.'

'Thank you,' Camille said.

'But that was years later,' Rosie said, trying to get her testimony over with as quickly as possible. 'That first time I arrived in the UK, all I could see was that it wasn't Helen who was pregnant, it was her daughter Lucy. Helen admitted that she'd lied to Grandfather William on Saint-Marie that she was about to have her third child. And now I was there, she wanted me to stay until Lucy had given birth and then I had to promise to get the children out to Grandfather William in the Caribbean. I had to get them away from Freddie. That's what she told me. Especially Lucy. I now understand why, but I didn't at the time. Anyway, that's what she made me promise that day. That I'd tell anyone who asked that the new baby was in fact Helen's, and not Lucy's. And that I'd get the children out to the safety of Saint-Marie. And I could see how worried Lucy was. How scared. And I had no problems saying yes. I said I'd stay for the birth. And then I'd help her get the children out to Saint-Marie. But once I'd said I wouldn't let her down, that's when she got up and walked out of the house. And I never saw her again. Just like I told you.'

'So Helen really did walk out on her family on the day you arrived?'

'The very same day. The thirteenth.'

'And when was Matthew born?'

'Two days later. On the fifteenth. Just like you said. In Queen Elizabeth's hospital in Woolwich. I'll never forget it. I held Lucy's hand the whole time. She was amazing that day. So brave. So young.' Rosie took a deep breath to steady herself. 'And afterwards, after the birth, Lucy held her baby in her arms, and then she handed him to me. And as I looked into his eyes, I knew that this little baby was blameless. Lucy was blameless. I would save them both. And Tom of course. I'd save all three children. Just as soon as Helen returned.

'But she never did. So I told Lucy that I'd promised to take her, her new baby and Tom out to visit Grandfather William in Saint-Marie, and that Helen's plan was that we should continue to tell everyone that the baby was Helen's. I think Lucy would have agreed to anything at that point. She was so confused. So upset. And as for Tom, he was only four years old and still too young to work out what was really going on. Lucy and Helen had kept Lucy's pregnancy from him. But I acted as a go-between for William and Freddie while we sorted out passports for baby Matthew. And made sure that the three children remained healthy and well. And in all that time, Helen never came back. Never made contact. And you're saying it's because she took her own life?'

Richard nodded.

'I imagine because of the shame, then,' Rosie said quietly. 'That she'd failed her children. That she'd not protected Lucy from Freddie. And, I suppose, once she knew that I'd be taking them to Saint Marie...?'

A silence fell on the room, with no-one daring to speak.

'Then I'm glad I did what I did,' Rosie said with finality. 'I did the right thing that day.'

'But this can't be true,' Hugh said.

'I'm sorry,' Richard said. 'Not only could it be true, it has to be true. Helen died on the 13th of June. We have the Police report that proves it. Matthew was born two days later, on the 15th of June. And then, once the three children had arrived on Saint-Marie, the only two people who knew the truth were Lucy and Rosie, and they weren't telling.'

Richard turned to Rosie.

'And you didn't even break that promise after Freddie died.'

'I didn't think it was connected. Especially when I discovered that Lucy had been with you when he was shot. I didn't think that anyone else could have wanted to kill him.'

'But you started to wonder when Lucy died, didn't you?'

'I suppose. Only wonder, mind. I wasn't sure.'

'But that's why it wasn't enough that Freddie die,' Richard said to the family. 'Matthew has spent the last five years on his own fighting his feelings in a school that values the ideals of honour above all else. And yet, Matthew knew that his urges weren't honourable. And now that he'd learned the truth of his parentage?

'The shame, confusion and pain that Matthew must have felt would have been enough to sink most people, but we have to remember that Matthew isn't most people. All his life he'd been fighting the belief that he was somehow broken. And imagine how many times he must have told himself that he wasn't like his father, Freddie. Or even: he wasn't like his ancestor, "Mad Jack". But Lucy's confession broke the dam inside Matthew. He *was* like his father. He *was* like "Mad Jack". And I think the release was in some ways intoxicating for Matthew. He could now give in to the instincts he'd been suppressing ever since he'd eviscerated that bird. And that meant that Freddie had to die. And then, Lucy had to die as well. No-one could know the truth of his parentage. In Matthew's sick mind, it was the only honourable thing to do.'

'You knew,' a strangled voice said.

Everyone turned and saw Matthew looking at Rosie with wild eyes.

'You've known my whole life,' he said in a louder voice. 'You've always known!' he shouted, jumped to his feet and tried to run at Rosie, but Dwayne and Fidel pounced and knocked Matthew to the ground where they held him as he screamed and shouted abuse at Rosie. With his wrists already in handcuffs, Matthew tried to kick at the Police, only relenting when Dwayne yanked the killer's hands behind his back until the pain in his elbows and shoulders finally silenced him.

Dwayne grabbed Matthew by the scruff of his neck and yanked him to his feet.

'These are lies,' Matthew said as he panted to get his breath back. 'I can show you my birth certificate.'

'Your short one, perhaps,' Richard said. 'But that's the thing about the short birth certificate. It only lists your name, where you were born, and your citizenship. That's it. But what about your longer birth certificate? I bet you've never applied to get that, have you? Well, I have. In fact, I've got it here.'

As Richard spoke, he slipped his hand into his inside jacket pocket and pulled out a folded-over piece of paper. Unfolding it so everyone could see, he held up a black and white photocopy of a full birth certificate.

'Because I've got a copy of your long birth certificate here. And while it says father "unknown" – which is understandable, considering the truth – it can't lie about who your mother is. And it lists your mother as being Lucy Beaumont.'

With a wild howl of pain, Matthew tried to lunge at Richard, but Dwayne and Fidel had him in a vice-like grip.

Richard looked into Matthew's eyes and saw, in among the shame and fear, that there was also a look that was deeply unsettling. It was a glimmer of triumph. As though

Matthew was relieved finally to reveal his true nature to the world.

'Take him away,' Richard said.

Dwayne yanked Matthew by the shoulder and led him out of the shower room.

Once the room was clear, Hugh went over to Tom and wrapped him in his arms. Tom looked at his adoptive father and burst into tears.

Hugh held on tight.

Rosie remained sitting quietly. Richard could see that she was trying to process what had just happened. As for Sylvie, Richard saw that she was frowning.

'But why Tom?' she asked when she saw Richard looking at her.

'What's that?' Richard asked.

'I still don't understand why Matthew had to frame Tom for the two murders. What did he have against Tom?'

'Ah,' Richard said, 'you're right. He didn't have anything against Tom. Not really. But I remembered something that your solicitor said when she showed me Grandfather William's will. She said that when Freddie died, the trust would automatically be dissolved and would then be inherited in its entirety by Freddie's firstborn, assuming that that person was over the age of eighteen, of sound mind and body, and – crucially – *had no unspent prison time*.

'That's why Matthew worked so hard to pin the murders on his brother. Because the moment we arrested Tom, he'd be stopped from inheriting anything. And when Tom was then convicted of double murder – as I'm sure he would have been, considering the evidence against him, both direct and indirect – then he'd have ended up in prison. Tom would have been ineligible to inherit. The whole estate would automatically have passed on to the next oldest child, Matthew. And seeing as Matthew has always been on record as wanting to sell the plantation, it wouldn't have even begun to look suspicious when he then sold the plantation for five million dollars.

'So Matthew wasn't just killing the only two people in the world he thought knew his secret shame. He was also making sure he inherited five million dollars. And five million dollars is *always* an incentive to commit murder. Don't you think, Sylvie?'

A few minutes later, Richard emerged from the shower room to see Dwayne and Fidel already guarding the locked boot of the Police jeep where a handcuffed Matthew was sitting inside. From the way his shoulders were heaving up and down, Richard could see that he was crying. As for Camille, she'd taken Andy Lucas off to the shade of a palm tree and was talking to him.

'Detective Inspector?' a voice said from behind Richard.

Richard turned and saw Hugh standing by the entrance to the shower room with Rosie and Tom. As for Sylvie, she was already heading back to the main house on her own.

'I'm sorry,' Hugh said. 'That you saw our family...like this. That you saw what we're really like.'

Richard knew that there was nothing he could say that would make Hugh feel any better. Instead he watched as Rosie very gently put her arms around Tom and Hugh's waists. She then nodded once to Richard – in thanks, perhaps, or just to say that she was taking over now – and then she turned and said something to Tom. It looked as though she were suggesting they go home, and Richard watched as the trio turned and started walking back up the hill to their house together.

And still, Mount Esmée continued to loom over the plantation – as it had done for the last two hundred years.

Heading over to the Police jeep, Richard saw Camille take the handcuffs off Andy and then heard her tell him that they weren't going to hold him any longer. However, she added, they wouldn't be so tolerant the next time he tried one of his scams on Saint-Marie. In fact, seeing as he owned such a powerful boat, she thought that he might want to leave the island by the end of the week.

Andy thanked Camille, and Richard saw him promise that he'd be leaving Saint-Marie at the first opportunity. Richard then heard Andy say that he was going to turn over a new leaf.

Richard looked up at the sun in the sky high above him and took half a step to steady himself as a sudden feeling of queasiness nearly overwhelmed him. He was overheating in his woollen suit, and if he didn't get into the shade – and soon – he knew he might end up passing out from heat exhaustion.

As Richard strode over to the Police jeep and climbed into its cabin – while barking at his team to hurry up – he found the thought popping into his head that he'd have none of these problems if he wore more appropriate tropical clothes, just like his team had been saying to him. But he couldn't start changing the rules he lived by at his age, could he? Where was the honour in that?

And then, without consciously doing so, he found himself considering how Matthew had developed his sense of honour while attending a single sex boarding school. Just as Richard had developed his strict code of honour while attending a single sex boarding school. And while Richard was pretty sure that he could never commit murder, the parallels between Matthew's schooling and his own were a little too close for him to feel entirely comfortable.

At the very least, Richard found himself wondering if he really needed to be so rule-bound the whole time. After all, during the case he'd had a hunch that Hugh had continued to lie to them, and that gut feeling had proven correct. And when he'd torn up the rule book by developing the photographic plates before they were officially ready, he'd got great results then as well, hadn't he?

Maybe, Richard thought to himself – a bit like Andy Lucas – it was time for him to turn over a new leaf?

★★★

By the following morning, Matthew had taken his solicitor's advice that he'd get a reduced sentence if he pleaded guilty, and had, through his tears, confessed to both murders. But Camille had had to handle the whole interview on her own. Richard hadn't come in to work at all that day. Nor was he answering his phone. His team were utterly unnerved. Their boss had never vanished like this before.

At lunchtime, a rumour started to sweep the island. It began when a woman from Fidel's church rang her daughter who then told her boss who then rang Camille's mother, Catherine. Catherine couldn't believe what she'd just heard, so she rang her daughter.

'It can't be true, can it?' Catherine said.

'What can't be true?' Camille asked.

'Where's Richard?'

'We don't know. He's not come in to work today. Why? Do you know where he is?'

'That's the thing, Camille. Apparently, he's been seen at the Saint-Marie shopping mall.'

'At the mall?'

'That's right.'

'But what's he doing there? He's supposed to be here.'

There was a pause at the other end of the line while Catherine made sure that no-one at her bar could overhear her.

'I believe he's been shopping,' she whispered. 'Clothes shopping.'

'He's been shopping for clothes?'

'I know! I can't believe it myself. Apparently he's bought a pair of jeans.'

'But that's impossible,' Camille said, trying to imagine her boss wearing a pair of jeans and failing.

'And it's not just that,' Catherine said. 'He's bought T-shirts. In lots of different colours. And shorts. Cotton shorts. And a pair of sky blue espadrilles.'

Now it was Camille's turn to feel light-headed. This couldn't be true, could it? And when she told Dwayne and Fidel what she'd just heard, they were just as disbelieving as she'd been. But then something happened that proved to them that this was indeed an age of miracles.

Richard rang Camille and said that he wanted the team to come around to his house for a drink after work as he had something to show them.

Richard had never voluntarily invited his team round for a drink at his shack before.

And so it came to pass that, just after six pm, Dwayne locked up the Police station and he, Camille and Fidel got into the Police jeep and drove to Richard's shack on the beach just outside the town of Honoré. They only just resisted turning on the lights and siren to make sure they arrived there as fast as they could.

As they approached the shack, they could see that all of the windows were shuttered, as were the French doors. In fact, it looked as though the shack had been made secure for winter. Or was unoccupied.

'Sir?' Camille called out.

'Stay where you are!' Richard called from inside. 'Just give me a minute.'

Camille, Dwayne and Fidel looked at each other. If what they thought was happening was actually happening, then, as far as they were concerned, Richard could take as long as he wanted.

As for Richard, he was inside his darkened shack trying to keep control of his racing heart. And, as he looked at himself in his mirror, he knew he'd never felt so vulnerable in his whole life.

He was wearing light blue espadrilles, a pair of jeans and a T-shirt that had thin blue and white horizontal stripes going across it. He wasn't even wearing socks. That's how improbable the whole 'look' was.

He returned to the main room of the shack and saw his black suit neatly folded on his bed. His old friend. But the day of the woollen suit was over. After all, Dwayne and Camille were right. He couldn't continue wearing a thick woollen suit in the tropics, could he?

Outside on the veranda, Camille, Fidel and Dwayne were still on tenterhooks. Richard had remained inside for over five minutes since they'd arrived. When was he coming out?

'Chief?' Dwayne eventually asked, unable to wait any longer.

'Just coming,' Richard's voice called out from inside.

As Richard said this, his team heard a scraping noise

as the lock on one of the French doors was turned. Instinctively, Camille, Fidel and Dwayne all took a step back to give their boss room.

This was it.

The moment of truth.

The French doors swung open and Richard stepped out onto the veranda wearing black brogues, black socks, a thick woollen suit, crisp white shirt and a Metropolitan Police tie – and in his hands he was holding a full bin bag that was tied into a knot at the top.

'What…?' Dwayne managed to splutter.

'What do you mean, "what"?' Richard asked irritably.

'Well, it's just…' Dwayne said, before realising he didn't have the courage to finish the sentence.

'What's in the bin bag, sir?' Fidel asked.

'Oh, this thing?' Richard asked, holding up the bin bag as though it were of no consequence. 'Just taking out some rubbish,' he then added grimly.

As he spoke, Richard moved to the side of his house where there was an empty metal dustbin, and he stuffed the bin bag into it.

'I don't understand,' Camille said, going over to her besuited boss.

'What don't you understand?'

'Well it's just, you weren't in the station today.'

'I know.'

'So what were you doing?'

'Shopping.'

'Shopping? What were you shopping for?'

'Well, among other things, I thought I might have a barbecue,' Richard said, and then went back into his house.

Camille took half a step towards the dustbin, but before she could open up the bin bag to see what was inside, Richard re-emerged holding a heavy bag of barbecue coals and other barbecue equipment in his hands.

'But I heard a rumour that you'd been clothes shopping,' Camille said.

'Oh you did, did you?' Richard said as he dumped the barbecue equipment on the sand a few feet from the bin.

'Yeah. You were seen trying on a pair of jeans. And T-shirts. And shorts.'

'Me?' Richard asked as he returned to his dustbin and dragged it over the sand towards his barbecue equipment. 'I'd check your sources if I were you, Camille. Have you ever seen me wearing those sorts of clothes before?'

'Yes. When you went undercover to catch Andy Lucas.'

'But that was for work. I'm talking about whether you could ever imagine me voluntarily wearing those sorts of clothes.'

'Of course, sir. That's what everyone wears.'

'Yes,' Richard said as he poured barbecue coals into the metal bin and then laced the whole thing with copious squirts from his bottle of paraffin, 'but as you so often point out to me, I'm not everyone.'

'Anyway,' Dwayne interrupted, thinking of his stomach. 'About this barbecue?'

Richard pulled a lighter from his pocket and clicked it with his thumb so that a flame jumped up.

'I've changed my mind,' he said, and then touched the flame to the bin before recoiling as a fireball erupted.

'You're setting fire to your new clothes?' Fidel asked in amazement.

'What new clothes?' Richard said, but he couldn't hide the surge of relief he felt as he saw the flames engulf the contents of the bin.

His day-long crisis of confidence was over, as he'd realised only seconds before he'd been about to step out onto the veranda in his new clothes. Because it was all very well trying to dress like everyone else, but it wasn't who he was. And if that made him a repressed stick-in-the-mud who was closed off to new experiences, then so be it. And, anyway, wasn't this in fact the more adventurous way to approach life? After all, anyone could flop about in loose cotton clothes being relaxed. The far more daring path was to wear a suit in the tropics because you felt that Policemen *had* to wear suits – and then to test that resolve on a daily basis.

'But you've got some food, haven't you?' Dwayne asked. 'And maybe an ice cold beer? It's hot out here.'

Yes, it was, Richard thought, and then he realised that this was partly because he was standing in a thick woollen suit on a tropical beach next to a raging fire in a bin.

But he'd made his decision.

He was an Englishman, and he'd damned well wear his suit wherever and whenever he liked.

The phone in Richard's pocket started to ring. He fished it out and saw that the call was being diverted from the Police station. This was what happened in the evenings. They all took it in turns to be the Duty Officer and tonight it was Richard's turn.

As Richard lifted the phone to his ear, he took a couple of paces down the beach and looked out over the sparkling Caribbean sea at the distant horizon. The sunshine was dazzling his eyes, so he turned his back on the view.

'Good evening,' he said into his phone. 'This is Detective Inspector Richard Poole of the Saint-Marie Police Force. How can I help you?'

ONE PLACE. MANY STORIES

Bold, innovative and
empowering publishing.

FOLLOW US ON:

@HQStories